Ariel had offered him friendship.

She'd breezed in and shifted his perspective, shaken him from the emotional coma that had gripped him.

She'd given him gifts that had nothing to do with the attraction he'd felt toward her, gifts he was far too grateful for to repay by entangling her in the disaster his life had become. Because she deserved better.

To her, life was a grand adventure, and she deserved to fall in love with a man who saw the world as she did—full of hope and miracles. Damon saw all the harsh edges.

He gritted his teeth against the welling of something akin to despair. Well, it would be over soon. This visit, this space of time where he'd glimpsed magic through Ariel's eyes. It would be for the better. Everything back to normal, but nothing ever quite the same.

Dear Reader,

Welcome to Silhouette **Special Edition** . . . welcome to romance. Each month, Silhouette **Special Edition** publishes six novels with you in mind—stories of love and life, tales that you can identify with—romance with that little ''something special'' added in.

This month, we're pleased to present the conclusion of Nora Roberts's enchanting new series, THE DONOVAN LEGACY. *Charmed* is the story of Boone Sawyer and Anastasia Donovan—and their magical, charmed love. Don't miss this wonderful tale!

Sherryl Woods's warm, tender series—VOWS—will light up this Thanksgiving month. *Honor*—Kevin and Lacey Halloran's story—will be followed next month by *Cherish*. The vows that three generations of Halloran men live by create timeless tales that you'll want to keep forever!

Rounding out the November lineup are books from other favorite writers: Arlene James, Celeste Hamilton, Victoria Pade and Kim Cates. This is truly a feast for romance readers this month!

I hope that you enjoy this book and all the stories to come. Happy Thanksgiving Day—and all of us at Silhouette Books wish you the most wonderful holiday season ever!

Sincerely,

Tara Gavin
Senior Editor
Silhouette Books

KIM
CATES

A SKY FULL OF MIRACLES

Silhouette®

SPECIAL EDITION®

Published by Silhouette Books New York
America's Publisher of Contemporary Romance

To Ricky and Serena Coppula—
two very special miracles.
And to Sue, there are no words that can express how
much I respect you for the gifts you have given them.

SILHOUETTE BOOKS
300 East 42nd St., New York, N.Y. 10017

A SKY FULL OF MIRACLES

Copyright © 1992 by Kim Ostrom Bush

ISBN: 0-373-09777-8

First Silhouette Books printing November 1992

Printed in the U.S.A.

Books by Kim Cates

Silhouette Special Edition

The Wishing Tree #687
A Sky Full of Miracles #777

KIM CATES

is an incurable fanatic, addicted to classic tearjerker movies, Chicago Cubs baseball and reading and writing romances—both contemporary and historical. Married to her high school sweetheart, she divides her time between her writing career and enjoying her young daughter, Kate, from whom, Kim insists, she's learned everything she knows about the temperament of royalty.

Chapter One

Ariel Madigan believed in magic—Easter bunnies, the tooth fairy and the spirits that visited Ebenezer Scrooge on Christmas Eve. It helped. Especially on days when miracles were scarce. And today it seemed that the Good Witch of the North was on sabbatical, because the magic Ariel had hoped for most of all, on this, the last day of school, had not come to pass.

Moey Kincaid's father hadn't shown up. Again.

The little girl was alone.

Ariel raked marker-stained fingers through a pixieish mop of honey-gold curls. Aquamarine eyes, as wonder-filled as those of the children she taught, darkened with unaccustomed restlessness.

She sighed, oblivious to the pandemonium of chattering parents and students crowded all around her. They were laughing, teasing and devouring treats, as they leafed through the One Terrific Kid books that chronicled each child's sometimes painful, hard-won progress during the past year; a year that for each of them had followed some kind of trauma—divorce or the death of a parent.

Tonight was to have been a celebration. A rite of passage. A symbol that they had made it through. They were going to be okay, now. Not the same, but different, and still very, very special.

Ariel knew she should be content. The enthusiastic babble of the kids was more evidence of her success than any psychological testing could have been.

But all she could think of was the little girl seated so quietly in the room's shadowy corner, her dark hair parted into almost painfully precise braids. Sky-blue ribbons were tied at the ends, a perfect match with the party dress that had obviously been bought in a store so exclusive the price of the fingernail polish sold there would have made Ariel blanch. Patent-leather Mary Janes glistened as the child toed the scuffed-up tiles beneath her feet. The shoes held more sparkle than the huge, dark eyes peering solemnly across purple crepe festoons and tissue-paper flowers.

"Ariel." The soft sound of a voice at Ariel's shoulder made her whirl, her eyes locking with social worker Nancy Ames's steady green gaze. Platinum hair cut in a bob swayed with ageless chic around a face that would have done a woman in her thirties proud. "Stop it," Nancy said in her Bryn Mawr accent. "It's not your fault."

Ariel caught at her lower lip with her teeth—a dead giveaway that she was drowning in guilt. "Stop what?" she demanded, smoothing a wrinkle from the cherry-red jumpsuit she wore.

"Obsessing about Moey Kincaid."

"I'm *not* obsessing."

"Come on, Ariel. It's me. Nancy. That child has had your stomach in knots for a month now. Ever since she entered the program—"

"Eighteen days."

"What?"

"It's been eighteen days since you finally convinced Sister Thomasetta to process Moey into Abracadabra. I haven't even had three weeks to work with her, and now school is out."

"I did everything I could to facilitate Melissa's entry into the program. But these things take time. Evaluations, sessions with the classroom teachers. I even let you talk me into letting Melissa begin Abracadabra *before* we had the prerequisite parent-staff conference."

"By the time you get her father to commit to a school meeting, Moey'll be graduating from high school. We got the permission slip signed."

"I'm not here to argue technicalities with you, Ariel. I know you get impatient with all the bureaucratic red tape, but it is in place to protect the school system—"

Ariel groaned.

"And," Nancy went on, "it also protects the kids. Sister Thomasetta and I could have made a strong case for keeping Moey out of Abracadabra altogether until the start of the next school year. But because of your enthusiasm and Melissa's special needs, we made an exception for her."

"I know. It's not that I don't appreciate everything you've done. It's just that I'm . . ." Ariel tried to keep the hot lump of tears balled up in her chest. "I'm angry and confused and miserable. And I want to help Moey so badly, I feel like screaming. How could he do this to her? How could her father let her come to something like this alone when he knew—*knew*—that every other child would have a parent, grandparents, sisters, brothers, *someone* who loves them to make this day special?"

"I'm not very good at playing devil's advocate, but maybe there is a perfectly reasonable explanation for Mr. Kincaid's absence. His job carries a great deal of responsibility. And besides that, he has two younger daughters."

"I've read Moey's files, Nan. Father—Kincaid, Damon R. Internationally renowned efficiency expert with Kincaid and Jameson Enterprises. Graduated magna cum laude from Stanford on full academic scholarship. He's a genius. A whiz kid. But, unfortunately he just happens to be stupid when it comes to seeing that his little girl is miserable."

"Ariel, I'm only saying—"

"I know what you're saying. And who knows? Maybe you're right." A sick little laugh escaped Ariel's lips, and she winced inwardly as she saw Moey's gaze follow wistfully after Brandon Matthews, whose father had scooped him up to ride on a pair of broad masculine shoulders. "Maybe Damon Kincaid has a magnificent reason for neglecting his daughter this time. But what about all the other times? The notes I sent home, the messages I left.... No reply from Mr. Stuffy-Three-Piece-Suit. Not even a five-minute phone call."

"Maybe he's having a hard time dealing with his own grief," Nan said gently. "When you're looking into Moey's eyes it's easy to forget that Damon Kincaid lost a wife."

Eyes that could be warm as a summer day grew thunderous. "I'm not much interested in Mr. Kincaid's pain right now, Nan. Not when Moey is—"

"Ms. Madigan?" A diminutive grandmother with iron-gray hair and a gorgeous tan that whispered of wintering in Florida, stood, smiling up at them. "I just wanted to thank you for all you've done for our Tommy. He thinks the sun rises and sets in your eyes, dear. And looking at you, now, I'd not be surprised if he was right."

Ariel's smile was only a little forced as the irrepressible Tommy bobbed like a cork around his grandparent.

"I loved having Tommy in my room this year. I'll miss him next fall."

"You mean he won't be returning to the program?"

Ariel's smile warmed further, and there was a quiet pride, and a wistfulness as she smiled down into the little boy's freckled face. "No. Tommy has his wings. It's out of the cocoon for this butterfly."

"Yeah," Tommy said, hopping on one sneaker-clad foot. "But Miss Madigan said I can come and see her anytime I want. And talk to Houdini, an'—"

"Houdini?" the grandmother echoed, mystified.

"Her hat rabbit. An' I can sneak him bunny treats an' wooden carrots."

"How . . . wonderful for you," Grandmama said with admirable aplomb.

Ariel ruffled the boy's blond curls. "Speaking of Houdini, why don't you go check on him. I'm going to be drawing names soon to see who gets to take him home during summer vacation."

"All *right!*" Tommy enthused, grabbing his grandmother's hand, and dragging her at a killing pace to where the rabbit hutch stood in its place of honor, the cage cunningly formed in the shape of a magician's hat.

They had just disappeared when another enthusiastic parent started toward Ariel, but instead of meeting their eyes with her usual welcoming smile, Ariel turned, and began threading her way through the crowd toward the little girl who was still sitting in aching solitude a room's breadth away.

As Ariel approached, Moey looked up, and her eyes brightened a little—just enough to make Ariel certain that Moey Kincaid would be the most beautiful child she'd ever seen if her eyes truly ever sparkled, or her rose-pink lips curved in a heedless child grin.

"Hey, there, Your Royal Highness, how are things in the Crystal Kingdom today?" Ariel greeted the little girl in the teasing manner that had sprung from her discovery of Moey's rich fantasy life. A life filled with unicorns, magical dreamlands and princesses who never cried. "Any giants marauding? Dragons on the rampage?"

"No," Moey said, looking up at Ariel from beneath inky, curled lashes. "Today there's an evil sorceress, and she cast a spell around my daddy. She built a wall of invisible bricks, you see, so tall and so thick he could never escape."

Moey glanced toward the open classroom door, and the faint light of hope in her eyes made Ariel wince as the child continued. "I sure hope my daddy brought his enchanted sword. Then he could cut a door right into that wall, and he could escape and come to the party tonight."

Ariel swallowed hard, searching for the right words. "Well, even if that wall is too strong for your daddy, maybe you and I could stick together tonight. You could help me with Houdini, and we could eat cupcakes, and drink bug juice."

Moey smiled a little at Ariel's name for lemonade.

"I'm going to need you to check out the treats before I eat them, anyway, princess," Ariel went on. "After all, someone might have put a potion in one, and maybe I would fall asleep for a jillion years if I ate it."

Moey's eyes widened, and her cheeks grew pink with eagerness. Relief sluiced through Ariel, as she watched the child becoming lost in the game of make-believe. "Maybe Sister Thomasetta did it. She hides spooky stuff under her black dresses. There's lots of room there, an' Johnny Lewis says she keeps the bones of children she ate up. She's got 'em hanging right there in a frame in the principal's office."

Ariel tried to stifle a laugh, as she pictured the stern-faced, rigid disciplinarian who had been the principal of St. Genevieve's Catholic School for over thirty years.

An anthropology buff, Thomasetta had spent a lifetime gathering reproductions of great anthropological discoveries—the heads of Cro-Magnon man, Neanderthal man and various other objects.

Though the nun's love of such antiquities was well-known, Ariel could well imagine what her own childhood reaction would have been at being confronted with that collection of eyeless sockets and bared teeth. She would have believed, without a doubt, that Sister Thomasetta had preserved relics of especially incorrigible children there on the walls.

Ariel shook herself inwardly, aware that little Moey had gone on speaking in an adorably solemn whisper. "Yep," the child said with the sagest of nods, "if somebody stuck a potion in the cupcakes, I'd bet you anything it was Sister Thomasetta."

Love welling up inside her, Ariel gave Moey a hug, delighting in the summertime-fresh smell of crisp lace and satin ribbons. "I'll have to be extra careful, then," she whispered in Moey's ear. "How about if we creep over there, and see if any unenchanted cupcakes are left."

Moey linked small fingers with Ariel's and only a little sadness showed around her smile. "I know just the one to get you. The plate I brought today. The cupcakes with pink frosting and sprinkles shaped like teddy bears."

"How did you know pink frosting is my favorite?" Ariel asked, as they approached the table full of treats.

"I didn't know. My mommy did. She made them, special."

Ariel's heart turned over. "Your... mommy?" she said, uncertain if this was more of Moey's imaginary games, or yet another indication of the denial the child seemed blocked up in as firmly as the enchantress's invisible wall.

Guileless brown eyes looked up into Ariel's. "My mommy always fixes my favorite things. She laughs and smiles in the kitchen, and she gives me hot chocolate with tons of marshmallows and sometimes she reads stories to me."

"She used to read stories to you?"

A crease marked between Moey's brows. "My favorite is the *Rainbow's Unicorn*. She reads it to me every night, just before I go to slee— Oh." The child broke off in the middle of a sentence. Her gaze flickered away, the color on her cheekbones darkening. "I forgot. I'm not... not supposed to tell...."

Ariel hated the sudden withdrawal she sensed in the child. She stopped in the middle of the room, bending on one knee so she could look Moey straight in the eye. "I've always told you that you can talk to me about anything, Moey. There are no wrong answers in Abracadabra. No secrets we have to keep, unless we want to.''

Moey twisted the end of her braid. She stared down at the toe of her shoe. "I don't think I'm very hungry now," she said in a listless voice that broke Ariel's heart. "My daddy must have had a meeting or something and couldn't get here in time to come to the party. But I'm sure he'll be here to pick me up. I'm going to go and wait by the doors."

Moey extended her hand in a gesture that was at once achingly adult, and painfully childlike. "Thank you very much for the party, Miss Madigan. I had a wonderful time."

"Thank you for coming," was all Ariel could manage.

"Maybe summer will get over real fast, so I can come back again, and play with Houdini and try to figure out how you make him disappear."

Ariel was beset with memories of the little girl cuddling Houdini in her arms, whispering secrets into his floppy, furry ears. "You take care of yourself this summer," Ariel said, her throat thick. "Be sure and keep track of your adventures in the Crystal Kingdom. I'll want to hear about every one."

"I'm gonna miss you, Miss Madigan." Moey's voice was quavery. "Tons and tons and—" Suddenly the little girl flung herself headlong at Ariel, giving her a fierce hug. Ariel caught the child in her arms, eyes burning, heart aching.

In an instant, Moey pulled away. The child turned and ran out of the room.

Ariel stared at the empty doorway feeling helpless, hurting.

She didn't even notice Nancy approach, holding the empty punch bowl. "Can you give me a hand?"

Ariel shook herself inwardly, then moved to take the bowl. "No problem. You stay here. I'll run to the teacher's lounge and get some more lemonade."

"*We'll* run to the lounge," Nan said, maneuvering the container out of Ariel's reach and starting for the door. Ariel followed, the corridor closing about her, echoing with after-school emptiness.

"Ariel, you can't fix things for Moey." Nan's voice broke into the silence. "No matter how much you might want to."

Irritation stung Ariel, heightened by the sharp bite of her helplessness. "So you always tell me."

Nan didn't bother to take offense. "Call it fifteen more years of experience in the real world. I've seen a dozen kids like Moey Kincaid. They'll cut your heart out if you let them."

"I'd rather let them have it than keep it locked away in some—some dungeon somewhere." *Like you do yours,* was the unspoken accusation.

Nan paused while Ariel opened the lounge door for her, then walked to set the bowl on a table that still held relics from the final day of school—a newsletter, pointedly ignored, three detention slips, a coffee cup whose logo said Smile, Summer's Coming.

Nan flattened her palms on the table and turned her calm eyes to meet Ariel's turbulent ones. "It's no secret I wasn't crazy about working on a counseling program with someone who didn't have any training in psychology or social work. When Sister Thomasetta came to me with your proposal last fall, I fully intended to reject it out of hand. But I figured I had to read the proposal to come up with a logical reason to kibosh the whole thing."

"I know. We've been through all this before."

"I've told you I was reluctant, but I never told you what made me change my mind. What made me willing to go out on a limb with you, risk...well, there was an uncomfortably large margin of possible failure in a program like this. Even if it were run by professional counselors." Nan turned, her hands warm on Ariel's shoulders. "It was because of you, Ariel. You. Your enthusiasm, your excitement, your gift for working with children. When I read what you had written, I was enchanted with the idea of Abracadabra. And when I met you... Well, I knew then and there that if anyone could make the program live up to its promise, you could."

Ariel sucked in a shuddery sigh. "I appreciate the vote of confidence, Nan. I really do. But—"

"The only thing I was concerned about," Nancy interrupted, "was the possibility of your becoming overly involved with the kids. That can be every bit as damaging as being *under* involved, Ariel. Both to you and to the children. And the way you feel about Moey—along with the way she feels about you—can be the most dangerous problem of all."

Ariel felt a rare flash of temper firing. "Dangerous? How can it be dangerous to love the kids I work with? Especially when their own parents sometimes don't bother?"

"There are lines you can't cross, Ariel. Barriers that protect both the counselor and the child. Moey has already suffered the loss of someone she loved. She's looking for someone to substitute for her mother. To take her mother's place in her heart. And you—you're warm, wonderful, always listening."

"What's wrong with that?"

"You won't always be there for her. You can't be. I just don't want Moey to have to face the loss of someone else she's depended on."

"Then maybe someone should go and shake up that blockheaded father of hers. Make him see what he's doing."

"That is not your responsibility. It's not your job. You're a resource person to help get Moey through the school year, not a counselor for her father."

"So I'm supposed to sit back and let Moey go on suffering for the rest of the summer, because *it's not my job?*"

"What other alternative did you have in mind?" Nancy asked with infuriating calm. "Are you going to storm up to Mr. Kincaid's door and demand that he focus on his daughter? Or maybe you could call up Children and Family Services, and file a report of neglect—Mr. Kincaid did not show up at a school function, June 7th at 6:00 p.m."

"This is no joke, Nancy. The pain in that little girl's eyes—"

"Don't you think I know that?" Nancy demanded, her patience faltering into loving exasperation. "Ariel, I wish you could save the world. I really do. But you can't. All you can accomplish by getting more involved in the Kincaid affair is to get yourself, me and even the Abracadabra program in one devil of a lot of hot water. As your direct superior, I forbid it."

"You've never pulled rank on me before." Ariel's eyes blazed as hurt and a niggling sense of betrayal battled inside her.

"I've never needed to. As far as I'm concerned, this discussion is over. I know it seems harsh, Ariel, but believe me, it's for your own good."

Scarlet fury burned in Ariel's cheeks. "Don't you dare start pontificating about—"

"Miss Madigan? Hey, Miss Madigan!" Tommy's high-pitched voice echoed down the hall. He raced into the lounge, breathless.

Ariel bit down on the stream of harsh words. She sucked in a deep breath, pressing her hands to her face in an effort to cool what she knew must be a hectic color. "What is it, kiddo?" she asked with forced lightness.

"You promised we could have the drawing for Houdini. It's almost time to go."

Ariel glanced at the clock. "So it is. We'd better get back to the party, Miss Ames," Ariel said with a bite of defiance. She looped one arm around Tommy's shoulder.

"I wonder whose name'll be on the piece of paper you pick," the little boy said, skipping with delight.

"I don't know. We'll just have to wait and see. There are twenty-seven kids in Abracadabra, and every one of them has their name in Houdini's ha—" For just a heartbeat,

Ariel froze, an idea striking through her as if the tile beneath her feet had been charged with a thousand volts.

It was simple. Abominably simple. Perfect.

I wonder whose name'll be on the piece of paper you pick. Tommy's words echoed through her.

She could only hope that Damon Kincaid had a raging allergy to rabbit fur, and a tolerance for surprises. Because he was going to get both rabbit and rampage delivered to his doorstep before he could jet off to Timbuktu and leave his little girl alone again.

And there was nothing Nancy, Sister Thomasetta or the whole blasted school board at St. Gen's could do to save him.

Chapter Two

Damon Kincaid stepped out of the shower, steamy water running down his lean, hard-muscled frame. A year ago he would have been whistling, the off-key sound filling the enormous master bath as he grabbed up a plush black towel from the side of the spacious hot tub and began to dry his freshly shampooed hair.

But now the room was quiet, except for the low-pitched hum of the exhaust fan recessed in the ceiling. The steam-filled room seemed somehow too still, too empty, as if the whole house were waiting for something to go awry.

Damon pushed the thought away as he anchored the towel around narrow hips and, with eyes the color of warm sherry, caught a glimpse of himself in the mirror.

Lines creased his forehead, carving between heavy dark brows, marking his face with an underlying edginess that never left it anymore.

No, this time everything was going just as planned, he told himself, padding barefoot into the walk-in closet adjoining the bedroom. He was just jittery because it was one of those days when the whole square in the calendar was squeezed full. Dentist appointments, business engagements and Moey's end-of-the-year party with that teacher she adored had all but obliterated the red-inked reminder that today was Ellen's fifth birthday.

Everyone got harried on days like this. Even Amanda had....

His jaw tightened as he grabbed a fresh change of clothes, trying to ignore the yawning emptiness that had once been occupied by rack upon rack of his wife's things.

No, Amanda had never been harried. She'd handled the household and the girls with the effortless aplomb she'd brought to everything she'd done. The house had always been immaculate, the girls as pristine as if they were posing for an ad for fabric softener. There had been no voices vulgarly raised, no jelly prints on the walls, no copious bouts of tears because braids were uneven and ribbons were crumpled.

The Kincaids of Worthington Drive had been a picture-perfect family. Perfect until the day Amanda's car had careened into an overpass, and the picture had shattered.

"Stop it, for God's sake," Damon grated aloud, trying to blot out a score of painful memories and gnawing regrets. "There's nothing you can do about that anymore. Nothing...."

He pulled a crisp white shirt over his broad shoulders, ignoring the haunted look that had sprung into his eyes. Regrets. Yes, he had plenty of them. But tonight wouldn't add any more to their weight.

Tonight was going to be different. He'd seen to that.

He'd bundled Moey off to her school party half an hour ago—rigged out in her prettiest dress. And even though it would have been simpler just to pull back her hair with a headband, he had tamed Moey's curls into the braids the child had wanted. He'd fixed her up with ribbons and rubbed a scuff out of one of her patent-leather shoes.

And when Moey had begged him to drop her off at school early so she could talk to that teacher she idolized, he'd buzzed her over to St. Genevieve's in the spit-shined BMW, while their live-in nanny, Mrs. Applebea got Ellen and Sarah ready, and put the finishing touches on Ellen's birthday cake. As he'd let Moey off at the door, he'd promised her that the whole family would join her at the school by six-thirty. And for once—he thought glancing at the clock on the nightstand—they might even be a little early.

Yes, he'd remembered everything. Not a mean feat for a man who had stayed up until two in the morning wrapping gifts, and had been at his desk at Kincaid Jameson three hours later. He'd blitzed his way through a mountain of work in record time so he could take off early. Then he had rushed out to make last-minute preparations for the birth-day party and Moey's last day of school.

His mother-in-law had made it patently clear that she did not think him capable of handling Ellen's party at home as it had always been done before. And that in her opinion they should forgo Moey's school function and cater Ellen's birthday out to a service that dealt with children's parties. But Damon had been adamant. Moey would attend her Abracadabra celebration, and as for Ellen's birthday—he was paid exorbitant amounts of money to organize entire companies, for God's sake, how difficult could a child's party be?

Resolute, he had plunged into planning with his usual determination. He could have had Mrs. Applebea wrap the gifts, and hang the gold-foil birthday banner that had been a family tradition since Moey's first birthday, but Damon had wanted to do as much as possible himself.

He'd cursed himself for a fool in the wee hours of the morning, as he'd fought to make certain that the ballerina bears frolicking across the paper were lined up with a pre-cision a general would have approved of. But in the end he had even managed to smile when he'd looked at the stash of toys he'd bought on his way home from the airport the day before yesterday.

Yes, tonight everything was going to be different.

The buzz of the cordless phone made him start, and he grimaced, shoving his legs into dark gray trousers before he went to pick up the receiver.

"Kincaid," he said brusquely, trapping the phone between his ear and his shoulder while he shoved his shirttail into his waistband.

"Hey, Damon, this is the Jameson half of Kincaid Jameson. How you doing, bud?" When Joe Jameson's voice was that bright and cheerful it was time to look for nuclear fallout, and God knew, the company had suffered enough meltdowns to rival Chernobyl lately. Damon gritted his teeth in aggravation.

"I'm getting ready to go to school for that program of Moey's, and in an hour and a half my mother-in-law is going to descend on the house for Ellen's birthday party. If you're looking for the information on the Bonhaven Chemical Plant, I gave it to Lucy—"

"No, no. I looked over the Bonhaven stuff hours ago. Looks great. But then, what can one expect from a genius?"

"Can it, Joe." Damon maneuvered a tie around his neck, and began the difficult task of achieving a perfect knot while balancing the receiver. "Listen, I've got a helluva lot to do, so if this is a social call, I'll see you in the morning."

"No! I mean, no." Joe's voice softened. "It's real important, or I wouldn't have called you at home."

"Important?" Damon's stomach muscles tensed.

"You remember Haley Enterprises, that company based in Melbourne?"

"Sure. We're supposed to go down there next month sometime. They were gathering up the information we'd need, so we can go through it."

"Well, that info you wanted turned up a rat. It seems that next month might be too late to pull the company out of a tailspin. They want us there now."

"Well, *now* I'm on my way to Moey's school, and then I'll be having Ellen's party at eight."

"You're having a million five-year-olds descend on you at eight o'clock at night?" Joe's voice was incredulous enough to set Damon's teeth on edge.

"Eight o'clock happens to be the only time left, after work and Moey's school function. And as for having a bunch of kids over—not this time. It's going to be a family party—just Eve and the girls and me."

"I can't wait to hear what Ellen thinks of that."

"Ellen wants the party just the way her mother did it, down to the teddy-bear napkins, and Amanda wasn't big on having a dozen preschoolers tearing apart the house. I—" A dull throb intensified at Damon's temples. Why the blazes was he talking about this with his business partner, anyway? "Joe, the bottom line is that I'm not going anywhere for the next month. We both agreed that there was no reason why I couldn't work in the home office for that length of time. You said you understood that the girls had to be a priority. And I took you at your word and gave the nanny the rest of the month off. Mrs. Applebea hasn't had any real time off since a month before Amanda died, and her daughter just had a baby."

"Babies are boring. All they do is sleep and scream. Give her a bonus and she'll be back in her apartment over the garage so fast your head will spin."

"She's already gone—she was out the door the minute I got back from dropping off Moey."

"What about your mother-in-law? I'll bet she'd just love to get her hands on the girls while you're away. They could pack their little suitcases and—"

"I've told you a dozen times that I'm not going to have the girls dragged from place to place when I have to be gone. If I don't have someone to stay with them in their own home, I don't go. Now, I agreed to go to Austin last week with the understanding that I could have a month-long block of time at home when I got back. Something I haven't had since Amanda's funeral. The girls lost their mother a year ago. I'd like them to know they have a father.''

''You're a terrific father. Those girls have everything they could imagine. Hell, they live in one of the best neighborhoods in Naperville, have their own nanny to take care of them and a swimming pool out back. And when you give them each a charge card for their sixteenth birthday, they'll be glad as hell that you worked all these hours. Besides, it's not good for kids to be too dependent. That's parenthood according to Jameson, my man, and I guarantee it's good advice.''

Joe's babble faded into a dull buzz, Damon's thoughts whirling. There had been a time Damon had ascribed to much the same theory. Years of watching his divorced mother working three jobs to support him had drummed into his head early on the vital importance of becoming a good provider. It had made him successful. Ambitious. Driven. Damon had done all in his power to insulate his family behind a cushion of prosperity, to insure that none of the hard-edged poverty that had characterized his own childhood could mar that of his little girls.

But in the end the wealth he had worked such long hours to accumulate for his daughters had not been able to protect them from an even worse pain than he had known—and he was certain that Moey, Ellen and Sarah would have traded every toy, every tricycle, even the roof over their heads, just to have their mother tuck them in bed one more time.

And the months Damon had spent eating hotel food and wrestling with gargantuan corporate disasters had made him all but a stranger to the children he loved more than his own life. The problem was, he didn't even know how to begin to work past their pain, to reach them.

Searing words that had flown between him and his mother-in-law, Eve Laughton-Smith at Amanda's funeral made his stomach burn, the refrain playing yet again in his head.

What do you know about being a father? A real father? You couldn't be bothered by your wife and children when Amanda was alive. Why burden yourself now that she is dead? Amanda wouldn't want the girls to be raised by a flock of hired baby-sitters. She'd want me to have them. Me...

There was enough truth in the words to make his throat tighten. Mrs. Applebea had been a godsend in the time since Amanda had died. Hired three months before the accident, so Amanda could "get out more," Alice Applebea was an experienced nanny with sterling references and a brisk no-nonsense approach to child rearing—but she was still hired help. And with the trouble Kincaid Jameson was embroiled in, Damon had been forced to be away from home more than ever.

How many times during the past year had he wondered if Eve was right? That keeping the girls with him was selfish? That if he wanted what was best for them he should pack them up and take them to the tasteful Georgian-style Oak Brook mansion where Amanda had grown up?

A dozen times Damon had come within a whisper of picking up the phone and punching out Eve's number. But then he would slip into Moey's room, and watch her dreaming, or he'd tuck restless Ellen's bare foot under a coverlet, or Sarah would call for him to take her to the bathroom in the middle of the night.

Her hair would be all tousled, and she would snuggle into his shoulder, all warm and soft and sweet smelling. And he wouldn't care that it was 3:00 a.m., and the rest of the world was sleeping. He wouldn't care that he was exhausted and frustrated and raked with self-doubt. He would stand by his daughters' bedsides for hours, just watching them, wishing he could be as certain he was doing the right thing in the hours when they were awake.

Tonight—packed with Moey's party and Ellen's birthday—was the perfect opportunity to prove to both Eve and himself that he'd finally managed to pull it together. That he could be a father to the girls. Give them what they needed in a way he'd never managed to give it to Amanda.

The desolation stole across him again, fiercer this time. He became aware of the sound of Joe's voice, had no idea what his partner had been saying. Truth was, he didn't give a damn.

He shook himself inwardly and glanced over at the time. So much for being early. He dug a brush out of a drawer and raked it through his hair. "Joe, I have to leave now."

"But we have to come to an agreement on this Melbourne project. It's vital. I'd go in a minute, but much as I hate to admit it, there would be a good chance I'd muck it up. I'm great with fixed figures, but if something unforeseen turns up we both know I'm not as good at thinking on my feet as you are. And we need this client and the bucks he'll bring in. Badly. After Antigo Ironworks..."

Damon's hand clenched on the receiver. He'd been working on the Antigo project the month after Amanda had died. And despite his grief and guilt, he had believed that he'd planned the project with the same thoroughness that had made Kincaid and Jameson one of the most sought after international troubleshooters. He had handed the project over to Joe and Jameson had implemented Damon's plan with a vengeance, totally confident in Damon's abilities.

But for once it seemed that grief had blinded Damon—dulling his almost psychic instincts regarding the real root of the company's problems—the fact that a particularly creative embezzler was fleecing the company's owners.

Twice Joe had called, mentioning that possibility. Twice Damon had been furious that Joe had questioned him. Already raw with grief, numb with shock over the death of his wife and the morass of decisions he was being forced to make, the one thing Damon had clung to was his total confidence in his work.

By the time Joe had managed to convince Damon to listen, the company had been in such a mess, it had taken three months to straighten things out. Three months that both Damon and Joe were to have spent working with another, far more influential client who had bailed out in frustration, taking their badly needed money with them.

The drain on Kincaid Jameson's bank account had been considerable—and Damon had never stopped blaming himself for that deficit.

"I'll be in the office in the morning."

"And on a plane tomorrow night? I hate to push, Damon—"

"Then don't. Goodbye." Damon jammed his finger against the phone's disconnect button. He shoved his feet into his shoes, glanced at himself in the mirror, then grabbed up his suit jacket.

He was halfway down the curving stairs when he heard Sarah wail.

Ariel checked the address she'd scrawled on the tummy of a panda bear-shaped notepad, and then looked up at the house crowning the hillside of the exclusive neighborhood. All planes and angles, wood, stone and glass, the house had all the warmth of a magazine ad, not so much as a tricycle or a jump rope giving any evidence a real flesh-and-blood child might live there. But the address checked out perfectly—along with the tasteful brass nameplate on the mailbox at the street. Kincaid, 411 Worthington Drive.

Ariel thought about the rambling Galena farmhouse she had grown up in, its lawn littered with toys and jackets, abandoned sleds and boards she and her brothers and sisters were using to build their latest creations—spaceships or castles or sorcerer's lairs. And she couldn't help feeling sorry for the little girl with the perfectly shined patent leather shoes and the dresses from exclusive stores.

Ariel's hands felt damp on the steering wheel, and she rubbed them on the thighs of her jumpsuit to dry them. Unease rippled through her, along with the memory of Nancy's warning about becoming more involved in the Kincaid matter.

Even Ariel had to admit to herself that a man who lived in a house like this one would probably not take kindly to a scruffy-looking schoolteacher criticizing the way he was parenting his daughter.

Even if he did let her in—presuming, of course, that the man was even home—how many words would she get out of her mouth before he showed her out the door? Hadn't that been partially what Nancy had warned her of? The futility of this visit? The danger in it?

What was it Nancy had said about her initial doubts regarding the Abracadabra program itself? That the risk of failure had been great? Comparing that risk to the one Ariel was about to take was like comparing a soggy match to Smokey the Bear's worst nightmare.

Ariel's stomach fluttered, and for an instant she was tempted to throw her car's lackadaisical transmission into gear, and speed back to the safety of her own apartment. But with a grimace of self-disgust, she stifled her nervousness, hating the fact that her resolve had wavered even for a heartbeat.

What was the worst Kincaid could do to her? Slam the door in her face?

Get her fired?

Well, there were other jobs, other schools. But there was only one Moey Kincaid, and she deserved to be loved and cared for. Deserved to stop hurting.

Ariel climbed out of her car, then reached through the boxes full of clutter from the school year to draw out the wriggling Houdini. She supposed she should leave him in his cage, but maybe the feel of him, warm and soft and furry, would help to diffuse the waves of frigid propriety that would no doubt freeze her when Mr. Kincaid opened the door.

Ariel grimaced, able to picture him perfectly; his suit impeccable, the thinning strands of his hair combed back from pop bottle-thick glasses, his face pasty white from huddling over a desk all day.

Cradling the bunny in her arms, she walked up the curving pebble and concrete steps and stopped at the massive door. She used the point of her elbow to ring the doorbell. A symphony of muted chimes echoed through the doorway. In spite of herself she couldn't stifle a nervous giggle. A butler named Jeeves would probably open the door and sweep her off the stoop with a silver-handled crumb brush.

Instead, there was an ungodly racket—something that sounded like a most uncivil bellow. Brow crinkling in puzzlement, Ariel pressed the doorbell again.

She was ready to buzz it a third time when the door exploded open, and every preconception she'd had about this visit disintegrated into wild confusion. The man whose tall frame filled the doorway looked as if he'd battled every dragon in Moey's Crystal Kingdom single-handedly—and lost.

In an instant Ariel took in disheveled sable hair, brown eyes that were more than a little desperate, a mouth that was twisted into a hard line of frustration and fury and something that could only be described as battle fatigue.

"We don't need any cookies, lawn-care services, aluminum windows or pamphlets predicting the end of the world," the man said, yanking at a tie whose knot had already been mangled. "Although, if the world *did* end at the moment, I wouldn't raise much of an objection."

"I...uh, I think the world's safe for the time being," Ariel managed to choke out, her grip tightening on the rabbit. "I'm Ariel Madigan. Moey's teacher."

"Moey's...teacher?" Dark eyes flashed from the unruly tangle of Ariel's curls, to Houdini's wriggling nose. The deeply tanned, undeniably gorgeous face washed dull red. One lean, well-formed hand groped for the tie in an effort to straighten it, and Ariel got the distinct feeling that this man had rarely, if ever, been caught in such a state of disaster.

She flashed him a nervous smile. "I'm in charge of the Abracadabra program at St. Gen's. I was hoping we could talk for a little while."

There was a thud from somewhere inside the house. Kincaid flicked a distracted glance over his shoulder, and jammed his fingers through thick hair. "Miss Madigan, I'm afraid this is not a good time."

"And when is a 'good time' Mr. Kincaid?" she inquired with forced sweetness. "I've sent home half a dozen notes regarding my concern for Melissa in the past month. Two of them I sent through the mail to be certain they couldn't get lost on the way home from school."

"Notes? I don't remember any notes." There was an ominous whitening at the corner of lips that were far too full and sensual for the daddy of three little girls. Dark brows crashed together. "I've been gone a great deal the past two months, but I'm certain my housekeeper would have brought any such communications to my attention."

Ariel flashed him her most winning smile. "Well, since I have your attention now, why don't you invite me in, and we can—"

"Daddy?" The piping little voice made both adults start, and Ariel looked down to see a small hand tugging on Kincaid's expensively tailored, but thoroughly rumpled gray trousers. A cherubic toddler stood like a miniature Lady Godiva, soaking strands of long hair clinging all the way down to her round little bottom. Rivulets of water ran down her bare tummy and sturdy bare legs to pool on the parquet floor beneath, while a black towel trailed, uselessly in her wake.

"Daddy, it still itches." The little girl's lower lip trembled. Face washing an even deeper hue of red, Damon Kincaid swept the child up into his arms, whisking the towel around her, as embarrassed as if he had been the one caught parading around in the buff. The very thought of that lean, hard-muscled body glistening wet was enough to make Ariel's pulses do a tap dance.

Kincaid's gruff voice made her flush as guiltily as though he could read her astonishingly lascivious thoughts, but it was his daughter to whom that quelling tone was directed.

"Sarah Jane, I told you to stay in the tub!" he said exasperatedly. "Dr. Walters says—"

"Dr. Walters smells like cabbage. An' you promised you'd come right back and put soda on me."

"Soda?" Ariel echoed, her less than proper thoughts quashed as her heart was captured by the winsome tyke who was regarding her father with enough righteous indignation for seven little girls. The child scratched at a red rash speckling one chubby arm.

"I *am* coming right back," Kincaid assured her. "Just as soon as Miss Madigan, here, leaves—"

"Miss Mad Again?"

"I'm Moey's teacher. And you must be . . ."

"Sarah. I'm three. You gots a rabbit there." Inquisitive dark eyes fixed on Houdini. "Moey brought a kitty home once, but Mommy made her give it to the pound people 'cause they get hair everywhere. I'm 'llergic, you know."

Ariel grinned, well used to getting mental whiplash from children's abrupt changes of subject. "And what are you allergic *to*, Miss Sarah Jane? Kitties? Rabbits?"

"Chocolate," Kincaid supplied.

The little girl put on a tragical face. "It's my most favoritest thing in the whole world." Sarah sighed with such ecstasy, Ariel laughed aloud.

Seemingly encouraged by the show of amusement, Sarah squirmed out of her father's arms, and Ariel was stricken by how delicious another sight appeared—that of Damon Kincaid's hard-muscled chest, its ridges clearly defined by the clinging fabric of his now-soaked shirt.

She swallowed hard, attempting to fix her attention upon the far safer vision of the man's daughter.

"There it was," Sarah was lamenting. "My most favoritest thing in the whole world smeared all over Ellen's cake. So I just ated it. But then..." The imp glanced up at her father, and grew a trifle subdued. "Then I had to go to the doctor's noffice."

"That's too bad."

"Moey's cryin' 'cause we didn't get to go to the Dabra party at school. She's cried ever since we picked her up after going to the doctor's. An' Ellen's not talkin' to me 'cause the birthday cake gots finger holes in it. An' daddy has to keep me in soda so the spots will go away. I'm in *b-i-g* trouble, Miss Mad Again. An' I think you better go afore you get in trouble, too."

Ariel's cheeks heated. Damon Kincaid was taking great pains to avoid meeting her eyes. In her years of teaching, Ariel had endured more than her share of "disaster days," and she was astonished to find herself feeling mildly sorry for the man who stood, so patently uncomfortable before her. But she quashed the emotion, reminding herself that no matter how good his excuse was for missing the party this time, there were a dozen other instances of his neglect to account for.

"If you'll excuse me," he said in a strained voice. "I'll have my secretary set up a meeting between us as soon as—" he sucked in a deep breath, exhaled. "I may be flying out to Melbourne tomorrow, but as soon as possible, I'll contact—"

A sudden horrific crash and the sound of shattering glass made Ariel all but drop Houdini. With an oath, Damon wheeled, just as child sobs split the air.

Instinctively Ariel bolted after Kincaid, slamming the door behind her as he charged toward the sound. She got fleeting images of exquisitely decorated rooms as he wound through the house to where a stark white kitchen was now flooded with grape juice.

Shards of glass glittered in wicked points all around little bare feet. What had once been a white sailor dress looked as if the Easter bunny had dumped it in a vat of purple egg dye. A girl of about five stood in the center of the disaster, her hands thrust behind her back, her eyes wide with horror.

"Ellen, don't move!" Kincaid's voice was low, firm.

"D-D-Daddy, I'm s-sorry!" the child sobbed. "I didn't w-want to pester you. The pitcher s-slipped."

"Just stand still." Kincaid began picking his way through the glass toward the girl, and Ariel noticed for the first time that his long, narrow feet were encased in nothing but a pair of gray socks. Didn't anybody in this family wear shoes?

"Mr. Kincaid, let me," Ariel began, stepping in front of him. She thrust Houdini into the man's arms, and Kincaid looked as if she'd handed him a snake. Grape juice soaked into the sides of her sandals as she picked her way through the maze of glass toward the little girl—a child whose woebegone face was now set and stubborn, her eyes narrowed with suspicion.

"Don't want you! I want my daddy to get me."

"Your daddy has bare feet just like you. We don't want him to cut his feet," Ariel said in soothing accents. "My sandals will crunch that glass right up."

"I made a big mess." Ellen still glared, but her lower lip trembled. "I'm always making messes."

"It's all right, Ellen." Kincaid's voice. Gentle. But threaded through with the same pain as his daughter's. Ariel glanced back for a heartbeat, and was stunned to see those dark, masculine eyes filled with the same haunting anguish that had drawn her to Moey Kincaid weeks before.

Ariel tore her gaze away, feeling as if something sharp and hot had lanced her heart. She fixed her attention on the child before her.

"You know what, Ellen?" Ariel said in a low, soothing voice. "My brother Jesse did this same thing to our kitchen floor once. He poured a whole six-pack of cola on the tile. But he did it on purpose."

Ellen regarded her, suspicious, but her face brightened just a little at the tale of such naughtiness.

"He—he did it on purpose?"

"Yep. He wanted to use it like a water slide. It worked terrific, too. I think that almost made up for the fact that he had to clean out the shed all by himself as punishment."

She scooped up the little girl, grape juice and all. Ellen Kincaid held herself stiffly, but she rested one small hand upon Ariel's shoulder.

"He must've been the baddest little boy in the whole world," the child said in awed tones.

"If he wasn't, it wasn't for lack of trying," Ariel said, beginning to make her way across the slippery floor. "Maybe we should submit his escapades to the *Guinness Book of World Records* and find out."

A bellow made Ariel jump and it was all she could do to keep her balance as a blur of white rabbit streaked through the air. In a great escape worthy of his namesake, Houdini bolted from Damon Kincaid's grasp, and straight onto the nearest available surface—the glass-topped kitchen table whose center happened to be crowned with an elaborate chocolate birthday cake.

Ariel cried out in dismay, and the man roared a curse as he dove toward Houdini.

There was a sickening crunching noise of glass being stepped on, followed by a soft, smooshy sound as Houdini planted his big back feet smack in the center of gooey chocolate frosting, and swirly blue lettering. Ellen gave a piercing wail, all but deafening Ariel.

In a flash, Houdini made a break for it, zigzagging across the white tile, and onto the cream-colored carpet beyond. Dark smears of frosting left a trail from one end of the room to the other. From beyond, a voice—Ariel recognized as Moey's—cried out in surprise, the rabbit obviously having stumbled into the child's path.

Still holding Ellen, Ariel sloshed through the rest of the grape juice, then raced into the living room. She plopped the little girl safely on the white sofa, and made a lunge for Houdini, but the rabbit's favorite pastime was eluding would-be captors. Despite the combined efforts of Ariel and Moey, Houdini streaked around the room in unadulterated bunny glee.

The rabbit was just making another pass across a white brocade chair in an effort to bolt into the kitchen when Damon upended the empty kitchen trash can, and slammed it down over the animal.

For an instant, Ariel thought Kincaid would strangle the bunny, but when she met the man's eyes she got the sinking feeling that she should be the one on the run.

Hurricane Houdini had struck with a vengeance, and if pictures of the devastation he'd left behind him had been sent to the Center for National Disasters, the Red Cross would have been beating down Damon Kincaid's door. Chocolate was smeared from one end of the room to the other, purple sandal prints marking the path of Ariel giving chase. The grape juice from Ellen's dress had seeped into the cloth of the couch where Ariel had dumped her, the child's eyes round and horrified in her tear-streaked face.

Moey stood gasping a few feet away, her gaze locked on a crystal vase that had been knocked over sometime during the mayhem, its two fresh roses lay bruised on the table, water trickling merrily across a tattered boxed set of J. R. R. Tolkien's *The Lord of the Rings*.

"Your...your books, daddy... " Moey choked out. "Your special books. They're ruined... "

He stalked over to the table, snatching the volumes out of the spreading puddle, the picture of the hobbit Frodo on the cover seeming incongruous framed by Damon Kincaid's large hand. Ariel knew a moment's astonishment that something so filled with fantasy could belong to a man like Damon Kincaid.

She stared at him, but for once in her life she had no idea what to say.

It was Sarah who broke the awful silence. "Daddy," she said, hunkering down to poke at one of the smears on the carpet. "I wonder if the rug is 'llergic..."

"Melissa." Kincaid's voice was terrifyingly level. "I want you to take your sisters upstairs. Now. It seems that Miss Madigan and I are going to have our discussion after all."

Ellen's lower lip quivered, at odds with the belligerent thrust of her jaw. "But what about my birthday party? Nana's coming, an'..."

"I'll call Barringdons, make reservations. It's what I should have done in the first place."

"I want to have my party here!" Ellen shrieked. "Mommy always had it here! And you promised!"

"Ellen, look at this place." There was a hopelessness in Kincaid's voice that wrenched at Ariel's heart. "Honey, I know you're disappointed, but there's nothing I can do—"

The little girl scrambled off the couch, shooting Kincaid a glare filled with anger and hurt. "Nana's right. You never keep your promises."

Ariel saw Damon Kincaid wince as if the child had struck him. He took a step toward Ellen, but the little girl skittered out of his way, flinging herself into Moey's arms.

Ariel's heart broke as she heard Moey crooning to her sister, comforting her, when Moey herself was in such dire need of solace.

"We'll make our own party tomorrow," Moey said. "I'll imagine it all for you—crepe paper and balloons. And it will look like a circus with a lion just like Roary. We'll bring him down from your bed, and..."

Ariel glanced back to Damon Kincaid, who stood, as if barred from the children by one of Moey's invisible walls. And she felt a sudden need to go to him, to comfort him just as Moey was soothing Ellen.

Those dark eyes met hers for an instant, and Ariel couldn't bear to see his pain. She looked down, hastily, her gaze locking on his stocking-clad feet, and all thoughts of comforting Kincaid and his daughters were lost in horror as she noticed another stain on the carpet—bright red blood.

"You cut yourself," she said.

Kincaid held up one hand, weary. "That's the least of my worries. Now if you would be so kind as to get out of here so I can...can do something about this." There was the tiniest crack in his voice, and he ground his fingertips against his eyes.

He looked devastated, overwhelmed, and Ariel knew instinctively that it was not an emotion Damon Kincaid had experienced very often.

She chewed at her bottom lip, feeling agonizingly responsible. "Mr. Kincaid, this was all my fault."

"Unfortunately, it doesn't much matter whose fault it is, does it, Miss Madigan?" He glanced at his watch. "I'll just have to call my mother-in-law and tell her...tell her the party will be at the restaurant. It'll give her one more thing to tally up on her list of my myriad sins."

"No! No, don't move the party! Ellen seems to want it here so much. And I'm sure if we all pitch in, we can get things thrown back together in no time!"

"Miss Madigan, there is absolutely no way to get this place looking liveable in half an hour. And as for the birthday cake—your rabbit finished what Sarah started."

"We'll get another birthday cake—have it delivered. Please, Mr. Kincaid."

"We can do it, Daddy! Honest!" Moey insisted. "Miss Madigan is magic. She can make the mess from pudding paints disappear just by saying 'Abracadabra.'"

A muscle twitched in Kincaid's hard jaw. "I don't care if she single-handedly patched the hole in the ozone. Moey, there is no way—"

"At least let me try," Ariel said. "The trunk of my car is full of stuff left over from the party at school, and there's something that can cover— Oh, never mind. There's no time to explain." She turned to the girls. "Moey, take your sisters upstairs and help them get ready. Plunk Ellen in the tub, and help Sarah dress.'' The girls bolted up the stairs.

She turned back to see Kincaid regarding her as if he'd rather resign himself to this disaster than dare to hope. Ariel crossed the room to where he stood. ''Mr. Kincaid, I know I haven't exactly made a great impression in the five minutes since we've met.''

Kincaid arched an eyebrow with understated eloquence, his lips twisting in a wry grimace. Ariel wondered what it would be like to see them curve with real enjoyment, what it would be like if the tiny creases fanning out from the corners of his eyes crinkled with laughter.

''Despite your first impression, I really am quite competent. I know you don't want Ellen to remember this birthday as the disaster where she spilled grape juice and her party was spoiled. No child deserves to be saddled with such a rotten memory.''

Something haunted, vulnerable crept into those dark eyes.

''My little girls have already suffered enough *bad memories* to last them until they're eighty, Miss Madigan. Ellen's fourth birthday last year among them. If you can...can work a miracle, somehow...I'll make it worth your while.''

Ariel reached up, impulsively smoothing her fingertips across that iron-hard jaw, as if it was the baby-soft cheek of his daughter. She felt him stiffen—but no icy aloofness hardened his features. Rather he looked surprised, unsettled, as if he hadn't expected the simple touch, didn't know how to react to it. The thought made Ariel sad.

''That's what is so wonderful about miracles, Mr. Kincaid,'' she said. ''Miracles are free.''

Something kindled in those dark eyes. Something that made Ariel's heart lurch, her fingers tingle where they were pressed against Damon Kincaid's skin.

''I need a miracle, Miss Madigan,'' Damon Kincaid said softly. ''More than you'll ever know.'' He drew away from her and Ariel watched him limp up the steps, his long, strong fingers still clamped about the set of books, the face of the Ring Bearer visible between his long, strong fingers.

And suddenly Ariel wanted a miracle more desperately than she'd ever wanted anything in her life—not only a miracle for Ellen, and Moey and little Sarah. But for this man with his hard-angled face and his dark eyes that were robbed of dreams.

Dreams. She closed her eyes for a moment, remembering Moey's words to Ellen, the circus party Moey had promised to "imagine" for her. A smile curved Ariel's lips.

She spun toward the door, racing out to where her car was parked, its back seat loaded down with a hodgepodge of party goods. She'd never set a deadline on a miracle before, but she had exactly thirty minutes to pull a happy birthday for Ellen Kincaid out of her hat.

Chapter Three

Damon sat on the edge of the tub, the mirrored walls flinging his reflection back at him, multiplied a dozen times. His fingers clenched, white knuckled where he was applying direct pressure to the ugly gash in his foot, but he knew that it wasn't the wound that had made his face so taut, so pale, or that smudged the dark shadows beneath his eyes.

It had been Ellen's accusations, and Moey comforting her in a way Damon knew he might never be able to. It had been that woman, Ariel Madigan with sunshine in her hair and eyes as bright and innocent and filled with hope as the students she taught.

She looked as if she should be locked away in a schoolroom somewhere—giggling over football stars and groaning over geometry assignments—not running the classroom herself.

Just the sight of her, her cotton-candy lips warm with her smile, had made him feel unutterably old, irreparably jaded. He had never cared for the casual social caresses people were often so free with—mere acquaintances embracing you in the middle of a shopping mall or bussing your cheek at an airport.

But when Ariel Madigan had touched him, with that silky feminine hand, he hadn't felt that instinctive need to draw away, to chill her with an aloof stare. Instead, he had felt an absurd urge to drag her into his arms and bury his face in her hair.

In spite of the fact that his house had been turned into a disaster area and his daughters had been clustered around, he had been excruciatingly aware of the scent of Ariel Madigan, the way that ridiculous cherry-red jumpsuit clung to her small, firm breasts and long, coltish legs. She had reminded him of candied apples, wholesome and sweet, with just the tiniest sharp tang.

Had reminded him of all the simple dreams he'd had when he had lain on his back on the fire escape outside of his mother's apartment, and had stared up at the sky. Before he'd noticed the dirty, crumbling brick of the tawdry apartments above him. Before his mother had taught him the shabbiness of his existence, and made him hunger for this other world he'd fought so hard to become a part of.

He let his lashes drift down, shutting out the face of the man staring back at him from the silvery surface. The man who wasn't certain of anything anymore.

A high-pitched giggle and the sound of feet running down the hallway startled him from his thoughts, and he shook himself, grabbing the first-aid supplies he'd brought from the medicine chest. Dragging the bloodstained towel away from his foot, he examined the gaping cut that stretched from the ball of his foot to his heel, the bleeding scarcely slowed at all by the minutes he'd elevated his foot and put pressure on the wound. He ground his teeth in frustration. There was nothing to be done about it. He'd just have to make do so he could go downstairs and help Miss Madigan put the house to rights.

Grabbing the bottle of peroxide, he unscrewed the lid and held his foot over the tub. Gritting his teeth, he dumped the contents onto the cut.

White-hot pain seared up his leg, his jaw clenched so hard that it ached. After a moment, the agony dulled, and he grabbed a wad of cotton gauze, fashioning a makeshift bandage so that he could cram his foot into his shoe.

With his luck, the blood would overflow the sides, but he'd deal with that later.

Jamming on his shoe, Damon attempted to stand, but his face, a ghastly gray color, swam before him in the mirror. He reached out to steady himself for a moment, then limped out into the hallway, and down the stairs, feeling more than a little woozy.

He kept his eyes trained, unwaveringly, upon the steps, but they seemed to be moving like those in a carnival fun house.

He had just reached the lower landing when he dared to raise his eyes. His jaw dropped, his hand freezing on the stair rail as his gaze swept the room.

The elegant white-upon-white motif that Amanda had cultivated with such ardor looked as if it had been doused in rainbows. A huge, round circle of silk was spread across the floor, concealing the damaged carpet with a dozen vivid colors. The furniture had been draped in what appeared to be sheets decorated with florescent kids on skateboards. A cage formed like a magician's hat was stuck in one corner, that hell-spawned rabbit looking out across the room with satanically docile eyes. While bright, if somewhat crumpled, crepe paper was looped and twisted and taped in wisps of color; it seemed that Ariel Madigan had left scarcely an inch of paint uncovered.

Fat balloons dangled in a cluster from the ceiling lamp, and were crammed in the corners of the room. Stuffed animals, doubtlessly rummaged from the girls' toy boxes, had been caged in front of the floor-to-ceiling picture windows at the far side of the room with twirling bars of yellow crepe paper forming a miniature zoo.

There were even ringmaster's hats, a sequined tutu and child-size clown noses, poufed red wigs and rickracked collars.

Mismatched letters above the door proclaimed Circus Of The Stars, while a tinfoil constellation sparkled below, each star carrying one of the girls' names.

Even the stash of presents Damon had been so proud of was displayed to the best advantage—atop a table made to look like one of those stands where elephants balance on one foot.

Moey had claimed that Ariel Madigan worked magic. And looking around the room, he half expected to find the woman wriggling her nose like the witch on the 1960's sitcom.

How had she done it? Taken the shambles that had been his living room, and made it more festive than his hours of preparation had?

God knew it was flamboyant and gaudy enough to give Eve heart failure, but it was worlds away from the total destruction of half an hour ago. Why was it that the mere sight of it made Damon feel aggravated, oddly frustrated and more inadequate than ever?

He gritted his teeth against the emotions, knowing that logically, he should be singing hosannas to the woman for what she'd managed to do. But he couldn't help hoping that, like that television witch, she had vanished the moment the house was put together again. That way he could send her a plant and a generous check and spare himself the unsettling sensation of looking into those fairy-tale eyes to thank her.

"Daddy! Daddy!"

He staggered as Moey and Sarah barreled into him like human cannonballs. Damon glanced down to see his daughters looking every bit as tasteful as the room. He had a fleeting impression of tumbled outfits and hair ribbons set askew on half-combed curls. And yet he couldn't remember the last time he had seen his children's faces lit up with such delight.

"It's a circus! She made it a circus!" Moey whirled around, with enough energy to light up the whole city of Chicago.

"Did you see the nephalants an' lions?" Sarah bubbled. "Be 'tareful, Daddy, or they're going to eat you up!"

"Sarah knows they're only pretend, Daddy," Moey explained hastily, her eyes holding a shadow of wariness that troubled him. "Sarah gets to be the animal trainer, because Ellen doesn't want to."

"I don't know what I want to be yet." Damon glanced over to see Ellen standing near the crepe-paper cage that held her much-adored stuffed lion, her chin stuck out at that mulish angle that had become so familiar since Amanda had died. "I didn't say I wanted a circus birthday. Moey was just imagining it."

Frustration jolted through Damon, Ellen's characteristic stubbornness eating away at his patience.

"Ellen, look at this place," Damon said, trying to infuse his voice with enough enthusiasm to sway the child. "I've never seen such great decorations."

But instead of drumming up enthusiasm, his words only made Ellen's scowl darken. "Mommy never had circuses and stuff at our birthday. I liked hers better."

Damon went over to where Ellen stood, and knelt down. "Ellen, Mommy can't be here anymore." He swallowed hard. "There's nothing you or I can do about that. We just have to do the best we can."

It was Moey who slipped up beside Ellen, stroking her hair just like Amanda had sometimes done. "Ellen, Miss Madigan says that Mommy will be a part of us forever. That we can't ever lose her, because there are all kinds of pictures of her inside of our hearts. Maybe you could imagine that Mommy was the trapeze lady, and she's wearing that sparkly blue dress with all the diamonds on it."

Ellen's gaze fixed on Moey's face. Her lip stopped trembling. "You mean the dress she wore when Daddy took her to the ballet?"

The words were a knife thrust to Damon's gut. The ballet. The last time he had been with his wife. Amanda's eyes had been puffy and reddened beneath her perfectly applied mascara. He had tried so damned hard to get her to talk to him, to tell him why she'd been crying. She'd asked why he should care....

He levered himself to his feet, and turned away to hide his anguish. But as he faced the archway that led to the kitchen, he saw a splash of vivid red jumpsuit, a fairy-princess face framed in a mop of gold curls. Saw blue eyes that were soft and aching. Aching for his children.

And it made him angry that she had somehow pried her way into their emotions, touched parts of them that were raw with grief. How could she understand what his children had suffered? What he had been through? How dare she even presume to stand there, looking at them with such empathy in those glowing eyes?

He straightened his shoulders, determined to hurl up a shield of aloofness, of distance, between this woman and his children. "It's amazing what you managed to accomplish. A hired birthday service couldn't have done any better."

She smiled, not at all touched by the chill in his voice. "It's the least I could do, considering that it was my rabbit who trashed the place. The cake even arrived a few minutes ago. If I could just find some candles, we'd be all set."

She swiped one hand against the hip of her jumpsuit as if to rub off a bit of dirt. Smudges that had to be grape juice dappled one of her sleeves. A bit of crepe paper was stuck in her hair.

She looked mussed and rumpled—worlds different from the elegant, perfectly groomed women who graced executive suites and strolled down Worthington Drive with their Shar-Pei puppies on rhinestone leashes. Damon was stunned to feel a swift, sharp stab of desire—an emotion that hadn't touched him in the year since he'd buried his wife. The power of the need stunned him, unnerved him. Because even in the years since he and Amanda had discovered sex in the back of his rattletrap car, he had never felt this kind of physical jolt.

"Mr. Kincaid?" It was the voice Ariel Madigan would use on an eight-year-old caught daydreaming, and it grated on his nerves. "Do you have some more candles stuck away somewhere, or should I run up to the convenient mart to grab some?"

"Candles?"

"Birthday candles. There were some on the cake Houdini smashed, so the rest of the box must be around here somewhere."

"I don't have the slightest idea where my housekeeper would have put them. And there's no point tearing the kitchen apart searching. We're lucky Ellen has a cake. Candles aren't important."

"But I have to blow 'em out, or I won't get a wish!" Ellen wailed in a voice bordering on hysteria. "Birthday wishes always come true. Always...."

"For God's sake, honey, that's just a superstition," Damon said, exasperated. "Your grandmother is going to be here any minute. And besides, with all this circus stuff you won't even notice the candles are missing."

"Mr. Kincaid, the candles must be here somewhere," Ariel Madigan said in soothing accents. "I just didn't want to go rummaging around in your drawers without asking. I'm sure I can find something—"

Damon wheeled, the sharp pain in his foot only hardening the glare that had made the presidents of international corporations back down. "Miss Madigan, I told you that candles are immaterial."

"Maybe to you," the woman said, eyes darkening, not with nervousness, but with anger. "Ellen apparently doesn't feel the same way."

"Well, there's nothing I can do about it. I can't pull candles out of thin air."

The muted orchestra of chimes made Damon's fist clench, and he spun toward the front door. Ellen was whimpering, little gasps that were a certain precursor to a bout of wailing loud enough to be heard at Wrigley Field. Ariel Madigan was glaring at him as if he were Simon Legree, and now Eve would be flying in on her broomstick, doubtless stirring things up with her sickly sweet sympathy, all the while, her eyes glittering with pleasure at being proven right—*again*.

He closed his eyes, and for one moment, pictured the serenity and elegance of a high-priced hotel in Australia. Guilt was swift, crushing, and he cursed himself as a coward.

The doorbell sounded a second time, and Damon started toward it, but he was cut off midstride as Ariel flung him a look of blatant defiance, yanked a crystal candle tree off a table and snatched five of the eight scented candles from their holders. Then she wheeled and stalked into the kitchen.

Damon's jaw tightened, indecision racking him. He wanted to stomp after her, snatch the candles out of her hands—tell her that one did not stick room candles on a birthday cake. He wanted to take hold of the arm encased in that slim red sleeve, and tell her to get the hell out of his house. He wanted to demand to know what to do—how to make Ellen's birthday a decent one, when he had already made so many mistakes.

Instead he limped to the door and tugged it open.

Eve Laughton-Smith stood on the stoop, her perfectly coiffured head turned so that she could stare at the somewhat disreputable pink bug parked in front of her gray sports car. The astonished disdain on features regularly touched up by the highest priced plastic surgeon in Chicago was so comical, it would have made Damon laugh if he hadn't been so stressed.

Suddenly the thought of table candles on Ellen's cake didn't disturb him, as he thought of the pleasure he could take in Eve's reaction.

"Hello, Eve," he said in his most civil tones.

Amanda's mother spun around, and he was struck again by how much Eve and Amanda had looked alike—Eve's favorite tale was the recounting of how often they had been mistaken for sisters. Only their eyes had been different— Eve's a chilly gray, while Amanda's had been a soft green that made Damon think of some timid woodland creature, despite his wife's outward aura of elegance.

"Damon, what is that... that *thing* in front of your house?"

"I don't know what you mean. What *thing?*"

"That—that car! It's an abomination. Amanda would have been struck dumb in horror to see it there, spoiling the landscape of your house. You must instruct your help to park somewhere less conspicuous."

"The car doesn't belong to my *help,* Eve," Damon said, surprised at the slight grin tugging at the corner of his mouth. "It belongs to Moey's teacher."

Eve looked as if she'd choked on a gob of caviar. "Don't even begin to tell me that a nun at St. Genevieve's would be seen in such a thing."

"Miss Madigan isn't a nun," Damon remarked wryly. "If she were, I doubt the convent would still be standing."

"Well, whatever she is, perhaps you might tell me what she is doing here, at your home, at this ungodly hour?"

"Conducting a torrid affair in front of the children." Damon couldn't help but goad her. But at the stricken expression on the woman's face, he relented. "Come on, Eve. It's hardly three in the morning. Miss Madigan merely stopped over to discuss some things about Melissa, and—" He hesitated for a moment, hardly willing to recount the happenings that had made Ariel Madigan stay on. But it seemed God had decided to spare him that, because, at that instant, Eve's face washed scarlet.

"My God in heaven," she gasped, one perfectly manicured hand pressed to her heart as she stared into the room beyond. *"What have you done to Amanda's living room?"*

"Made it into a circus," Damon said, his face deadpan.

"A—A *what?*"

"You know, a circus. Lion tamers and human cannonballs and clowns riding bicycles across high wires."

Like one in a trance, Eve wandered down through the entryway to the room Ariel had splashed in hues as vivid and varied as those in a child's paint box.

"Of all the... the ridiculous... It looks like some tawdry hooker's gown! My God, it's the most tasteless thing I've ever laid eyes on."

"Well, then," a spritely voice came from the door to the kitchen, "you've obviously never been to my apartment."

Eve spun around, and Damon turned to see Ariel hurrying out of the kitchen, her face lit by a welcoming smile. She extended a juice-stained hand toward Eve. "You must be the children's grandmother. I'm Melissa's teacher, Miss Madigan. But everyone calls me Ariel."

"Ariel?" Eve echoed, her eyes all but popping from her head. Lines of disapproval creased her face, and she pointedly ignored the hand Ariel had offered to her so openly. For some reason, Eve's flagrant scorn set Damon's teeth on edge.

Blatantly unaffected, Ariel stuffed her hands in her back pockets, and flashed Damon a grin, those aquamarine eyes brimming with amusement and sympathy, her dimpled smile speaking volumes regarding her opinion of Eve.

"Mr. Kincaid, thank you so much for allowing me to talk to you tonight," Ariel said. "I know my timing was not exactly convenient, what with all your preparations for Ellen's birthday."

Damon battled to keep a straight face, but there was something irresistible about the twin imps twinkling in Ariel Madigan's eyes. "Don't mention it, Miss Madigan," he said, the corner of his mouth twitching with a repressed grin, as he said in a low voice. "Don't mention *any* of it. Ever again."

The woman's face positively glowed with delight as she extended her hand to him. "Believe me, I won't." He enfolded that juice-stained hand in his, a strange wrenching sensation deep in his chest as he felt the warmth in it, saw that the nails on her fingers were bitten like a child's. He dropped her hand as if it had burned him.

"Well, I'd best be on my way." Was her voice a trifle unsteady, or had he imagined it? "Mr. Kincaid . . . can we talk some more before you leave on your business trip?" There was such a hopeful, trusting light in her eyes that Damon could only nod.

"Of course."

At that instant, Moey spilled out of the kitchen. Eve opened her arms to the little girl, but Moey charged past her, flinging herself against Ariel, little Sarah bundling along in her sister's wake.

"No, Daddy, no!" Moey cried. "You're not going to let Miss Madigan go home!"

"She gots to help me tame the lions!" Sarah tugged on his pant leg until he looked down into her thick-lashed eyes. "She gots to, Daddy, or they'll eat me up, an' then you won't have a Sarah Jane anymore."

"Don't be absurd, girls," Eve cut in, her voice edged with irritation and just a shadow of hurt. "Melissa's teacher hardly belongs at a family birthday party."

Ariel hunkered down, drawing the children close. "It's sweet of you to invite me, but your grandma's right. You can tell me all about it, later."

"But the lions . . . !" Sarah squealed. "They'll gobble me down in a single gulp!"

The smile Ariel bestowed on her was like sunshine. "Your daddy's big and strong. A real tough guy." She shot Damon a teasing glance. "I'm sure he can keep them in line."

"No, he can't." Ellen stood, framed in the doorway to the kitchen. The tears that had threatened a few minutes ago had been replaced by that steely determination Damon had always found so astonishing for a five-year-old. "He doesn't know anything about lions. He never took us to a single circus."

Damon winced inwardly as the words cut deep, joining countless other slashes this blunt, rebellious little tintype of himself had inflicted in the past year. "Ellen, I—"

"It's *my* birthday," the child said, hands on hips. "*I* want her to stay."

"Sweetheart, you can tell me about it later," Ariel said, hustling over to the child, attempting to take Ellen in her arms.

But Ellen tugged away, glowering up at her from beneath lowered brows. "Sarah likes hugs, and Moey's the sweetheart. I'm the stubborn girl, and I say I want you to stay."

Damon was stricken by the child's perception of herself, saw in Ariel's face the same quick flash of concern.

It was Eve who spoke. "This kind of behavior is what comes of leaving children in the charge of hired help. Ellen, this is no way for a young lady to—"

In that very instant, Damon decided. "It's Ellen's birthday," he cut in, more shaken by the child's words than he cared to reveal. "If she wants Miss Madigan to stay, then she stays...unless," he added as an afterthought, "unless you have other plans, Miss Madigan?"

Those blue eyes swept from his face to Ellen's and back to his. "I... Well, actually..." She hesitated a moment. Then smiled. "I'd love to stay."

Favoring his uninjured foot, Damon went to Ellen and tipped her chin up. "Would you like that, Ellen?" he asked. She nodded, with a fierceness that would have been adorable, were it not for the wariness in her eyes.

"Then Miss Madigan can be your guest. As long as you realize one thing, Ellen Kincaid. You're *my* sweetheart." He trailed his fingers over her short dark curls.

She yanked away. He'd said something wrong. He knew it as he watched her join her sisters—Moey glowing with happiness, Sarah bubbling over with excitement, Ellen, triumphant, but holding none of a child's usual birthday glee.

"Damon, this is the most...most absurd thing I've ever heard of! You're spoiling that child. She'll be completely unmanageable, if she's not so already."

"Come on, now," Ariel interceded. "Granting a child's birthday wish can hardly be called spoiling—"

"Miss Madigan—is that your name? This is no concern of yours. I am certain that when Amanda researched schools and found St. Genevieve's, she had no idea it would be staffed by people like you. I have half a mind to call your superiors."

Damon saw Ariel's face pale, her smile fading. Irritation at his mother-in-law stirred through him. "Eve, this is none of your affair. You'll not interfere."

"Interfere? If I don't, these children will be ruined!"

Ariel stepped between them, laying a hand on Damon's arm. "The only thing that is going to be ruined tonight is Ellen's birthday," she said softly, gesturing to where the child stood, staring at them from across the room. "Please. This isn't a time for adult disagreements."

"H-how dare you presume," Eve began to huff, Damon's own cheeks heating.

He straightened. "Miss Madigan's right, Eve. God knows, we can talk about this later."

"Later. Always later," Eve couldn't seem to resist getting in a parting shot. "You mark my words, Damon. You'll live to regret the way you are dealing with these children."

Damon turned to join Ariel Madigan as she bustled over to rig the children out in clown noses and ringmaster hats. But as he fastened the sequined tutu about Ellen's small waist, Eve's words echoed in his head.

He stared into the belligerent face of his little daughter and wondered if his mother-in-law was right.

The lions were tamed, the clown act was over, the cake with its circus motif was nothing but a plateful of crumbs.

Ariel leaned against the fireplace, as far away from Eve Laughton-Smith as possible and watched as Ellen and her sisters played with the stash of birthday toys while Damon limped around, gathering up the wrapping paper and boxes.

The presents Ellen Kincaid had received had probably cost more than Ariel's last paycheck. And yet, as Ariel looked at the children, she couldn't help remembering birthdays from her own childhood. There had been far fewer presents, bought at the local dime store instead of at some exclusive toy shop. But there had also been far more delight, squealing and squabbling in the midst of her multitude of brothers and sisters.

Damon Kincaid's children played quietly, carefully, almost as if they feared the toys would break. And whenever Ellen or Sarah bordered upon boisterous, Ariel noticed that it was Moey's hand that stole out to hush them, or the slightest shake of her head that made them quiet down.

It was sad, somehow, to watch them. Sad to watch their father, as well. In the faculty room at St. Gen's, Ariel had been determined to view Damon Kincaid as a monster—a neglectful jerk who ignored his children. It had been easier that way. But this man—who had looked so desperately uncomfortable when Ellen had wanted to paste the ringmaster's fake mustache on him, this man with his eyes shadowed with confusion, and what must be grief—was worlds away from the Yuppie Three-Piece-Suit Ariel had expected to confront when she had knocked upon the Kincaid door.

It made her uncomfortable. Set her off balance. And she caught herself watching him time and time again as the party wore on. His hair was tousled by restless fingers, his face, a strong one, a hard one, with a stubborn, square jaw, and lips that whispered of pirate captains and highwaymen in the romances Ariel loved to take with her to the beach.

There was an edginess about him that never seemed to fade, as if he were waiting for something to happen. And

Ariel kept having the urge to reach out her hand, to stop him.

Stop him from what? she thought wryly, as he carried the garbage out to the kitchen.

"Ellen, quit that." Eve's voice broke into Ariel's thoughts. "You'll rip that dress."

Ariel glanced over to see that the dress in question belonged to Ellen's birthday doll—the child engaged in that inevitable rush to strip away all the plaything's finery to see what lay underneath. Ellen pouted, but continued to tug at the golden-curled doll's ruffled petticoats.

"She's going to be a trapeze girl," Ellen said. "Moey's going to make her a suit out of toilet paper."

Eve blanched, and went on scolding, but Ariel was pleased to see Ellen Kincaid holding her own against her dictatorial grandmother.

Ariel glanced at her watch, knowing that it was time she should be going. Shoving herself away from the fireplace, she traced Kincaid's steps into the kitchen. The room was empty, but there was a rustling from beyond a half-open door at the far end of the spacious kitchen.

Ariel went to it, and pushed the door open. Kincaid's head jerked up, and he shifted on the wooden bench where he sat, jerking his leg down from where he had it propped up on the edge of the sink. One hand still gripping his foot, he angled himself away from her, as if he were trying to hide something. His face was ghastly pale against a backdrop of winter coats and mittens, ski equipment and laundry supplies, but a dark flush crept along his cheekbones.

"Mr. Kincaid . . . is anything wrong?"

"I'll be out in a minute," he said hastily. "Just wait in the kitchen—"

"It's nothing important. I just wanted to say that I'm leav— Oh my God." Her stomach lurched as her gaze fixed on what he'd been attempting to hide. Bloody towels lay in the sink of what looked to be a mudroom. The leather of the shoe he'd discarded moments before was stained dark and wet. The sock he'd stripped away had enough blood stains to satisfy the star of a slasher movie.

One of Kincaid's hands was pressing yet another towel against the bottom of his foot, and the pale cast to his features took on a whole new meaning.

"Your foot," Ariel said, stunned. "You said it wasn't bad."

"It isn't," he said between gritted teeth. "In fact, I'd be ready for a set of tennis if the damned thing would just quit bleeding."

Ariel dropped down, Indian-style, onto the tile in front of him, and peeled his fingers away from the towel.

"Miss Madigan, it's hardly necessary—"

"The shark in *Jaws* didn't leave this much blood. Now let me look at it." She stared him down, determined. And after a moment, he released his hold on the towel.

Gently Ariel unwrapped the cloth, baring a long, narrow foot. It was warm in her hand, somehow intimate, despite the circumstances. And she felt her palm tingle where it brushed against his skin. Squelching the feelings, she angled his foot so she could get a good look at its sole, and what she saw there made her stomach pitch.

A deep gash gaped like a sickening grin from his heel to the ball of his foot, the skin surrounding the wound an angry red and purple, doubtless from all the walking Kincaid had done in the two hours since he'd hurt it. Hollows and creases had been pressed into the surrounding area and the whole foot had begun to swell.

"Mr. Kincaid, from what I read in Moey's file, you're supposed to be some kind of whiz-kid genius," Ariel said, exasperated. "I don't suppose that it occurred to you when you were making all those trips in here to mop up the blood that you might—just might—need stitches in this thing?"

He blew out his breath, and ground his fingertips against his temple. "I figured it would be all right. The pressure of the shoe and my walking around on it slowed the bleeding down some. Ellen was already so upset...."

"She might be even more upset if you passed out from loss of blood, or got gangrene and wound up losing a foot. Of all the idiotic male stupidity—" Ariel scolded, but she was oddly touched by his words, surprised, yet not surprised, that he had endured the pain rather than risk dealing Ellen any further disappointment.

"I figured once the party was over, I could jerry-rig a butterfly bandage, or tape it up, or—"

"If you gathered up every monarch in Illinois you wouldn't have enough butterflies to hold this cut together. Looks to me like you're going to be visiting the emergency room."

"No," he said so sharply, Ariel's gaze flew to his face in astonishment. His mouth was a white line, his whole body tense.

"Mr. Kincaid..." she began, unsettled. "A doctor has to see this cut, and the only place you're going to find one on duty at this time of night is the hospital. I've seen enough playground accidents to know when someone needs stitches. This cut looks like it's clear to the bone. Leave this wound open, and you'll be in serious trouble."

He looked away, his fist clenching.

Heavenly days, was the man *afraid* of getting a few stitches? Her brother Jake had always been a little squeamish when it came to blood. The rest of the Madigan brood had teased him unmercifully.

Ariel couldn't help but smile. "Getting stitches won't be so bad, Mr. Kincaid. I speak with the voice of experience."

"I don't give a damn about the stitches," he said with a savagery that made her stare.

"Then what is it?"

A muscle in his jaw worked, but he said nothing.

"Is it the girls? Do you need someone to watch them? I'd be happy to stay while your mother-in-law drives you—"

"Eve can't . . . I won't let her go there."

"Okay. I'll take you."

"I can drive myself."

Confused, aggravated, Ariel climbed to her feet. "Pale as you look, you wouldn't make it to the end of the block, mister. Not to mention the fact that if you tried to use the brake with that foot, you'd probably go through the roof." She crossed to where a clean towel lay folded on top of the dryer. "Be reasonable. Get your foot wrapped up in this, and—"

"No. I'll put on my shoe."

"You've already mashed your foot in there once. Why you would want to do something that crazed again, I can't imagine."

Every sinew of his body fairly reeking with obstinacy, he grabbed up his shoe and jammed his toes into the opening.

Exasperation, anger flooded Ariel's veins as she heard his low groan, saw his features whiten as he worked to pull the shoe over his injury. He hadn't said a word, but if a psychic medium had been within a radius of a hundred miles, the person would be bouncing off the walls with the vibes Kincaid was throwing off.

"You're just going to hurt yourself more," Ariel warned, disgusted.

With a savage curse, he gave a fierce yank on the leather, his head arching back as his heel slid into place. Beads of sweat clung to his upper lip, trickled from his temples down to the angular jut of his jaw.

"Lady, if I want to cut my foot off at the ankle, it's none of your business," Kincaid snarled.

Ariel's mouth dropped open, outrage boiling up inside her as she stared at this man who had briefly, ever so briefly touched her with a shading of vulnerability, of sensitivity— qualities that could never have existed in such a hard-edged face. He must have been possessed by an alien during the time he had smiled, caressed his daughters. "Mr. Kincaid," she said in deadly measured accents. "You can take your attitude and—"

"Miss Madigan, I appreciate all you've done for Moey and Ellen. And the truth is, I do need a ride to the emergency room. But if you're going to spend the drive lecturing me on proper first aid, I'd rather walk.''

"The way you're acting at the moment, Mr. Kincaid, it would serve you right if I let you.'' Ariel glared at him, her own anger blazing hot. She had half a mind to let him be a typical idiotic male, ignoring how hurt he was, but the memory of three small faces made her leash her temper.

"Fortunately,'' she said, "unlike you, I don't have the temper of a grizzly bear. So I won't say another word, as long as you get your buns into my car. Now.''

Kincaid's eyes widened, the rich brown glittering with anger and frustration, but Ariel didn't wait to hear his retort. She spun and stalked out of the room, battling to get hold of her temper.

"Mrs. Laughton-Smith?'' she said as she approached the woman sitting stiffly on the edge of the couch. "I'm afraid Mr. Kincaid and I are going to have to slip out for an hour or so.''

The woman's eyes went positively arctic. "Excuse me?''

"There was a little accident before you arrived, and it seems that he cut his foot. He patched it up himself so he could make it through the party, but it's going to need stitches.''

"Daddy...hurt?'' Moey's voice was small, sick, and Ariel felt the child's hand grasp at her leg.

"Is my daddy going to get dead?'' Sarah demanded, tears trickling down her cheeks.

"Oh, for heaven's sake,'' Eve Laughton-Smith snapped. "Don't be ridiculous! He's been walking around all evening.''

But as Ariel looked down into the children's small faces, the force of the terror she saw there slammed like a fist into her stomach. It was as if they were expecting their father to vanish, disappear just as their mother had. Had Damon Kincaid seen that expression on their faces before? If so, Ariel wouldn't have been able to find it in her heart to condemn him, even if he'd tried to conceal a compound fracture.

"Your daddy is going to be just fine!" Ariel scooped the little girl into her arms. "It's nothing serious. Just a little cut. But we want the doctor to look at it."

"He cut himself on the pitcher, didn't he?" Ellen asked, stricken. "The pitcher I dropped."

"Yes," Ariel said honestly, "but the reason he stepped on the glass was because of my rabbit. So if it's anyone's fault, honey, it's mine."

Ellen looked so relieved, Ariel had to smile.

"Now, if your grandmother will just baby-sit you guys for a little while, I can get your daddy to the hospital and get this over with. Just between us," she said, conspiratorially to the girls huddled around her, "your daddy is about as cranky as Oscar the Grouch the day after Telly Monster cleaned out his garbage can."

She was rewarded with soft giggles and tremulous smiles from Ellen and Sarah, but Moey looked into her eyes, her little brow still creased with worry.

"Daddy doesn't mean to be crabby, Miss Madigan," Moey said softly. "It's just that he has this big hurt inside him."

He has this big hurt inside him...

Ariel let her hand drift down to caress Moey's cheek, and she wondered how someone so small could be so infinitely wise.

Chapter Four

Cosgrave Memorial Hospital rose up out of a maze of concrete highways, the arteries that carried endless streams of traffic from the suburb into the heart of Chicago. Damon stood on the sidewalk where Ariel Madigan had dropped him off on her way to park the car, and stared up at the sprawling red brick building before him. He knew he should just walk through the plate-glass doors, cross into the waiting room and join the rest of the Friday-night revelers whose celebrations had taken an unexpected turn. But he couldn't seem to make himself move as his eyes locked upon the red neon sign blinking on the building above him.

TRAUMA CENTER. The words glowed against the aged brick, as sickeningly familiar to him as the scene of a recurring nightmare. The only differences were the light bulb behind the letter *U* had been fixed and a raft of magenta petunias had replaced the marigolds edging the shrubs at the entryway.

But there was an eerie sameness about the place, a chilling feeling of having stepped through a window in time.

Damon shifted his gaze to where the ambulances stood ready in a parking garage across the way. The paramedics were replenishing medical supplies while celebrating the Chicago Cubs' dramatic ninth-inning rally against the Mets.

But in his mind's eye, Damon could hear the sounds of that other night, feel the clawing terror in him, the sick sense of helplessness as he charged through a maze of medical personnel racing about, desperately trying to deal with the victims of the three-car pileup on a rain-slickened overpass.

A violent shudder worked through Damon's body, and he shook himself, trying to banish the images from his mind. But if he lived to be a hundred, he knew he would never forget the smell of blood and fear and death. Would never forget wading through the aftermath of the accident— looking for Amanda among the other victims and their terrified families.

And he would never forget the hideous sense of foreboding he had felt when a solemn, bespectacled intern had drawn him into a secluded area and told him his wife was dead.

Damon raked a shaking hand through his hair, the memories crowding agonizingly close. The intern had taken him down to the morgue where fatalities were processed. And Damon had been forced to identify Amanda.

He had reached out, closing her fingers in his own, and they had been chilled, lifeless; the way her eyes had been for longer than he could remember.

And as he let Amanda go forever, all he'd been able to think about was his daughters, tucked up safe in their beds, fully expecting that when morning came Amanda would be there to braid their hair and feed them breakfast and listen to their endless chatter.

And of all the guilt he had carried the past year, the most crushing of all had been the undeniable truth that it had not been his wife who he mourned, a wife he'd somehow lost years ago. Rather it had been the mother of his children—Moey's loss, and Ellen's and Sarah Jane's—that had devastated him beyond imagining.

The click of footsteps on concrete intruded on his thoughts. He turned to see Ariel hurrying toward him with a graceful stride, her curls in a windblown disorder, a purse the size of the state of Montana slung over her shoulder. Her lips were compressed in patent disapproval.

"Mr. Kincaid, I dropped you off here so you could get off your hurt foot, not stand here, bleeding all over the sidewalk."

Anger raked quick, harsh, over the rawness in Damon's chest. And he wanted nothing more than to drive this woman away from him, and not let her or anyone see how just the sight of this place shook him deep inside. He schooled his face into hard, cold lines.

"I know that you are accustomed to working with children who can't even find their way to the bathroom without help, Miss Madigan. But I'm not a third-grader. I assure you, I'm quite capable of handling the rest of this myself."

Her cheeks paled visibly in the ring of light cast down by a nearby street lamp. "You're right, Mr. Kincaid. You're obviously not a third-grader. A third-grader would have had the sense to go inside. Now let's just go and—"

"Let's not," Damon said firmly. "*I'll* go on into the hospital. *You* go climb back into that car of yours and go... well, go wherever it was you were supposed to spend Friday night in the first place."

"I was supposed to be celebrating the end of school with a bunch of my friends—and believe me, Mexican food and margaritas wouldn't have given me half the indigestion your temper has. But unless you want to walk home, I'd better stay."

"Ever heard of public transit? I'll take a cab."

"You'll—"

The sharp wail of a siren sliced through Damon's nerves like a machete. Within moments, an ambulance careened up the driveway, pulling to a stop in the roofed entryway. Paramedics spilled out of the vehicle, emergency room personnel bursting out of the door.

Damon stared, mesmerized in horror as they slid the stretcher out of the back of the ambulance.

"A DWI," one of the paramedics barked out to a trauma nurse with bright red hair. "Slammed into the back of a semi."

"Ah, the joys of being the closest hospital to half the accidents in the city," the nurse flung back at him, already busy with some medical procedure. "How bad is it?"

"Oh, I think the guy will make it long enough to swill down another gallon of gin."

The automatic doors opened as they pushed the stretcher into the hospital. Damon stared at the doors, unwilling to face the woman who stood, now so quiet, beside him.

"It was here, wasn't it?" she asked softly. "This was the hospital where your wife..." She paused for a moment, and he could feel her empathy as if it were a living thing. "No wonder you were acting so strangely."

"Yes, Miss Madigan, no wonder I'm acting so strange," he said in a harsh voice. "Now just go home and leave me the hell alone."

Jaw clenching against the throbbing in his foot, Damon limped into the sterile hospital, leaving Ariel Madigan and her soft angel eyes behind him.

Ariel perched on the edge of a brick planter, watching the stars in the piece of sky visible beyond the hospital's towering walls. Her father had always told her that stars were wishes, dreams that were so bright and beautiful they lit up the heavens. And some of her favorite memories were lying on her stomach in the night-dark hayloft and looking out, trying to imagine the people who had sent those dreams up to the sky, what their wishes were, their hopes.

But as she watched a shooting star streak across the sky tonight, she wondered if Damon Kincaid had any dreams at all. Any wishes except to be free of the pain that seemed to burn deep inside him, making his sensual, full lips edged with hardness, his dark eyes intense, not with passion or pleasure, but with a kind of soul-weary despair.

Leave me the hell alone. His words echoed in her memory. She had been tempted to take him at his word, to climb into her car and drive away... away from the havoc he wreaked on her senses, away from the dangerous magnetism of his eyes, his face.

But in the end she hadn't been able to bring herself to leave him. Alone. So alone.

Alone as he struggled with tending to his daughters. Alone as he wrestled with the reality of his wife's death. Alone as he dealt with his mother-in-law's obvious disapproval and subtle sabotage of the relationship he had with his children.

He had been such a study in contrasts as he had stalked through those gleaming metal doors—his shoulders so broad and strong—heavily muscled beneath the fabric of his shirt. His whole physique was powerful, his very essence one of driving ambition, hard-won success.

Only the faintest hint of vulnerability had lurked beneath the high-tech businessman facade. The shape of his hands and the intensity in his eyes seemed more fitting for an artist or a poet than the fast-track executive she had been more than ready to dislike on sight. She had wanted to go to him, slip her hand into his strong one. She had wanted to brush her lips across his, soften the hard line of his mouth with hers.

In comfort—she protested inwardly. *Only in comfort.*

Her whole life, Ariel had been as free and open with her affection as the children she taught. But Damon Kincaid was no eight-year-old who was hurting. And the soothing caresses Ariel had lavished on her small charges would be a radically different experience if she were to reach out to Damon Kincaid.

The shoulders that would lie beneath her encircling arm would not be narrow, fragile, but rather broad, encased in a thick sheath of muscle. The cheeks would be roughened with the merest hint of stubble. The scent of bubble gum and baby shampoo that wreathed the kids Ariel adored would be supplanted by the subtle, expensive cologne that mingled so perfectly with Kincaid's own rawly masculine scent.

She closed her eyes, imagining a totally different kind of caress...envisioned that beautifully shaped, sensual mouth beneath the soothing whisper of her own.

And the mere thought made her heart lurch while a strange tingling sensation burned in the curves of her lips.

She pressed her fingertips against her mouth as if to crush the feelings, hide them, her mind roving back to the faculty room and Nancy's warning, which seemed a lifetime ago.

It was unprofessional to get involved with one of her cases outside of school. It wasn't her job. Wasn't her place. It could cause far more damage than good.

And Ariel knew, even now, that in the grand scheme of things, Nancy was probably right. In most instances, such involvement was neither necessary nor beneficial. But this time Ariel hadn't been able to stop herself from crossing that imaginary line between caring for Melissa Kincaid and loving her. What if she was just as clumsy about shielding her emotions when it came to the child's father?

Don't be ridiculous, Ariel berated herself sharply. *After tonight you won't ever have to see Kincaid again...except,* she thought wryly, *at school functions.* And Ariel couldn't think of a more effective way to douse an inferno of desire than to be beneath the sharp eyes of Sister Thomasetta.

Ariel felt the hint of a grin tug at her mouth as the image of the daunting nun rose in her mind.

No, the stirrings of attraction Ariel felt were only natural. She *was* human, after all—far from immune to a nice pair of biceps. She would just wait here until Damon Kincaid was finished, and take him and his biceps back to Worthington Drive.

She glanced over her shoulder through the plate-glass door, checking the entryway for the dozenth time. The entrance to the trauma center's rooms was just visible from where she sat. Watching the stream of patients being processed, treated and released provided some small diversion. The usual Friday-night crowd of knife wounds and drug overdoses would have depressed her unbearably, had it not been for the few cases she found vaguely amusing.

A boy of twelve had exited an hour ago, chattering delightedly with his much-abashed father about a play at home plate in the father/son game the two had evidently been involved in. It seemed that the father had been a hero. And Ariel had wondered if the man thought that those hard-won laurels had been worth the price of the cast that encased his arm.

A four-year-old, whose neck was garbed in ropes of gaudy costume beads had evidently attempted to complete her dress-up ensemble by shoving a particularly lovely bead into one nostril.

For over an hour, now, Ariel had watched the stream of patients—all of them being bullied or cajoled, scolded or fussed over by someone who loved them. Even the druggies and gang members had been accompanied by someone—the policemen who had collared them on the street.

It seemed unfair that only Damon Kincaid had gone in there alone.

Alone, when his injury wasn't half as painful as the emotions that must be raking through him. Alone, as she sensed he had been a year ago, when he had come here searching for his wife.

Ariel ran her fingers lightly through her tousled curls, unable to stop herself from attempting to picture the woman who had been married to Damon Kincaid. Amanda Kincaid must have been polished, elegant. And beautiful, if she'd looked anything like her mother. Maybe a gorgeous white-blonde with a model's high cheekbones. Tall, willowy, the perfect foil for Damon Kincaid's dark good looks.

Ariel grimaced, remembering the expression on the man's face when he'd opened the door to see her standing there earlier that evening. She must have looked a sight—her hair windblown, Houdini in her arms, her jumpsuit the color of a matador's cape. Damon Kincaid was probably used to women who demanded Dom Pérignon with pizza. No doubt his wife...

No, that wasn't fair, Ariel thought, disgusted with herself. The woman was dead, for God's sake. Her daughters were grieving. And as for Damon Kincaid, himself—the emotions she'd seen in his eyes, the pain she'd sensed clawing inside him even after a year had passed, could only be spawned by a great love. Love as intense as the promise of fire in Kincaid's dark eyes.

Suddenly restless, Ariel slid down from her seat, and jammed her hands into the pockets of her jumpsuit. It was none of her affair. Not Kincaid's grief. Not his relationship to his wife. The only link she had to the man should be through the little girl that she taught. Her single focus should be on Moey Kincaid's grief, the fact that the child wasn't coping....

Out of the corner of her eye, Ariel caught a glimpse of pewter gray, and turned to see Kincaid at the desk. He was balanced on crutches, his foot heavily bandaged. Even from this distance, Ariel could see that his features were pale. The receptionist behind the desk was putting a phone up on the counter for him to use.

Ariel made a face. He'd probably be about as overjoyed to see her as he would be to contract a heavy-duty case of bubonic plague. Well, tough. He could just spend the whole trip home grinding his dental work to dust in frustration.

Steeling herself to do battle, Ariel hurried into the building just as Kincaid began punching out the number. Slipping up beside him, she pushed the button that disconnected the call. Irate at the interruption, the man glared up at her, but the instant his gaze locked on her face, anger gave way to astonishment.

"Miss Madigan?" he said, his voice more than a little muzzy. "I thought I told you to go home."

Ariel couldn't suppress a smile. The man was obviously half-drugged on pain medication, and he was still trying to order people around. "I'm afraid my lowest marks in school were always in citizenship, Mr. Kincaid." She dropped into sotto voce. "'Ariel needs to be more careful in following instructions.'"

She was surprised when the corner of his mouth lifted in a half smile. A smile that was a little crooked, a little sleepy, and a lot sexy. "Damon. Call me Damon," he ordered her.

"Okay. Damon."

"And I'll call you Ariel."

"All right."

"Ariel...sounds like some kind of...of fairy princess or something. Not a one-woman demolition squad."

Ariel grinned. "Watch it, mister. Flattery will get you nowhere."

"Know what, Ariel? I'm glad you're rotten at following directions. I have to pick up a prescription at the hospital pharmacy, and some bandages. And they gave me this shot that made me groggy as hell."

"Really?" Ariel teased. "I never would have guessed."

"Yeah, really. And I don't much feel like waiting around for a taxi to show up."

"Well, how about if we go get your paraphernalia and get you home to bed."

"Yeah. Bed." Was she imagining it, or did something flicker in those hazy brown eyes?

A hospital directory was bolted to a nearby wall, and Ariel quickly busied herself finding the arrow that pointed toward the hospital pharmacy. Steering Damon in the right direction, they started down the hall. But the man was obviously unfamiliar with walking with the aid of crutches, his progress slow and unsteady enough to make Ariel nervous. She cupped her hand around his arm in an attempt to steady him, all the while realizing that if the man did start to topple, there would be nothing she could do to stop him—as big as he was in comparison to her petite frame.

Not that she'd be aware he was falling until he crashed into the floor, she thought grimly. The feel of his muscles beneath her fingers, the sinews flexing and shifting beneath the smooth, tanned silk of his skin, made her feel as if she were the one zinged out on medication.

Relief stole through her when they reached the pharmacy counter, and she was able to lean Damon against the far more stable support of the wall.

A grandfatherly man bustled up to the window, a smile lighting his face. "So what can I do for you, cutie?" he asked Ariel.

"Pain medication," she said, indicating Damon. "He had a fight with a rabbit and lost."

Damon grumbled, and the man laughed aloud.

"A rabbit, huh? Haven't heard that one before. Have you got the prescription?"

Ariel turned to Damon. He was leaning against the wall, his eyes closed. "Hey, could you wake up long enough to tell me where you stuck the prescription?"

"In my...pocket." He made an attempt to reach into the front pocket of his tight-fitting pants, but between the awkwardness of the crutches and the wooziness of the medication, Ariel could tell there was no hope.

"Never mind," she said with a grimace. "Go back to never-never land. I'll get it."

Flattening her hand, she slid it beneath the flap of his front pocket, her teasing mood vanishing as she felt the steely muscles of his thigh beneath her hand. The pocket was empty, but as she drew her fingers free, she felt as if she'd carried away all of the heat that had pulsed beneath the thin layer of cloth. She moved to the other pocket, her cheeks on fire, her hand more than a little shaky, but the prescription wasn't there, either. What *was* thoroughly disconcerted her, the firm bulge her fingertips skimmed at the bottom of the pocket making her mouth go dry.

She yanked her hand out as if her fingers were on fire. "Damn it, Damon, where did you stick the prescription?" she demanded. But he didn't say anything. She looked up at his face, sensing a change in him, a tautening. The medication must be wearing off. If they didn't get the capsules into the man soon, he'd be in for some serious pain.

Gritting her teeth, she slid her hand into the pocket that was pulled tight over the curve of his granite-hard buttocks, and she almost cried with relief as she heard the crackling of paper. She withdrew the scrawled note, and shoved it beneath the glass window.

Ariel saw the pharmacist's grin mirrored through the reflection of her own fiery red cheeks.

"Be just a minute," the man said, as he went off to fill the prescription and get the rest of their needs.

By the time he returned, Ariel had managed to compose herself.

"That'll be forty-eight dollars and twenty-three cents," he said briskly as he began stuffing the items in a white paper bag.

"Forty-eight..." Ariel echoed dubiously. She'd intended to hit the money machine before she went out with her friends. At the moment, she'd be hard-pressed to spring for an order of French fries, let alone this prescription. And yet, if she put her hands in the man's pockets again, the paramedics were going to have to come out and jump-start *her* heart.

"I—I don't..." she stammered.

"I've got it."

She looked up at the sound of Damon's voice, clearer than it had been since the moment she'd found him by the phone.

He withdrew a leather wallet and awkwardly got it open. Ariel stared at a picture revealed beneath a thin layer of plastic as he withdrew some bills. A stunningly beautiful blonde stared out from the image, her hair perfectly styled, a gorgeous black dress accenting her flawless complexion. Ariel felt as if someone had slugged her in the stomach. The woman in the picture was young, beautiful, everything Ariel had imagined and more.

She remembered the quick, unnerving flutter of attraction she'd felt for Damon Kincaid. Even if she were tempted, there would be about as much chance of a man like Kincaid becoming involved with her as there would be of the man indulging in a torrid affair with Raggedy Ann.

Her thoughts were interrupted by the sound of Damon's gruff thank-you and the pharmacist shoving the package of supplies beneath the glass. Damon reached out to take it.

"Better not, son," the pharmacist said. "You'll have all you can do to manage those crutches. Let that pretty little wife of yours take care of you."

Ariel froze, stricken, her gaze flashing to Damon's face. His fingers were still gripping the wallet, the knuckles standing out, white, against his tanned skin. "My wife is... She's not here." Kincaid said, then turned and began to make his way down the hall.

Ariel grabbed the bag and hurried after him. "Damon," she said, uneasily. "I'm sorry. About... about what he said."

"Understandable mistake."

"I know, but... I'm just sorry." They had reached the automatic doors, and the glass panels opened, the hot summer night washing over them as they exited the building. Ariel chewed at her lower lip, feeling compelled to explain. "This is all my fault. Your party being ruined, your foot— everything."

"The party wasn't ruined. You did far better than I ever could have. You're terrific with kids."

"It's what they pay me the big bucks for," Ariel made a feeble attempt at teasing him.

They had reached the parking lot, and she moved to unlock the car door.

"I'm not good with kids."

His words made her hand pause for a moment in the motion of turning the key.

"I never was."

His voice was soft, and so weary that it broke her heart.

"You did great tonight," she said, and meant it.

"Miss Madigan, I—"

"I thought we agreed that you were going to call me Ariel." She couldn't resist reaching out, laying her hand on his arm. "Come on. Lighten up on yourself. You barely batted an eye when Ellen glued that mustache on you. And there aren't many fathers that I know who would go through a child's birthday party with their foot cut from here to Kansas."

"I couldn't stand for Ellen's party to be ruined. Not again." He looked away, and Ariel knew that he was staring at the stream of traffic marked by a river of blurred headlights on the highway nearby. "Amanda died three weeks before Ellen's fourth birthday. I was—we were all still in shock. Couldn't seem to cope. There were presents Amanda had bought for her, all hidden in behind the winter coats. Watching Ellen open them, knowing that Amanda had...had shopped for them weeks before, that she had wrapped them, and..." His voice trailed off.

Ariel swallowed hard, not knowing what to say.

"It tore me apart," he said, his voice hushed. "Damn, it still does."

He opened the car door, and lowered himself into the seat, attempting to drag the crutches in with him. But they were too long, too ungainly for him to manage, and Ariel tugged them from his grasp. She leaned across him, arranging the crutches with some difficulty, through the gap between the two front seats.

She was just starting to ease herself out of the doorway, when she felt a hard hand close on her wrist. Damon Kincaid's face was close, nerve-janglingly close, his breath warm and moist against her face. His dark hair was rumpled, and his mouth solemn.

"Thank you," was all he said, but Ariel felt her pulses riot, felt as if she were drowning in those melting-dark eyes.

"You're welcome," she said, gently but firmly withdrawing her hand from his grasp.

She closed the door and walked around the car to slip into the driver's seat. The engine sputtered to life and she all but stripped what remained of the gears as she threw the transmission into Drive.

A gritty rock song filled the silence, followed by a mellow ballad and a golden moldie that should have been buried six feet under the day it was released. The night-shrouded city blurred past, and Ariel kept stealing glances at the man beside her.

His head leaned back, his lips were parted. Dark lashes had fluttered down to lay in thick drifts on his cheekbones. There was a gentling of the hard planes of his face, as if the medication had cleansed away pain that had nothing to do with the slash in his foot. A lock of black hair had tumbled across his forehead, just dusting the straight black lines of his eyebrows. There was a boyishness about him, something sensitive about the shape of his mouth, something vulnerable about the way his cheek was pillowed against the cracked vinyl seat. And she wondered if this was the only way Damon Kincaid ever felt peace.

Her heart twisted as she dragged her eyes back to the road.

When at last they pulled to a stop in front of the Kincaid house, it seemed a crime to wake him, to bring him back to the reality of the ache in his foot and the anguish in his heart. But she had no choice. As gently as possible, she got out of the driver's side, and grabbed the sack of medical supplies, running them up to the front porch. A brass-and-smoked-glass fixture lit the doorway, the glow of a lamp from inside setting the draperies beyond the window aglow.

The muffled sound of classical music drifted out, Eve apparently indulging in the top-of-the-line stereo Ariel had seen in the living room.

For a moment, Ariel considered knocking on the door, and enlisting the woman's help, but she couldn't stifle the instinctive dislike she'd felt for Damon Kincaid's mother-in-law, couldn't seem to bring herself to subject Damon to the woman's caustic tongue before he'd had a chance to wake up at least a little bit.

Returning to the car, Ariel maneuvered the crutches out of the cramped cab. Carrying them around to his side, she leaned them against the rear fender, and opened the door.

"Damon?" she said softly, grasping his shoulder and giving him a gentle shake. "You're home."

"Tired . . ." he murmured, but his lashes didn't stir.

"Come on, Damon. I'd carry you if I could, but you'd give me a hernia. Just wake up enough so I can get you to your room, and I promise you can go back to sleep. Your bed will be a heck of a lot more comfortable, believe me."

"No . . ." he said in that groggy, devastatingly sexy voice. "Not . . . comfortable. Empty. So damn . . . empty."

Ariel was stunned to feel her eyes burn, and she stroked the lock of hair back from his forehead. "I know," she said, through a throat thick with tears. "I know it is. But we have to get you inside. The girls will be looking for you first thing in the morning."

That seemed to rouse him. She could almost see him fighting off the waves of drowsiness, dragging himself forcibly to awareness. "Girls," he echoed her as his eyes fluttered open. "Be looking . . . for me."

"That's right. Now, if you can just get yourself turned around, I'll help you climb out, and get the crutches."

"Yeah. Okay, yeah. Crutches."

A wave of tenderness swept through Ariel as she helped him, just the fact that he leaned on her so heavily serving as a testament to how much effort this was costing him.

If he'd been less than steady on his crutches in the hospital, now he was swaying like a California bridge in an earthquake.

Instead of relying on the crutches, Ariel slipped one from beneath his arm, and wedged her own shoulder in its place, supporting most of his considerable weight.

She badgered him, cajoled him, the distance from the car to the front door seeming endless. She figured he wouldn't even remember this in the morning. Figured that even once she enlisted his mother-in-law's help, they'd be lucky to get him to the living room couch, let alone into bed.

They had just reached the front porch when he spoke, his words unexpected, oddly disconcerting.

"Your eyes are . . . blue."

"Yep," Ariel replied, intending to prop him against the wall so that she could ring the doorbell. "Blue eyes, blond hair. Awfully unimaginative combination, isn't it?" She shifted him so his back was toward the wall, and started to untangle herself from the crook of his arm, but he held on to her, the heat rippling out from wherever he touched her making her suddenly, excruciatingly aware.

"Pretty," he whispered. "I like blue eyes."

"Terrific. You have nice eyes, too. Now why don't you let go of me, so that I can get you inside where you can close them again."

But his eyes were open, now, hazy, not from the medication, or from exhaustion, but rather with something that made Ariel's heart smack into her ribs. His arm tightened where it held her, the single crutch he'd been using to support his other side slipping from beneath his arm, clattering to the concrete.

He stumbled back against the wall, dragging her with him. She thudded against the hard plane of his chest, struggled to right herself. But his other arm had closed around her now, melding her against him.

She craned her head back to look up into his face, demand that he let her go, but her lips had scarcely opened, when hard ones, masculine ones, crashed down upon them.

Ariel gasped, a jolt of pure flame licking through her, the world reeling crazily as Damon Kincaid kissed her—not the usual tentative first kiss she'd experienced with other men. But rather a soul-searingly fierce one, a bone-meltingly intimate one, so powerful, so devastating, she felt pieces of herself shattering deep inside, the sensation more terrifying, more wonderful than anything she'd ever known.

This was insane, she thought wildly. She should push him away, stop...

But at that instant his tongue swept the crease of her lips, forced its way into her mouth, and she opened to him, threading her fingers through the dark silk of his hair.

She could feel the need pulsing through him, a kind of choked, desperate sound low in his chest, as if all the pain, all the loneliness, all the grief that had been simmering so near the surface all night had suddenly broken free.

She felt him shudder, his hands roving, hungrily up and down her back, urging her closer, tighter against him, and she felt that part of him she'd brushed with her fingertip when she'd searched through his pocket tightening insistently against her.

Good grief, the fleeting thought wisped through her mind, if the man could kiss this well half-conscious, what would it be like to be in his arms when he was fully aware?

Her fingers stilled in his hair, her whole body stiffening as reality forced its way through desire-numbed senses. She dragged her mouth away from his and wedged her hands against his chest to push him away.

"Damon, stop," she managed in an unsteady voice, as he tried to recapture her mouth with his. "Stop," she said more firmly.

"No...no, please..." he grated, his hands still devouring her.

The sound of the door cracking against the wall made Ariel jump back in a desperate attempt to pull away from him.

She wheeled, to stare, horrified, at Eve Laughton-Smith, framed in the doorway. The woman's face was ashen, sick, but not half as sick as Ariel felt as she raised a hand to her breast, fully aware of how both she and Damon appeared, their lips kiss reddened, their cheeks flushed, even their clothes rumpled from their embrace.

"Mrs. Laughton-Smith . . . I can explain. . . ." Ariel said in a shaky voice. "It's not what it looks like. The medication they gave him . . ."

"It's exactly what it looks like." The woman's voice vibrated with scorn, her eyes filled with disgust and a sobering pain. "Just a repeat of what happened every time he left town—left his wife and his children while he gorged himself on expensive women halfway across the world."

"Eve, that's not true." Damon's voice was agonizingly clear, and Ariel could see him battling to shake off the effects of the medication, and the even more dizzying ones of the kiss they had shared moments before. "I was never unfaithful to Amanda. And this . . . with Ariel, I . . ."

"You were unfaithful! I know you were!" Eve shrilled. "I always suspected it was true! Why else would Amanda have been so unhappy?" Eve wheeled and stormed into the house, returning a moment later with her purse.

"You disgust me. Both of you! You're not fit to teach children, and you—you're no more fit to be a father than you were to be a husband. I told Amanda . . . warned her before she married you. Warned her that someone with your background . . . that you would be just as common and as vulgar as that mother of yours! But she wouldn't listen. Amanda wouldn't listen."

"Don't bring my mother into this." His voice was steely, cold.

"It's true! All of it! True! You should have stayed in that filthy apartment you grew up in! I wish you'd rotted there!"

Eve's voice broke, and she wheeled, all but running down to where her gray sports car was parked.

The silence nearly suffocated Ariel as she watched the vehicle speed away. She couldn't bring herself to look into Damon Kincaid's face. The man had lost his wife, lost his hope, and now, because she hadn't had the sense to pull away when he'd tried to kiss her, he'd been subjected to a scene as cruel and crippling as anything she'd ever witnessed.

"Oh, God," she whispered. "I'm sorry."

A sharp breath hissed through Damon's teeth as he limped over to retrieve the crutch lying on the ground, and then scooped up the white paper package Ariel had placed on the porch. He turned and limped through the doorway.

Ariel followed him, and saw the living room, denuded of its crepe paper and decorations. The wreckage Houdini had created hours before now lay bare for all to see. Ariel's sick feeling of guilt magnified.

A fatalistic sigh rose from Damon's chest, and he closed his eyes, shaking his head.

"Damon," she said softly, "I—"

"I know. You're sorry." The hardness was back in his face again, harsh lines of guilt and grief intensified a thousand fold. "Good night, Ariel," he said quietly. "I can make it the rest of the way alone."

She nodded, and slipped out the door, closing it behind her. Outside, she leaned against the wooden panel a long time, terrified of the emotions raging through her, wondering where the reckless course of her actions tonight would take them.

Chapter Five

Banners of fuchsia and mauve unfurled against the dawn-gray sky, a handful of intrepid runners sprinkled about the neighborhood in jogging outfits more coordinated than Ariel's entire wardrobe. She watched as a particularly perky brunette cruised past her car, everything from the band catching up her long hair to the insignias on her running shoes colored the same shade of pink.

Ariel grimaced, aware that *she* was the one who looked as if she'd run the Boston Marathon. She hadn't slept ten minutes all night, raked with guilt as she was. And even with the aid of a prescription, she doubted Damon Kincaid had slept, either.

"Oh, God, Madigan, when you make a mess, you make a mess," she muttered to herself, hating the confusing feelings racing through her.

With fingers clenching the doughnut box she held on her lap, she looked through her windshield up at the porch where he had kissed her the night before. The scene had played over and over in her head through the sleepless hours—the surrealistic quality of the entire evening making her feel as if she'd been trapped in the Twilight Zone.

A hundred times during the night, she had heard Nancy's voice, warning her about becoming involved with the Kincaids. She had heard her superior predict the direst of consequences for both Ariel's own career and the future of Abracadabra. She had heard Damon Kincaid's mother-in-law's threats to contact Sister Thomasetta and apprise the nun of Ariel's lack of professionalism. And it didn't tap any of Ariel's imagination at all to picture what would happen if this matter were to be brought before St. Gen's school board.

She could just see the more conservative members joyfully penning their signatures on her termination papers.

Maybe she had been foolish to disregard Nancy's orders, but in her wildest of dreams, Ariel had never expected to fall with Houdini down a rabbit hole to rival Lewis Carroll's—one inhabited by three adorable, troubled little girls, and a man as gorgeous, as devastatingly sexy and as tormented as the hero in any romance novel Ariel had ever read.

She had paced her studio apartment, trying to reason out what to do, trying to pen a letter apologizing to Damon for the damage she had caused. She'd promised herself a dozen times that she'd never go near the Kincaids again, except in the neutral confines of St. Gen's. Had promised the Fates anything, if she could just keep her job, just smooth things over for Damon with his mother-in-law. If she could just start last night over again, and leave Houdini in his cage in the car.

She could have spoken to Damon about Moey—like a professional, as she'd intended—and then she could have exited stage right, before Eve Laughton-Smith had climbed off her broomstick.

It would have been better—far better for everyone concerned, if she had taken the first plane to Timbuktu the minute school had been officially closed for the year.

Or would it have been? She wouldn't have had a chance to alert Damon to the problems Moey was having—and after last night, there could be no doubt Kincaid was no neglectful, uncaring parent. The man loved his daughters fiercely.

Even if Ariel had never shown up on the elegant Worthington Drive doorstep, Sarah would still have had the allergic reaction, Ellen would still have broken the pitcher of grape juice, Eve would still have been seething with resentment toward Damon. And the pain—the pain in those sherry-dark eyes would still have been there—the haunting vulnerability, the confusion would still have tainted the beautifully carved lines of Damon Kincaid's face.

In the end, she'd trashed the letters of apology that she'd drafted, reasoned that whatever damage had been done to her career was already done, and admitted that she couldn't bear not seeing Damon for herself, assuring herself that he was all right.

The doughnuts had been a last-minute idea—after all that had happened, Ariel figured the least she could do was provide a treat for the girls.

And yet, even after she'd pulled up in front of the house over twenty minutes ago, after she'd mentally rehearsed a hundred times what she was going to say, she hadn't been able to make herself get out of the car and climb the stairs she had taken last night with her arm locked around Damon Kincaid's taut waist. She couldn't bring herself to knock on the door where he'd appeared when she'd arrived earlier that night—his shirt plastered wetly to a well-defined masculine chest, his hair tousled, his lips twisting with exasperation and a wry humor that had delighted her the moment he opened his mouth.

She'd simply sat in her car, staring at the windows that had been glowing with light even before she'd arrived. And all the apologies, all the condolences, every word she'd ever known had evaporated beneath the heat of the memory of the kiss they'd shared.

A kiss that still made Ariel's knees feel like ice cream that someone had forgotten to put back in the freezer.

Did Damon remember it as clearly as she did? Or was it just an image out of focus, skewed by the prescription he'd been on, only the traumatic ending of the kiss, with Eve in her fury, seeming real to him?

What would the man say—think—when he found Ariel on his doorstep at eight in the morning? How would he react to what had happened the night before?

What could she even begin to say to him?

"Well, either get your buns up those stairs and find out, or drive away before the man looks out the window and sees you skulking around out here like you're casing the joint," Ariel scolded herself roundly.

She swung open the door, and climbed out, slamming it behind her. Without giving herself any more time to think, she dashed up the steps, her heart giving a funny hop in her chest as she pressed the doorbell.

She expected to see the effects of last night still evident in Damon's face, expected to see him pale with pain, adorably tousled in a rumpled, yet no doubt expensive robe, exhausted, disheveled. She wanted to set a plate of doughnuts in front of the girls, and make up a pot of coffee for their father—decaffeinated coffee. God knew, he was so stressed he didn't need the added jolt of caffeine.

She would sit with him, talk to him, try to make him break into that bone-meltingly sexy smile. And maybe...just maybe she would touch his hand. See if just the feel of his skin under her fingertips could really have sent such lightning bolts of sensation sizzling through her.

Heat flooded her cheeks as she became aware of the muffled sound of footsteps approaching from behind the door, the latch giving a hollow metallic click. But when the panel swung open, it was all Ariel could do not to gasp in astonishment.

The infinitely touchable man of the night before had vanished, in his place a high-power businessman who looked as if he'd stepped out of an advertisement in some high-brow men's magazine.

Cool, confident, Damon Kincaid was the very picture of success—a man who exuded an aura of power from the high-polished toe of his single dress shoe to the red silk tie knotted to perfection beneath that square, clean-shaven jaw. Only the fact that he was leaning on crutches and his injured foot was encased in a thick black sock made Ariel certain that last night hadn't been some kind of twisted nightmare.

She swallowed hard, searching that impassive face for some hint of the man whose pockets she'd searched the night before, some whisper of that gravelly, sexy voice that had spoken words that had wrenched her heart. But even the warm gold sparkles of wry humor were gone from those eyes, and his mouth curled with a mingling of confidence and arrogance that made Ariel suddenly feel like a grubby third-grader caught making copies of her hand prints on a company photocopier.

Come on, Ariel, she cautioned herself inwardly, *you know that everyone deals with emotions in different ways. The man was left totally vulnerable last night. Not a comfy feeling for someone like Damon Kincaid...*

Not a comfy feeling for anyone, she thought, remembering the raw sensation in her own chest.

"Good morning," she managed, forcing a smile despite the fact that she was agonizingly aware she looked like something that had spent the night sleeping under a rock. Her gold-print leggings had a smear of powdered sugar from the doughnut shop, the baggy purple sweatshirt she'd pulled on this morning was big enough to fit Kincaid's broad shoulders. Her hair had been pulled back in a cloth band, and she hadn't even bothered with the slight touches of blush and lipstick she usually swiped on in the morning.

Something unreadable flickered in Damon Kincaid's eyes.

"Miss Madigan." His eyebrow arched. "I hardly expected to see you here this morning."

The words were formal, his voice like chilled champagne. And somehow that hurt Ariel more than any tirade she'd ever suffered.

"I wanted to see if you were all right. How your foot was, and..." She sounded idiotic. The man who had kissed her yesterday would have put her at ease with a dry jest. This Damon Kincaid gave her no such quarter.

"As you can see, I have everything under control," he said in that ice-sliver voice. "The only thing I was concerned about was that rabbit you forgot here last night. Now that you're here to retrieve it—"

"I'm not here about the rabbit. Moey won the draw to keep him for the summer."

"That animal? Here for the summer? I think not."

Ariel peered into his eyes, searching for some hint, any hint that this was just his way of dealing with what had happened. But it was as if he'd drawn a shield across those eyes that had been so revealing the night before. As if he'd erected the invisible wall Moey had been babbling about during the Abracadabra party. A sorceress's wall, the child had called it. But Ariel wondered how much pain, how much sadness had forced Damon Kincaid to close himself off so effectively.

The thought of that pain made her risk saying, "Damon, I understand that you're feeling off balance about...well, about kissing me last night. But you were under a lot of stress, and with all the medicine they'd pumped in you...what happened was...well, it was no big deal."

Did she imagine it, or did the line of his mouth tighten further still.

"I hardly care to conduct this conversation on the front stoop." His voice was crisp as he gestured for her to come inside. When she hesitated, he glanced pointedly across the yard, and Ariel was chagrined to see a portly woman with curlers in her hair and enough diamonds on her fingers to

stock the most exclusive jewelery store retrieving her morning paper from the mailbox.

"Don't you think we gave my neighbors enough to gos-
sip about last night, Miss Madigan?"

Ariel's breath caught, as if he'd suddenly struck her. She
felt her own spine stiffen as she stalked across the thresh-
old.

She was so distracted by her mounting aggravation, she
all but tripped over a set of luggage stacked beside the
doorway.

Kincaid's hand shot out to steady her, his touch so im-
personal, she felt as if she'd been frostbit. The memory of
those same hands, urging her against his hard body, his lips,
warm and welcoming and desperate, seemed a million life-
times away.

"The limo is picking me up for the airport in about
twenty minutes—" he bit out the cursory explanation "—so
if you could get your rabbit and leave, I would appreciate—"

"Airport?" Ariel echoed.

"Yes, Miss Madigan. One can reach Australia by ship,
but it takes a good deal longer—"

"You're going to Australia?"

"I fly out at eleven-fifteen."

"I know you said something last night about the possibility of a trip, but I thought... Well, with your foot the way
it is, how can you spend so many hours on a plane?"

"That's why doctors invented pain pills, Miss Madigan."

Ariel felt heat steal into her cheeks as she remembered in
vivid detail her search for that particular prescription. It was
almost as if the man wanted to embarrass her into leaving,
he regarded her so intently.

"Well, what about the girls, then?" Ariel demanded.
"They didn't even mention you were going."

His features grew even colder, but Ariel saw his fist
clench. "The girls didn't know. The trip came up rather

unexpectedly, but business is like that.'' Was there the slightest hint of defensiveness in his voice? "They're used to my leaving on short notice."

"I see." Ariel scrambled desperately to reconcile this diamond-hard executive with the exasperated, yet wonderfully warm man on whom she had watched Ellen paste a mustache the night before.

"*Do* you see, Miss Madigan? I'm very busy. I've been on the phone since six o'clock with the baby-sitting service, trying to arrange for the girls' favorite substitute sitter to come, not to mention having to call my secretary and instruct her to contact carpet and upholstery cleaners, my housekeeping service and various other people to clean up the aftermath of last night. At the moment, I need to call the baby-sitting agency back to see if they've located the woman I requested."

Ariel glared at him, fuming. She was being summarily dismissed—treated with exactly the dictatorial arrogance she had expected the first time she had knocked on Damon Kincaid's door. But after what had passed between them last night, the behavior made her feel bruised, battered. Infuriated beyond imagining.

"I'll tell you what, *Damon.*" She accented his first name on purpose, wanting to jab him with the reminder that she was not some lackey he'd never seen before. "You call the agency, I'll give the girls the treat I brought them and then, until your *limo* arrives, you and I can spend the time discussing what I came to see you about in the first place— Melissa's difficulty in adjusting to her mother's death."

"I fully intend to deal with Moey. She'll have the best child psychologist money can buy. I've already instructed my secretary to make inquiries."

"That's fine, but it will take Melissa some time to bond with a new counselor. She needs someone to talk to now. I'd like to keep working with her. Listening to her. Maybe I can speed up the process—"

"Of leaving her life in shambles?" He started to rake his hand through his hair, then stopped as if realizing it would muss it up. "Miss Madigan, I don't mean to sound ungrateful. But my daughter is too important to me to rely on some teacher-turned-shrink whose sole credentials are a degree in finger painting and reading the latest issues of pop psychology magazines. Now, from what Corrin Michaels told me when she recommended your program, you are quite remarkable, as far as it goes. But surely you understand that I would want what is best for Melissa."

"Do you? Or do you want what makes *you* feel better? More in control? Your daughters aren't corporations for you to organize and put on a shelf until it's convenient. And not even clothes, books, schools ... or shrinks with high price tags are going to guarantee their happiness. Don't you care if—"

With savage suddenness he rounded on her, the chill gone from his eyes. In its place was a blaze that made Ariel want to take a step back.

"You think you understand everything about me, don't you? Have me slotted in your mind as just one more parent who can't be bothered with his children. But you don't know anything about me, or Moey or Ellen or Sarah. I'd sell my soul just to see my children smile, just once the way they did before their mother died. I'd pay anything—"

"That's the trouble with children's smiles. You can't buy them with anything except time." She was shaking with fury, on the verge of tears, but she stood toe-to-toe with Kincaid, the man towering over her. "I know you're still upset about last night," Ariel said. "You've been through a rough time. But after all we went through together, I don't think I deserve to be treated this way—no matter how much you happen to be hurting."

Damon stared at her, suddenly quiet. His grip tightened on the crutches and he turned away from her, stumping over to lean against the wall. His reflection caught in the mirror, and Ariel saw a flicker of regret, weariness, before he turned again to face her.

"You're right. You don't deserve this. I'm not very good at—at dealing with scenes like last night. I'm a very private person."

Ariel was surprised to find her lips curving into a crooked smile. "I live for scenes. I seek them out. I revel in them."

"Why do I believe that?" He shot her a sideways glance and heaved a sigh. "Listen, I'm sorry about being a jerk. And about last night—I really am grateful for your interest in Moey. I'll handle things now that it's been brought to my attention."

"From Australia."

"What?"

"You'll handle it from Australia."

"Where I choose to handle it from and how I decide to handle it is none of your concern. It will be taken care of."

"Right." It was Ariel's turn to sigh. "I'd like to document some of the behavior I've seen, some of the things Moey has said that disturb me. Ways I've found to draw her out."

"That would be fine if it would make you feel better."

Ariel was astonished to feel a thick lump of something like tears in her throat. She turned away, her arms already aching with the emptiness of knowing that someone else would be soothing Melissa Kincaid's tears from now on. Someone else would be listening to the child's tales of the Crystal Kingdom and the invisible walls that were holding her daddy prisoner.

If only the high-priced professional Damon Kincaid hired would truly listen to what Moey was saying. If only the counselor wouldn't dismiss the rich fantasy life the child had used to insulate herself from her pain. If only the counselor would see the blatant reality that lurked beneath even Moey's most remarkable tales.

Ariel hugged her arms to her chest, trying not to feel the emptiness. "Moey seemed to respond best when she was cuddling Houdini. Sometimes it's easier to talk to a bunny than to a person who will talk back.''

''Moey's talking to the rabbit?'' Concern flashed in Damon's eyes. ''Is that what has you worried?''

''I talk to Houdini sometimes myself. He never criticizes you, never laughs at you, never tells you to quit being a baby or that you have to take some bumps because life isn't fair. He only snuggles close and wiggles his nose at you, his eyes all soft and warm.''

She fell quiet, and was stunned to hear footsteps approaching her. A hand, warm and hard, hesitated for a moment a few inches away from her shoulder. Then she felt Damon Kincaid pat her, with an awkward gentleness that made the tears well in her eyes.

She quashed them, and dodged away from the touch that was suddenly too painful.

''The thing that concerns me most of all,'' she said, ''is that Moey seems trapped in denial—that she hasn't accepted the fact that her mother is gone, is never coming back. Now and then, she slips and says something about her mother brushing her hair or baking cupcakes or reading her a story.''

Damon's brow furrowed, and he tugged at the knot of his tie. ''I would think that was natural enough—talking about what she and Amanda used to do.''

''Not *used* to, Damon. Melissa talks as if they are still doing these things now. At the party last night, she told me her mother baked the cupcakes she brought as a treat. That her mother made them have pink icing, because she knew how much Moey loved it.''

The hand fell away from Damon's tie, as if he'd gone numb; his face paled, his eyes filling with anguish. ''Oh my God. I never even suspected. Damn it, why didn't I see something? Know...'' He raked his fingers through his hair. ''Moey's always seemed so levelheaded. The one who appeared to be dealing with Amanda's death the best. When I was falling apart, and Ellen and Sarah were so devastated, it was Moey who..." He ground his fingertips against his eyes. "What you're telling me is that all this time, she has been pretending away her mother's death."

"I think so."

"But why didn't I pick up on that? Never once has she said anything like that to me. I would have remembered, for God's sake."

"Maybe she did say something, in the beginning, when you were still . . . still deep in grief. And maybe she saw how much it hurt you. Maybe she's slipped, and said something to the baby-sitter, and the baby-sitter scolded her, or tried to force her to see reality. At the party at school, Moey told me she's not allowed to talk about this time she spends with her mother. That it's supposed to be a secret."

"This is crazy. I can't believe I didn't know."

"Your wife has been dead over a year now. None of Moey's teachers picked up on the fact that she was having problems until just recently. And they're trained to identify difficulties the kids might be having." She was echoing Nancy's excuses, but found that she couldn't bear the self-recrimination in Damon's features.

"I'm her father. I should have known."

"You're not a superhero, Damon. You don't have X-ray vision. The thing to do now is to try to help Moey as best you can."

At that moment the man looked as if he'd do anything to help his daughter. "Amanda is dead. She's never coming back. Moey has to be made to understand that. I'll talk to her myself, even before the psychologist."

"No! No, please." Ariel grasped his arm, a jolt of fear going through her. "The worst possible thing you could do would be to bully her into admitting her mother is gone forever. Moey's such a gentle child, so sensitive. If you force her to open up, you'll bruise her, Damon. So deeply you may never be able to reach her again. She's already hiding so much of the way she feels. If you go charging after her, she'll retreat even farther into her fantasies. Worse, still, you'll never again be able to coax her to reveal them. You won't have a clue as to what is going on inside your daughter."

Kincaid's face was harsh. "What? You think I would hurt Melissa? Bellow at her about all this?"

"It wouldn't take bellowing. It would hardly take anything at all to make her close up. When I was a little girl, I wanted to take a flower to my teacher on her birthday. My mother had roses. Roses that won prizes at three state fairs. I had watched a particular bud for almost a week, waiting for it to open. I was just sure it would blossom in time. When it didn't, well, I got frustrated, and I picked it anyway. I took it to my room and tried to peel the petals apart. Nothing I could do could put that flower back together again once it had been torn. Whenever I work with a child like Moey, I remember how that rose looked, with its petals all shredded and bruised."

Damon limped over to a window, stared out, his shoulders just a little slumped beneath the rich fabric of his suit coat. "All right. Your point is well-taken. I won't—how did you say it?—bully Melissa into confiding in me. I'll just try to be patient. Listen to her and let the psychologist do his job."

Ariel let out a breath, surprised to find that she'd been holding it. Hope stirred inside her as she watched him strip off his suit jacket and toss it onto a chair. Good heavens, was he staying? Staying home with his little girls instead of jetting off on his business trip? Her pulses tripped, her heart seeming to swell inside her chest with something warm and wonderful. And she felt an almost untamable urge to go to him, fling her arms around him in an exuberant hug.

Ever since she was in college, everyone from psychology professors, to supervising teachers, to guidance counselors had cautioned her that only rarely could she change the pattern of a student's life outside the classroom. But they were wrong. Wrong.

From the look on Damon Kincaid's face, there wouldn't be any more missed school parties or neglected notes. There wouldn't be any more business trips when his daughters needed him.

If she lost her job tomorrow, it would be worth it, just to know that Moey Kincaid would have someone to love her.

Ariel swallowed hard. "If it's all right with you, I'd like to talk to Moey about Houdini before I take him home. I wouldn't want her to wake up and find him gone."

"She's not asleep. The girls are all outside, playing on the swing set."

He gestured out the window, to where three small figures sat on a piece of playground equipment so elaborate, it would have made the park board's mouth water.

But instead of the rambunctious free play Ariel had seen so many children indulge in in the past, the Kincaid girls were all subdued. Moey sat on a swing, drawing patterns in the sand with the toe of her sneaker. Ellen was whacking a fallen branch against the support post of the clubhouse, while Sarah sat at the top of the slide, her little legs dangling over the edge.

And Ariel wanted nothing more than to run outside and gather them into her arms. Wanted nothing more than to tumble them all into the living room to play circus again, to paste a fake mustache on their father's lip and make him smile.

But it wasn't her job, wasn't her place, as Nancy was so fond of reminding her. If only such sage reminders could penetrate that part of her that was an incurable meddler, that part that believed the slipper always fit Cinderella, and that a single kiss from Beauty could change the Beast into a handsome prince.

She absently shifted the box of doughnuts she was still holding from one hand to the other. At least this time she could see that the Kincaids were going to find a happy ending. That things would be at least a little bit different from now on.

She was startled from her thoughts by the sound of Damon's voice.

"Listen...Ariel." He used her first name, and she turned to see shadings of that sensitive, exasperated man again. Somehow the sight only increased the lost sensation that had gnawed at her ever since he had opened the door. "I really do have to call and try to finalize arrangements with the sitter, but you go ahead and talk to Moey for as long as you like."

"The sitter?" Ariel felt as if he'd punched her in the stomach.

"The sitter. The person who is going to watch them while I'm in Australia. Remember? I told you when you got here that I'm having trouble finding someone."

"I remember. I just... When you took off your coat, and sounded so...so worried, I thought..."

Thought you would tell corporate America to take a hike. Thought you'd want to hold Moey yourself, talk to her about all that is troubling her.... I just believed in miracles.

She became aware of those dark eyes, intent on her face, that mouth that had kissed her curving into a frown.

"You thought I was going to cancel my business trip." The words were soft, but that didn't ease their sting.

She wanted to deny it, but she knew that the truth might as well be emblazoned in neon across her face.

"Ariel, it's not that simple—"

"No. Of course not." All she wanted was to get away from him, to deal with the crushing sense of disappointment and failure on her own. "I'd like a little time with Moey."

The restlessness was there again, the edginess in his dark-lashed eyes, but it was mingled with an earnestness that somehow tugged at Ariel's heart. He looked down at the floor, then back into her eyes. "Ariel, I know you care about Moey, and I thank you, for all you've done for her these past few weeks."

"I love Moey. It was a joy to have her." *It was only losing the little girl that was breaking Ariel's heart.*

"Be that as it may, I'd like to show you how grateful I am that you brought this to my attention."

He dug into his pocket and pulled out a money clip. "Let me reimburse you for all the work you've done. I know that teacher's salaries at private schools don't exactly keep you in caviar."

Disappointment fired into fury, and Ariel stared at the wad of money as if it were a snake. "If I wanted to eat fish eggs I'd scrape them off the bottom of the Mississippi," she snapped, the emotions roiling inside her tearing at the raw places in her heart.

He stared, obviously taken aback. "I didn't mean to insult you."

"Well you did. There isn't enough money in the mint to *reimburse* me for how much I hurt for the kids I work with. And an ocean of diamonds wouldn't be half as precious as what they give to me in return."

Kincaid's long fingers clenched about the money clip, and he returned it to his pocket. A dark red flush had stained his high cheekbones, his brows drawn down in a scowl. "Damn it, I said I'm sorry. I was only trying to—"

"To what? Pay for services rendered? Some things aren't for sale. Thank God. Good luck getting your baby-sitter, Mr. Kincaid. Give her a generous salary and it might even salve your conscience just a little."

"My conscience?"

"Yeah. That little voice inside you that tells you you're wrong to be leaving them right now. The one that it seems you've grown so adept at ignoring."

The ring of the phone sounded like cannon fire, cutting the thick waves of tension that seemed to be suffocating them both.

Damon cursed, and Ariel was glad of it. He started to speak, but the phone buzzed again. With an oath, he stalked over to the table and snatched up the receiver.

All her life, Ariel had been free with her emotions—an emotional merry-go-round, with bright hues of happiness and hope that dipped only rarely into the shades of sorrow. Like quicksilver she experienced every range of feelings, glorying in them. But not until this instant had she felt the merry-go-round spin out of control. Not until this instant had she wanted to get off....

With a final glance at Damon Kincaid, she dumped the box of doughnuts on the counter and ran out to where the children were waiting.

The cries of excitement at the sight of her might have calmed her anger, soothed that raw feeling in her chest, except that she kept picturing his stricken features as she had delivered her parting verbal blow, kept envisioning the haunted aura in his eyes, emotions hidden so deeply, she was certain the man believed that no one would ever find them.

It was Moey who reached her first, racing across the lawn to fling herself into Ariel's arms. Ariel caught the child up, felt those warm little arms twine around her neck.

"I wished you here, Miss Madigan," Moey said in a quavery small voice. "And it worked."

"I guess it did."

"Miss Madigan," the little girl whispered. "My daddy's going away."

Ariel buried her face against Melissa Kincaid's silky hair, knowing that there was one consequence of her job she hadn't confessed to Damon Kincaid.

Sometimes...just sometimes the children broke her heart.

Chapter Six

Damon set the phone receiver back in its cradle, frustration pulsing through him. The search for the favored substitute sitter—a woman by the incredible name of Miss Turnipseed—had proved fruitless, and to make matters worse, none of the other sitters the girls were familiar with were available on such short notice. There was some college student named Kimmie that the agency insisted could watch the girls, but there was something about leaving his children with a person who still used an *ie* after her name that made Damon uneasy.

Grandmotherly types like Mrs. Applebea, who had already managed to survive raising children of her own, inspired far more confidence. And at the moment, the last thing he needed was to be stranded in Australia, imagining his daughters in the hands of a teenager—suffering hearing loss because of the heavy-metal music pumping from the stereo, dining on a steady diet of pizza and sodas and getting an education far too advanced for their ages if this "Kimmie" person's boyfriend came over to "play."

There was always the possibility of calling Eve, asking her to take the girls for the week he'd be gone. But ever since Amanda died, he'd been careful not to rely on his mother-in-law as a baby-sitter, realizing that any such requests only gave Eve further ammunition to use in her battle to get him to give her permanent custody of the children.

But this time, he thought grimly, he might not have any other choice. He glanced at his watch, teetering on the razor's edge of indecision.

Hell, he'd have to do it. Enlist Eve's help, or else call Joe and tell him the project was off, that they'd have to release the account to someone else. And if he called Joe, he couldn't even begin to think what it would cost the company.

The memory of Ariel Madigan's wide aquamarine eyes brimming with hope rippled through him, leaving a wave of fresh guilt in its wake.

Damon gritted his teeth. No, it wasn't that simple, just as he'd told Ariel. He had been attempting for months to cut down the time he was away from home, but he couldn't just turn his back on his job. This Melbourne project was his responsibility. Owning your own business was gratifying, lucrative, but it could also be scary as hell. There was no one else to blame for failure.

Damon's fingers tightened on his crutches as he remembered the conversation he had had with Joe the day before, when his partner had alluded, none too subtly, to the account Damon had blown the year before.

Some might claim that Joe was out of line, that he was being manipulative by bringing up that disaster. And yet Damon didn't see it that way. The bottom line was that Damon had fouled up and it had cost the company big bucks.

Damon yanked at the knot on his tie, loosening it at his throat. He might not be able to bring the girls' mother back to life, but the one thing he could control was seeing that they had everything else their hearts could desire. Every dress, every doll, no matter how much it cost.

Some things aren't for sale, Ariel Madigan's words drifted back to him. His jaw clenched. That sounded good, when spouted off the lips of some idealistic, dewy-eyed dreamer like her. Damon had seen enough of the hard edges of life to question that it was true.

The slam of the back door made him look up to see Ariel and his three daughters entering the house. Sarah was sitting on purple sweat-shirted shoulders that seemed too narrow and delicate to bear her weight. Moey was clinging tightly to Ariel's hand. The sad, solemn expression that had been on the child's face ever since he'd told her he was leaving had deepened into a kind of resignation far too old for her years. Ellen trudged along behind them. When she caught a glimpse of him, she glared as if he had just set fire to her toy box.

"*You* said the bunny can't stay!" Ellen accused, her little face as threatening as a thundercloud.

Aggravation ripped through Damon. What had the woman done? Run out there and told his daughters that he was the bunny equivalent of Simon Legree? A scene with Ellen was all he needed.

"Ellen," he began, exasperated, "we can't have a rabbit—"

But Ariel had already swooped Sarah off her shoulders, and set the child on her feet with a loving pat. All patience and understanding, Ariel knelt down in front of his stubborn little girl, and laid a hand on each of Ellen's shoulders. "Sweetheart, I explained to you why I had to take Houdini home. Miss Turnipseed will want to take you three to the park and to the zoo, and where else was it you said you liked to go?"

"The museum. To look at the dinosaur bones," Ellen said grudgingly. She slanted her father a fulminating glare. "They have great big skeletons of them put together like blocks. Someday I'm going to knock them right down."

"Ellen!" Damon groped deep inside himself, trying to dredge up some of his dwindling supply of patience.

"It'll be okay, Ellen." Moey's voice. Dull enough to send guilt slicing through Damon. "Miss Madigan says she'll bring Houdini over next Saturday, and we can play with him on the lawn. That way, he won't shed all over the furniture."

"Melissa Kincaid, I didn't say a word about the furniture," Ariel corrected hastily. "I told you that Houdini likes to play in the yard. He can nibble on clover there."

"There's no clovers in *our* yard," Ellen said. "They're *weeds*. The lawn man kills 'em every year before Moey even gets to make one flower crown."

Trust Ellen to make simple lawn care sound like mass murder.

"Girls, the rabbit is the least of my worries at the moment. Now make yourselves scarce while I try to figure this out."

"What's wrong, Daddy?" Moey asked, concerned.

"It seems that Miss Turnipseed, as well as all the other baby-sitters you've had the past year have dropped off the face of the earth."

Sarah's eyes widened in horror, even Moey and Ellen looked aghast.

"Did they drop off the ears or the noses?" Sarah asked, awed. "I didn't know the earth had noses."

"That would make maps look pretty funny, wouldn't it sweetheart?" Ariel intervened. "I think that your Daddy means that the ladies that usually take care of you are going to be busy while he's gone."

"Daddy, you promised we could have Miss Turnipseed!" Ellen shrilled.

"I promised I would *try* to get Miss Turnipseed. I can't help it that the woman is busy. I'll find you another sitter, honey. Or maybe you could stay with your grandmother."

"Nana's leaving for Florida tomorrow," Moey said, and Damon's heart sank. So much for that option.

"Yeah. And she said she won't bring me an alligator head," Ellen complained. "I'll probably get some stupid doll."

Damon heaved a sigh. "Well, then, I'll just have to call the agency, try again." He reached for the phone, but Ellen flung herself on him, stopping his hand.

"No! I don't like new sitters! They make all kinds of stupid rules, and mix up our names and forget to close the closet doors at night so the monsters can't come out."

"Ellen, I'll tell the sitter to close the closet doors before I leave. And as for rules—you have to obey them even when Mrs. Applebea is here."

There were tears shimmering in his daughter's eyes. "I *won't* obey the rules. I'll be so bad, I'll make that new sitter go away!"

"What if it wasn't a strange person, Ellen?" Moey asked, hopeful. "What if it was somebody we knew."

Frustration made Damon's voice sharp. "I already told you, all the sitters you've had before have already been hired out. Melissa, I can't—"

"Miss Madigan's not hired," Moey said, looking up at him with solemn eyes.

Damon steeled himself against them. "Moey, contrary to popular belief, teachers have a life outside of school. I'm sure Miss Madigan has other things to do with her time."

"No she doesn't. I heard her talking to Ms. Ames on their way to the cafeteria last Thursday. She said she was going to lie by the pool and read books all summer."

Ariel gave the child an indulgent hug. "Moey, it's true I'm not working this summer, but your father... I think he feels more comfortable going through this baby-sitting agency he trusts."

"All the sitters except Miss Turnipseed and Mrs. Applebea are yucky," Ellen said.

"You're not yucky, Miss Mad Again," Sarah said, looking up at her with hopeful eyes. "You smell like flowers, and laugh and make circuses."

"Honey," Ariel began, "I don't think—"

But Ellen interrupted. "Yeah. And *you* wouldn't mind about the bunny. We could keep him and hug him and feed him carrots and *still* go see the dinosaur bones."

"I'd love to see the dinosaur bones, but . . ."

"Then stay! Please, Daddy, make her stay!"

"Ellen, I won't allow you to put her on the spot like this. It isn't fair."

"It isn't fair that you're going to 'Stralia, either," the child said, meeting him glare for glare. "You promised you'd stay with us when Mrs. Applebea was gone. And then you promised to get Miss Turnipseed. You were unfair two more times than me, Daddy."

Damon's head throbbed with the beginnings of a headache, every tick of the clock as it closed in on eleven-fifteen making him feel as if he were drowning.

Ariel Madigan baby-sit his children?

It was ridiculous. Impossible. And yet . . . he was running out of other options. Fast.

Damon regarded her seriously, her creamy complexion every bit as soft as his daughters', her lips that seemed fashioned to curve in that angelic smile. Even the clothes she wore—those ungodly shades of purple and gold—seemed like a splash of fun against the sterile backdrop of the expensively decorated room.

"Moey, take your sisters upstairs," he said at last.

Ellen thrust out her small chest. "I don't want to go! I want to play with the bunny."

"Go upstairs. Now," Damon said in a determinedly level voice, but he didn't take his eyes off Ariel as the girls left the room.

She straightened, wiping the palms of her hands on her leggings in a gesture that screamed of nervousness. "I'd better be leaving. You've got a lot to get settled."

"Maybe not. That is, except for whatever salary you might want to ask."

"Salary? I . . ." She gave an unsettled laugh. "Damon, I don't . . . this idea of Ellen's . . . it's—"

"Perfect. That is, if you really *were* intending to sit by the pool all summer."

"I was, but—"

"I have a pool. You could sit by it for the next week and get paid."

She backed away. "I don't think—"

"Don't you see? It's perfect. You said you wanted more time with Moey. Said she'd need some time to bond with a new counselor. You could work with her while you're here."

"And you said you wanted to hire a child psychologist. That you didn't want someone with an elementary ed degree that reads pop psychology magazines meddling with your daughter."

"I don't. Not permanently. But—damn it, don't you see?—this way we can compromise. I won't try to kid you. I'm more than a little desperate. But even so, I'm not the kind of father who is comfortable leaving his kids with just anyone. I've seen how great you are with the girls. And if Sister Thomasetta trusts you with a classroom full of thirty, I suppose it's safe enough to trust you with my three."

"I'm flattered that you would feel confident leaving them with me. Really I am. And I understand that you need a sitter badly, but—"

"I'd pay whatever salary you asked. Name your price."

Ariel gave an uneasy laugh. "I'd like to. I'd really like to stay, take care of the girls. They're adorable. They remind me of my nieces back in Galena. But if my superiors ever found out . . ." She sighed. "I've already crossed most of the lines they've drawn, just by coming here last night to talk to you. Add this early morning visit, and . . . well, even if they didn't know I had been . . . well, kissing the daddy of one of my pupils, I could be in a lot of trouble."

The reminder of the moments he had held her, kissed her, on the porch made Damon's blood heat. The kiss had been a mistake, made when his defenses had been lowered by the medication they'd pumped into him at the hospital. And yet, he was certain that even if he'd been knocked out cold he would never have forgotten how she had tasted, how he could feel the generosity in her lips, the openness of her heart.

He hadn't considered the fact that these incidents that had just disturbed his peace of mind might hold dire consequences for her.

"They couldn't object unless I complained, could they? About your coming here?"

"Not really."

"And other teachers get summer jobs, don't they? Tutoring kids that have trouble in some subject, or teaching summer school."

"I suppose so. But—"

"I bet some of them even baby-sit other kids during summer vacation. Watch them for working mothers who can't be home." Damon surprised himself by catching up her hands. The skin was so soft he couldn't resist skimming his thumb over the dainty ridges of her knuckles. He heard her breath catch, knew that his own pulse was racing. He told himself it was only because so much depended on her agreeing to stay. "This wouldn't be any different than that, Ariel."

Her fingers curled around his, the sensation of those small fingers, cocooning his large ones shaking Damon to his very core.

"It would be different," she said softly, "because of what happened last night." She tipped her head back, those aquamarine eyes seeming to stare straight into his soul.

"You said yourself that it was because we were both under a lot of stress. I was pumped full of painkiller. We were both exhausted. It was my fault, all of it."

"Not all."

"Yes, it was, damn it. But even so, it's not as if I'm going to be grabbing you by the hair and dragging you upstairs to have an orgy in front of the kids. I just want to hire you as a baby-sitter. For one week while I'm in Australia. Even if I wanted to, I could hardly carry on an affair from a continent away."

She caught her lip between her teeth, the little indentations only reminding Damon how soft those lips had been, how giving. And the breezy words he had tossed off a moment ago seemed ludicrous as he felt himself hardening beneath the potent mixture of the memory of the taste of her, and the image his careless words had conjured—of this woman lying like a tumbled angel in the middle of his big bed.

With astonishing clarity, he remembered telling her the night before that his bed was empty—and it had been, since Amanda had died. Not even one of the beautiful, sophisticated women who had offered themselves to him in the past year had even begun to tempt him. But this woman . . . with her winsome features, had made him feel the starvation that gnawed down deep in his soul, the unquenchable thirst to be touched, to be held, to unloose the passion he kept hidden beneath his aloof facade.

Afraid that Ariel would see his thoughts in his eyes, he released her hands and turned away. She was quiet, so quiet.

At last he spoke. "I don't want to pressure you. But I really am desperate."

"I should say no. That way you might stay with the girls yourself. It would be better for them if you did."

"I can't. I—"

"So you say. All right. I'll do it."

Relief rocketed through Damon, but for an unsettling instant, he wasn't sure why—whether it was because he was out of his baby-sitting jam, or because the thought of her here, with his little girls, suddenly seemed so right.

"I'll have to get some of my things. . . ."

"Can you take the girls? I hate to ask—" he glanced down at his watch "—but the time—"

"It's no bother. They can see how the other half lives."

He was amazed to find himself wondering what her apartment was like. He could almost picture it—vivid colors splashed about, a jungle full of plants. It would probably be a mess, with crayon drawings from her students taped to the refrigerator, and goo for pudding paint stuffed on the counters. And she'd probably play scratched jazz records on an old turntable.

Intuition had never been Damon's strong suit, and he was surprised at how certain he was that he had read her personality so easily. It made him wary, the possibility that she had somehow wormed her way past his customary reserve.

He retreated into his usual businesslike air. "I had already written out instructions for the sitter. I've also listed the girls' pediatrician and dentist and the number for poison control, just in case. There's a copy of their daily routine. And you know about the monsters in the closet."

Her lips curved into a smile. "Yeah. I know about the monsters."

"When I'm here, Mrs. Applebea has an apartment over the garage, but when I'm gone, she stays in the house."

"All right."

"Believe it or not, there isn't a guest bedroom in this place. The sitters usually take my room when I'm gone, so they can be close to the girls."

"Your... room?" she echoed, appearing nonplussed.

"The couch is hard as a slab of granite. My bed is a lot more comfortable."

As soon as the words were out, he regretted them. He'd never much thought about the other baby-sitters using his room. But the thought of Ariel Madigan there, her gold curls tumbled on the pillowcases, her long, dainty legs stretched out beneath his sheets made the ache in his groin more persistent than ever.

He clenched his fist on the handle of his crutch, trying to drive the image out of his mind. That would be all he needed—to botch things up now that she'd agreed to stay.

"If you want, Moey can sleep in my room," he amended hastily.

Ariel smiled, a rather pale copy of her usual beaming amusement. "What, and leave me in there with the monsters? No thanks."

Did she have any idea how many monsters lurked in Damon's own room? Pooled in the shadows, scraping their claws against his conscience, late into the night. They had haunted him so relentlessly, he had finally called the interior decorator, had her completely redo the master bedroom—gutting it, down to the very bed he'd shared with his wife.

But it hadn't mattered. The monsters were still there.

They were inside him.

And the only thing he had accomplished by redecorating the room was to implant the idea in Ellen's little mind that *she* should be the next person to have such a treat.

A fact that she never let him forget.

The blast of an automobile horn from the street below made Damon curse, and he stumped over to the window, to peer out onto the street. A stretch limo had glided to a stop directly behind Ariel's pink bug.

He turned back to find her directly behind him, that face that was so animated suddenly seeming far too still. Fragile.

"I'll be back a week from tomorrow," he said. "The number of the hotel, and the company where I'll be working are written in the instructions. And there's money for whatever you need in the top desk drawer."

"Of course." Did he imagine it, or was her voice just a touch sarcastic?

"I'll call whenever I can."

"We'll be here."

"Just let me tell the girls you're staying, and . . . and say goodbye."

He hurried out of the room, the crutch barely slowing him at all. Ariel listened to the uproar of the Kincaid girls as he told them—their squeals of delight, and excited chatter.

She should have felt better about her decision to stay, as enthusiastically as her charges were greeting her. But as she watched Damon Kincaid make his way down the front steps, crutches supporting his tall frame, his handsome face highlighted by the sun, she was suddenly certain she was making the biggest mistake of her life.

Chapter Seven

It had been a mistake to let her stay.

Damon had known it the moment he set foot on the plane at O'Hare. Had been certain of it every time, thereafter, that he had picked up the phone and called his children, only to feel that jolt, low in his stomach, when Ariel Madigan's voice had come through the receiver.

Not since Amanda had died had he been so distracted, having to force himself, time and again, to focus on business records, pay logs, examine a hundred different official records in an effort to discover who was attempting to take the Melbourne company down.

The very fact that his thoughts had been so scattered set off alarm bells so insistent they all but split his head, the memory of the consequences should he fail far too fresh in his mind to be ignored.

Instead, he'd done his best to ignore *her*. Block out that honey-sweet voice that held just enough smoke to make a man think of what happened the night *after* Cinderella married the prince.

He'd made it all the way to Tuesday by being distant and polite to her whenever he called the girls. But when a particularly grueling session with the company accountants had drained Damon of energy, he had made the mistake of calling home late.

It had been the last call he'd made while he was gone.

Ariel had been sleeping, her middle-of-the-night voice so incredibly seductive and warm, it had seemed to caress him, even though he was an ocean away.

Sarah was cuddled in bed with her—a very small monster having managed to slip beneath the crack beneath the closet door.

Ariel had laughed drowsily, spinning out for him the story of Sarah wandering in, her thumb stuck in her mouth, her treasured "blankie" trailing behind her.

Damon had closed his eyes, able to picture with painful clarity the little bundle of his daughter curled in the crook of Ariel's arms, Ariel stroking Sarah's curls, murmuring to her to soothe away the bad dream. Making the child feel warm, secure. Protected in that wonderful childhood way that was so fleeting.

It had made him ache, way down deep in his chest. Had made him wonder if those same hands could ease his night pain.

Through the phone, he heard Sarah give a contented little sigh, and he remembered those times he had wanted to draw his frightened daughters into the big bed with him and Amanda. How much he had wanted to cocoon them in the coverlets, far away from whatever had scared them.

But Amanda had never allowed the girls to do so, some parenting manual she had read having convinced her that if she allowed them to do it once, they would become clingy and dependent and expect to sleep there all the time.

The idea of his daughters—especially of his intrepid little Ellen—becoming clingy had seemed ridiculous to Damon.

And the nightmare issue had been one of the few times Damon had questioned Amanda. He hadn't been able to see any danger in letting a terrified child cuddle where she felt safe. Especially when there was no way to mistake the very real terror in her face.

But his wife had met his objections with a flood of her own tears, telling him that he knew nothing about children. That she was only trying to do what was best for them.

That had been true enough for him to quit arguing.

No, Damon thought, leaning his throbbing head back against the seat of the airport limo. He didn't know anything about his children except that he loved them so much it hurt.

And that they couldn't go on this way much longer.

Damon closed his eyes against the blur of rush-hour traffic, feeling raw inside. He should be elated to be back in the States, and only ten minutes away from Worthington Drive. He should be eagerly anticipating seeing his children and relaxing, however briefly, at home.

But with every mile he had traveled, the insidious sense of dread he so loathed had tightened around him—the knowledge that he would again have to confront the myriad problems that awaited him setting his stomach to burning, his head to aching.

Ellen's fits of stubbornness were getting worse all the time. Moey was retreating deeper and deeper into a fantasy world of her own, trying in a sad, pathetic way to fill up the empty space Amanda had left in her life. And Sarah . . . his little Sarah needed someone to love her. Someone to hold her hand while she toddled through the park. Someone to catch her when she shot off the sliding board. Someone to cuddle her close in the darkness and chase the monsters back into the closet where they belonged.

They needed someone to mother them. Needed it desperately. It was the one thing Damon couldn't give them.

The throbbing in his temples thrummed deeper, and he pressed his fingertips to his forehead. He'd failed as a hus-

band once already. He'd made Amanda unhappy, though
God knew, he would have done anything to change things.
And he would pay for that failure for the rest of his life.
How could he risk making such a terrible mistake again?
Risk opening himself to another woman, risk disappoint-
ing her, hurting her? Risk devastating his children when
things didn't work out?

Because they wouldn't. Couldn't.

The only kind of woman who could deal with the life-style
his job required would be a woman who was as engrossed in
her career as he was in his, thriving on the challenges and
frustrations, the excitement and the grind of the business
world that had always been the only place Damon truly felt
at home.

And that kind of woman would hardly be eager to sacrifice what little free time she had to take trips to the zoo, or
make a birthday circus out of crepe paper, stuffed animals
and a whimsical imagination.

No, his children needed someone who understood them
far better than their father did. Someone who knew what to
say to them when they ran in crying with a skinned knee.
Someone who knew how to comfort them when they experienced the far bigger bumps life would surely offer them.

Eve had said so a million times since Amanda had died.
And worse still, Damon had said so himself.

He should find someone—maybe a divorcée with a cou-
ple of her own kids to raise. A realist who understood how
damn hard it was to be a single parent. A solid, steady sort
of woman who would be willing to care for the girls in ex-
change for the material things Damon could give her and her
children.

Hell, he wasn't immune to loneliness himself. Wasn't
above wanting someone in his life, in his bed. He was a
normal man with a healthy enough sexual appetite. If this
hypothetical woman was good with his children, he was sure
he could manage to deal well enough with her as a lover.

It wasn't as if he was still looking for the earth to move when he touched someone. It wasn't as if he needed to feel that bone-melting jolt he'd experienced the night he had kissed Sleeping Beauty on his front porch.

Only *he* was the one who had come awake that night—excruciatingly awake, when he had wanted to stay numb, asleep forever.

Ariel.

He winced at the sudden clear image of her, tangled in his sheets, her winsome fairy face pillowed on the curve of her arm, those thick, astonishingly dark lashes fanned across her cheekbones. Vulnerable, idealistic, full of hope and life and love—things that Damon had never known, never shared.

He raked his hand through his hair. Yes, he needed someone. But he needed a woman who was safe—reliable. One who would keep his daughters' lives organized, the way his own childhood had never been. One who would deal with the long absences and the countless bouts of entertaining expected of him in his position at Kincaid Jameson.

Someone who would be content to handle all the responsibilities inherent in being his wife without asking more of him emotionally than he could give.

And Ariel Madigan was most definitely not that kind of woman. She was the most dangerous sort of all—one who would burrow into the most secret, closely guarded corners of a man's soul, if she ever chose to love him.

Love him? Where in God's name had that thought come from? He didn't want anyone to love him. Didn't want to feel so responsible for anyone's happiness ever again.

No. He would get home, pay the woman her salary and shove her bodily back into that pink sardine can she called a car. And then . . . then he would figure out what to do.

Yes. That was it. He'd organized billion-dollar corporations. Surely he could manage to get his life in order, as well.

Damon shifted in the seat, and cursed as his foot clunked into the crutch that was propped beside him. He was down to only one, but he'd come to loathe the crutch, hating the way it slowed him down when he had spent his whole life racing along at breakneck speed. By force of will, he brought his impatience under control. Another day or two at most, and then he'd be rid of the blasted thing.

The driver pulled off onto Worthington Drive, the familiar houses blurring past as he wound down the street.

Damon saw his house amid those of his neighbors, but the wood and glass of the architecture was the only thing that seemed familiar about the place. The lawn that had always been so pristine—a testament to being nurtured by the professional landscaping service—was now littered with toys. Three small pairs of tennis shoes were abandoned on the steps and a raincoat that looked like Sarah's was draped across a shrub, while a lemonade stand built out of crates sat deserted by the street. A sign, lettered in Moey's awkward, child script, priced the drink at fifty cents a glass.

He felt his cheeks heat with embarrassment at the thought that his daughters had been sitting there, peddling sticky sweet lemonade to his neighbors. The girls had been so close to the street, anything could have happened—they could have been hit by a car, or snatched by some crazy person.

Damon gritted his teeth.

Yes, the lemonade stand alone was evidence enough that leaving Ariel in charge had been a mistake.

The limo glided to a smooth stop, and Damon paid the driver, then climbed out of the car. He tucked the crutch under his arm, and slung his carryon bag over his shoulder, then started up to the front door, the driver following with the rest of his luggage. The front door was wide open, and Damon cursed at the certainty that the woman must be air-conditioning half of Naperville.

But as he walked in, his irritation changed to confusion as the smell of wet paint slammed into his nostrils.

Paint? What the blazes was the woman doing? Some kind of art project with the kids? But the smell was so thick, like wall paint—

Alarmed, Damon slung his bag to the floor along with his crutch and limped down the hall as fast as his half-healed foot would carry him. The sound of three little girls chattering at once above muffled music drifted down the stairs, the hubbub punctuated by shrill child giggles, and a warm laugh that could only belong to Ariel.

Gripping the railing in one hand, Damon made his way up the steps, blazing lights and the barrage of noise seeming to come from the direction of Ellen's room.

The paint smell was so strong he could hardly breathe, and his jaw clenched as his eyes locked on several open cans of paint sitting on newspaper out in the hall.

"Ariel? Girls?" he called out, but at that very moment, everyone in the room erupted in uproarious giggles that must have drowned out his voice, even Ellen laughing in a way he'd not known for a long time—since even before Amanda had died.

He paused outside the room, suddenly feeling like a stranger in his own home. The sensation made him angry, confused.

He limped to the open doorway, but he felt as if he could have set off the grand finale of the Fourth of July fireworks and no one in the room would have noticed. His head throbbed at the level of noise in the room, his eyes besieged by a rainbow of colors so vivid he was tempted to pull out his sunglasses.

The white-and-gold French-Provincial furniture Amanda had bought was clumped in the middle of the room, tented with clear protective plastic on which Sarah was happily painting a flying cat.

The off-white carpet was blanketed with drop cloths that seemed to be afflicted with some rare disease—spots of every color imaginable speckling and splashing the material.

Moey and Ellen were dabbing the pink paint on the tutu that banded the waist of an elephant dancing amidst a dozen other animal ballerinas upon one wall, the girls' small faces beaming beneath smudges of paint.

Lions and tigers twirled canes, their heads adorned with top hats, cravats at their throats. A toucan, rigged out in a garish waistcoat, bowed to a blushing giraffe, while a crocodile, eyes aglitter with amusing wickedness, balanced a huge carrot between his teeth, in an effort to lure one of the fluffy lop-eared bunnies doing a tightrope act to come close enough to be his lunch.

However, unbeknownst to the crafty reptile, another bunny brigade swung from the trapeze over his head, fishing lines in their paws as they attempted to hook the treat and pull it safely out of the crocodile's mouth.

High above all this mayhem, Ariel perched precariously on a ladder, painting red-and-white streamers that made the ceiling look for all the world like the top of a circus tent.

Her slender body was all but lost in a pair of denim overalls, an orange tube top banding her breasts. Her arms were bare, silky and smooth, her throat graceful, as she arched back to concentrate on the ceiling above her.

Music poured out from Ellen's tape recorder—one of those children's TV puppets singing that he loved trash.

Ariel was singing right along, her hips swaying to the music as she applied the paint with practiced strokes.

Damon's mouth went dry as he stared at the vulnerable undercurve of her arm, the fullness of her breast bobbing gently, enticingly beneath the thin band of fabric covering it. Glimpses of her skin showed beneath several three-corner tears in the overall legs.

Damon felt himself grow taut with the need to cross the room, press his lips against those sensitive, soft triangles of bared skin.

That sudden fierce need was enough to shatter the astonished daze that had gripped him since he climbed the stairs moments before. His hand was clenched and his voice rough as he snapped, ''What the hell is going on here?''

Chapter Eight

Ellen gave a yelp of surprise, Moey whirled around in horror and accidentally swiped a pink trail across Ellen's tummy while Ariel all but tumbled backward off the ladder. Only Sarah seemed patently unperturbed.

Not bothering to abandon the paintbrush clutched in her chubby hand, Sarah raced across the slippery plastic at breakneck speed, hurtling her paint-splattered little body against Damon to offer an enthusiastic hug.

"S'prise!" she chortled gleefully. "Daddy, it's a s'prise!"

Damon gritted his teeth against the anger pulsing through him, as he untangled his daughter's arms from his knees, the sticky paint smudging his dark blue trousers, trickling down his fingertips. Not so easily dissuaded, Sarah climbed up his legs like a little monkey, and proceeded to work the goo into his hair.

"Sarah, you're full of paint."

"Uh-huh." She sighed with consummate satisfaction. "It's all over *everywhere!* But I didn't eat any. Ariel said I couldn't taste it, even if it looked de-lish-iss."

"That's right." Ariel's voice was full of tender indulgence as she turned gracefully on the ladder. "And she didn't even taste a drop."

"Neither did Moey or me," Ellen added. "Paint would taste all yucky." She gave a skip of delight. "I wish I had a million walls to paint, forever and ever and ever. Isn't it beautiful, Daddy? Miss Madigan imagined it all for me. She said she'd help Moey and Sarah do their rooms too, if you said it was okay. Moey's is going to be the Crystal Kingdom, with princesses and knights and sorcerers that have magic wands that really sparkle. And Sarah's is going to be a funny flower garden."

"With ladybugs," Sarah cried, ecstatic. "'Ladybug, Ladybug, fly 'way home...'" She began chanting her favorite rhyme.

Damon struggled to get hold of his temper, only Moey— who was agonizingly silent—seeming to sense how close he was to losing it.

Ariel seemed oblivious. Her mouth was curved in a welcoming smile, one of the straps of her overalls slipping down her shoulder. The upper curve of her breast was just visible beneath the band of stretchy material—the effect totally artless and mind-shatteringly alluring. Damon felt like a wire about to snap.

"We didn't expect you home so early," she said in that sultry sweet voice that was already far too familiar.

"But you did know I'd be returning eventually, didn't you?" he inquired in a deadly quiet voice. "Or were you intending to rent an air gun and spray the whole room white again before I returned?"

She looked a little nonplussed. "You said Ellen could redecorate her room. However she wanted. You talked about it on the phone. I heard you."

"I was planning to hire an interior decorator. She did a fine job last time."

"It looked like that medicine Mrs. Applebea makes me take when I've got di-reah," Ellen piped up. "And it had lace an' stuff stuck all over. I *hate* lace."

"Ellen, there was nothing at all wrong with your room," Damon began.

Ellen's chin stuck out, the animation in her face stilling, her mouth setting in an ominous pout. "There was nothing wrong with *your* bedroom, either, and *you* got it all changed around!"

Damon winced, Ellen's verbal blow aimed as effectively as a knee slammed into his midsection.

"You took out Mommy's big mirrors and that sculpture thing. And you even took out Mommy's bed."

"Ellen, enough!" Damon's cheeks burned, the feel of Ariel's eyes on his face seeming to rake him with the certainty that his vulnerability had just been laid bare by his daughter's angry words. "My choice in redecorating the bedroom is an entirely different matter."

"It's always different when grown-ups do things. If *I* was a grown-up, I'd make *you* sleep under all that lace stuff an' see how *you* like it!" Ellen huffed. "It scratched my nose an' made my eyes feel boring."

Ariel jumped down off the ladder, and went to Ellen, looping one arm around the little girl's shoulder. Damon was surprised and not at all pleased to see Ellen lean close against those denim-clad legs.

"I think that what Ellen is trying to say," Ariel began, "is that white is very *bland*. I understand that this color scheme can look...well, elegant for adults, but kids need vivid hues to stimulate their minds, pictures to spark imagination—"

"The color combinations you have here seem most appropriate to stimulate nightmares," Damon growled under his breath. Louder, he said, "You girls go on and wash up— I do trust they don't have to take a bath in paint thinner?"

"Water will be fine. Just turn on the sprinkler, like I showed you yesterday, Moey. And be sure not to touch anything on your way out."

Ellen clung closer, and turned pleading eyes to Ariel. "You won't let him erase all the pictures, will you, Ariel? He *said* I could have my room fixed up. And I love Madame Poopsie and Wrigglenose Esquire and Mr. Crock E. Gator."

"We'll talk about it later, sweetheart. Go on, now."

Damon expected wails of fury, expected one of Ellen's full-scale tantrums. But though Ellen's chin jutted in its usual attitude of displeasure, the little girl clung to Ariel a moment more, and then, with a parting glare at her father, followed her sisters out of the room.

A crushing silence enveloped the room as Damon stood, waiting until he heard the back door slam shut behind the girls. Then he rounded on Ariel, furious.

"Of all the irresponsible, brainless—" He battled for a modicum of control. "How could you do this? Tear apart Ellen's room without asking my permission—without saying so much as a word about it."

Ariel's cheeks were pink, her smile vanished, and even the animals on the bedroom walls seemed to lose their vivid colors in response.

"You're upset."

"*Upset?* That's an understatement. I arrive home to find the walls of my daughter's bedroom scrawled with nothing less than a kindergartner's idea of graffiti, and you're surprised that I'm upset?"

"You told Ellen that she could have the room redone any way she liked it."

"So you just took it upon yourself to play interior designer? Of course. Whenever *I* hear any of my clients talk about refurbishing their houses, I immediately run for my paintbrush."

"It wasn't like that, exactly."

"Then tell me how it *was* exactly. I can't wait to hear your explanation."

She shoved her hands in the pockets of her overalls, and nibbled at her lower lip. "The night after you called last—Wednesday, I think it was—a storm front moved in. A pretty bad one. It sounded like the Fourth of July—thunder cracking, lightning flashing."

Damon's jaw clenched. He knew what was coming.

"The storm...it affected the children badly. Ellen was in a horrible temper—Moey was subdued. And Sarah...Sarah kept crying over nothing. She's such a sunshiny little bundle, it didn't seem right."

"I suppose you didn't think of renting a movie for the VCR, or taking them to the museum to distract them from the storm?"

"I could have come up with a dozen things to distract them. But it wouldn't have done them any good in the long run. The best thing with children is to find out just what it is about the storm that frightens them—the loud, sudden noises, the lights flickering when the electricity threatens to black out. Sometimes the lightning scares them. Or else they're scared because most monsters in creepy movies come out when it storms."

"I've explained what happens in a storm to them a dozen times in the past year. Even Sarah knows about hot- and cold-air masses and wind currents and—"

"This isn't about wind currents and air masses." Ariel's eyes were sad, soft. "It's about the night their mother died."

Damon felt as if the floor had just dropped open below him. Denial, self-recrimination flashed jaggedly through him. For months, he had been frustrated, confused about his daughters' behavior during storms. He'd dismissed it as just one more example of the usual childhood fears. He'd done what he could to remedy the situation, but in the end, had merely grimaced, and figured that the phobia was just something they'd grow out of, like the fear of the dark.

But in reality, the fear of storms had been yet another piece of the puzzle, yet another clue that his little girls were hurting. And he hadn't been able to see it.

He buried his face in one splayed hand, and paced over to the window to where Ellen and Sarah were even now running through the sparkling jets of the sprinkler system, while Moey stood still beneath one stream of water, earnestly scrubbing paint from her elbow.

Ariel's voice was quiet. "I'm sorry if I overstepped my bounds. But I just wanted to give them some other memory to replace the bad one. I thought that if we designed the murals and painted them on Ellen's walls—well, that when it thundered they'd think of Madame Poopsie dancing around in her tutu, and about the crocodile and how much fun we had painting them."

Damon remembered the children's enthusiasm when he'd first come in—how excited Ellen had been as she pointed out the characters on the wall. All three of his little girls had been positively glowing with excitement, their eyes sparkling, their cheeks flushed with pleasure. And their laughter... He had heard it drifting down the hallway, the sweetest music he'd ever known.

But he'd silenced that laughter within moments of appearing at the door—had brought that wary light to Melissa's eyes, that shading of belligerence to the thrust of Ellen's chin. Only Sarah had seemed unfazed by his less than jovial appearance, and that was because she was too small to read the warning signs of his threatening temper. Given enough time, Damon was sure he'd extinguish the welcoming light in her eyes, as well.

The images were so vivid, Damon couldn't seem to squeeze words past the knot in his throat.

He heard the sound of plastic crackling beneath Ariel's feet, felt her fingertips drift down to lie softly on his shoulder. "Damon, I would have told you what we were doing. I really would have. But you didn't call back, and I didn't want to bother you. I know you're busy, and if you got a message to call home, you probably would have been worried sick until you got hold of me. The girls and I were in and out all week, and I didn't want to risk it."

"Not to mention the fact that by not calling me, you avoided the chance that I would say no." He turned and peered into her face, certain, in that instant, that he was right.

Crimson stained her cheekbones, and she lowered her lashes, her lips firming into a line that twitched just a little. He was certain she was attempting to quell a self-deprecating smile.

"All right," she admitted. "It did occur to me that you might be less than thrilled. But I figured once we got started, well, there wouldn't be much you could say. Especially when you heard how excited the girls were."

"So you intended to blackmail me through my daughters."

"No. Not really. I just . . . I've learned enough about you to know that you really do love your daughters. That you want what is best for them. I was sure that once you saw . . . once I explained . . ." Her words trailed off. "I suppose I'm not very good at taking *no* for an answer."

"And you knew I'd say no."

"The truth is, when you quit calling, it was like a gift from God."

Heat stole into Damon's face as he recalled in vivid detail the reason he hadn't phoned again—the fantasies that had unsettled him with images of Ariel in his bed. But she didn't seem to notice his discomfiture, her own cheeks flushed as she continued.

"I figured we could have it all finished, the mess all cleaned up, and . . . well, once it was a fait accompli . . ."

"I could make you spray it all white again. I could call in the decorator and have her over here in five minutes."

"You wouldn't do that." Was that bravado in her voice? Conviction? Or was there just a little unease beneath her tone?

"Wouldn't I? I don't like being manipulated. No matter what pretty excuse you use to disguise it."

"Luckily for me, your pride isn't half as important to you as that little girl out there."

Damon stared at her, astonished. In the eight years since Melissa had been born, Damon had heard numerous times how he lacked as a father. That he didn't understand children. That he didn't know how to be a parent. There was something about the words Ariel had said that stunned him. She was confident—completely confident that no matter how angry he was, he would do what was right for Ellen.

That this woman who seemed born with an innate understanding of the enigmatic little beings should have such faith in him startled him more thoroughly than if she had stalked over and dumped a bucket of paint over his head.

His astonishment must have shown on his face, because she smiled. A smile that took his breath away. "My mom has warned me for years that I have a bad habit of acting first, thinking later. But even so, I've never been one to shirk paying the piper afterward. You don't have to worry about paying me for this week. Consider my salary a down payment on the pair of sunglasses you'll need to invest in for whenever you walk into Ellen's room."

He walked over to the dancing elephant painted on the wall, traced the line of her trunk with his fingertip. The absurdly long eyelashes on the animal were wet, the gigantic tutu half filled in with the paint Moey and Ellen had been so diligently applying when he'd walked into the room. But despite the fact that the picture was unfinished, there was an animation about the beast that made him almost able to feel those big galumphing feet banging into the floor, hear the music being played by the orchestra of turtles half hidden by the stage curtain.

"As for the rest of this," Ariel continued, "I'll finish it up as fast as I can. Have it all cleaned up, and back in order before I leave."

Leave? Of course she was going to leave. He'd only asked her to stay at all because he was desperate for a sitter. And she had only agreed to watch the girls for the week he was in Australia. Considering that, he was surprised by the tug of panic he felt deep down, at the thought of her walking out the door.

"You don't have to hurry," he said, far too quickly. "About leaving, I mean."

Her eyes widened, and there was a watchfulness in those aquamarine depths.

"These mural things look as if they take a great deal of time. Especially with children underfoot."

"They were a big help," Ariel said slowly. "Ellen was the one who thought of using the carrot for rabbit bait. And Moey has terrific color sense."

"I suppose you're going to tell me that Sarah is a master at painting in the details like eyelashes and crocodile teeth."

"Sarah's job is to look as adorable as possible."

"While smearing paint over anything that doesn't move." Damon couldn't suppress the hint of a smile.

"Chill out, Dad," Ariel teased. "There isn't any damage that I can't fix."

She had meant the words to coax a laugh from him, as certainly as Mr. Crock E. Gator was attempting to coax the bunnies down into his mouth. And yet her voice was just a little unsteady, her words causing him to still, his eyes intent on her face.

"You could almost make me believe that." The confession was quiet.

Blue-green eyes fixed on his for a breathless heartbeat, then flicked, like a white-hot flame to his lips.

She wheeled, scooping up paintbrushes, dumping them in a bucket of water, then busied herself gathering up the girls' abandoned tools. "Just let me pull things together here and I'll—"

"Ariel." Damon paced over to stand behind her, and saw the back of her neck flush prettily, wisps of golden curls clinging to her vulnerable nape.

He wanted to reach out a fingertip, smooth it down the delicate skin. He wanted to turn her around, and touch her—the soft, moist curve of her lower lip, the sprinkling of freckles across her nose, the eyelashes that curled like silk fans upon her cheeks.

She angled her face to look at him, and he felt himself being yanked into the vulnerability, the openness of her eyes.

He shoved his hands into his pockets to keep from reaching out to her and made a great show of examining the giraffe's hot-pink toenails.

"Ariel, about my reaction to the mural. I..." He sighed. "Let's just say I'm about as good at dealing with surprises as you are at taking no for an answer. Ellen really does seem to love the paintings. And if it makes her happy... well, I'll get used to it...*somehow.*"

Ariel grinned, and Damon felt as if he'd been blindsided by a three-hundred-pound tackle. "Sunglasses. That's what I'd recommend."

"Orange ones with purple lenses?" he asked with a crooked smile.

"Definitely not. Aviator glasses. Wire rims accented with leather and mirrored lenses so no one can see inside."

Damon averted his eyes, feeling as if a wall of solid lead couldn't keep this woman from probing past the outer layers of his defenses, touching the places he had spent a lifetime trying to hide.

She was watching him, her face suddenly solemn, as if she could sense his very thoughts.

He turned away, almost afraid that if she could see his face, she would know what she was doing to him. She would know how deeply she moved him, how much she confused him. How much he was suddenly afraid that he needed her.

In the middle of such emotional turmoil, he should have wanted to run, to block her out completely. But instead, he felt a part of himself opening to her, revealing, perhaps not what was really gnawing deep inside him, but another place that was raw.

"The whole time I was away, I did a lot of thinking. About the girls. About me. You were right. I don't spend enough time with them, and I want to do something to remedy the situation."

He could see a flicker in her eye, knew that she was fully aware he was skirting the subject of what was really troubling him. But he plunged on, anyway.

"I even planned an itinerary for tomorrow while I was waiting for the airport limo. I got all these brochures to see Chicago. Lincoln Park Zoo, the Museum of Science and Industry, Field Museum, the Planetarium and the Shedd Aquarium. I even figured out what time we'd have to be at the aquarium's main tank to see the divers feed the sharks. Ellen would love that."

"She'd adore it, Damon. So would Moey and Sarah." The words were all he could hope for, but there was something in the tone of her voice that made Damon look into her eyes. They were a little amused, and yet, vaguely troubled.

He raced on. "And then . . . well, I figured I'd take them for a walk on the lakeshore, so they could see all the boats, and if there was time, we could go to the top of the Sears Tower. Then I'll make reservations for dinner at Farraday's and get junior theater tickets."

He could tell that she wanted to say something, the corners of her lips twitching with an amusement so tender, he couldn't bring himself to be irritated. "What is it?"

"Nothing. It's just . . ." She touched his arm softly. "All these ideas are wonderful, Damon. But this itinerary might be a little . . . ah, ambitious, for just one afternoon. You don't have to do anything so elaborate. One of the things I love most about kids is the fact that they enjoy the simplest things. Old boards to make tree houses, doll families made out of pussywillows tucked into beds made of matchboxes.

They like to make castles or pirate lairs of refrigerator boxes and fight dragons that are disguised as their daddies. And sometimes they love to just lay on their stomachs on the grass and watch an anthill.''

"You make it sound so simple, but it isn't, Ariel. Not for me. I love my daughters, but I don't . . . I can't seem to understand them. I make mistakes. A lot of them."

"Everyone makes mistakes."

"You don't."

The tender laughter that trilled from those rosy lips made Damon's gut clench with need. "I'd love to see Sister Thomasetta's reaction if she heard you say that. I've spent my entire life richocheting from one disaster to another."

"But not with children, Ariel. Never where children are concerned."

"Let's see. How do I try the principal's patience? Let me count the ways. There was the time we did a taffy pull for a pioneer unit, and the taffy didn't set. There was gooey stuff everywhere—on the floor, on the walls. I think Father O'Boyle even found some in the sacristy. We didn't even go in the sacristy! And then, there was the time we did a Creepy Crawly Corner for science."

"A Creepy Crawly Corner?" Damon was stunned to find the tight coil of stress easing in his chest, the muscles of his face relaxing into a smile. "I'm almost afraid to ask."

"It's exactly what it sounds like. The kids can bring in anything to study that creeps or crawls. We have magnifying glasses, simple identification books and posters on the life cycles of butterflies and things. The only rule is that the creepy crawlies still have to be alive."

"I see."

"It was a great success. Every kid in the class participated. We must have had eight million bugs in mayonnaise jars sitting on the window ledge, two tree toads, a bullfrog and three garter snakes in plastic containers with holes in the tops. Unfortunately I didn't realize I also had a pint-sized, animal-rights activist in the third row. He sneaked into the school during recess and set them all free.''

Damon couldn't help but chuckle at the image.

Ariel arched one brow with understated eloquence. "Yeah, the entire staff thought that it was just a bundle of laughs. Especially since Cody didn't bother to take the critters outside first. We were finding snakes and bugs for weeks.'' Her eyes were sparkling as she scooped up a paint rag and began scrubbing the spatterings of vivid colors from her fingers.

"Of course, I'll always believe it was God himself who led one of my miniature serpents onto the chalk tray in Mrs. VandenHaus's room. See, we have this feud going—she believes my program is worthless, and I believe she should have retired from teaching at the age of twenty-three.''

Ariel blew at a strand of hair that straggled across her cheek, then when that failed to move it, attempted to nudge it aside with her shoulder.

Damon swallowed hard as he watched the soft curve of bare skin brush against the stubborn curl stuck to her cheek. But when she failed again to get the irritating strand out of her way, he stepped forward, unable to resist lifting the silky curl between his fingers.

He heard Ariel's breath catch as his fingertips brushed her skin, but the gesture he'd meant to be brief lengthened into long seconds as he stroked the golden strand with his thumb. It was soft, so soft, without the slightest stiffness of hair spray or mousse. She smelled like paint and sweet summer grass crushed beneath children's bare feet.

And he wanted nothing more than to bury his face in her hair, to sip the laughter from her lips. His pulse quickened, and he felt as if he were drowning as he looked into her face. The tiniest smudge of blue paint graced one high cheekbone, a blot of pink near the corner of her lips. Without a word, he took the paint rag from her hands. Curving his finger beneath her chin, he tipped her face up as if she were no older than Moey, and gently rubbed at the speck of blue paint.

He could hear her breathing, soft, shallow, could feel it, warm and moist against the inside of his wrist.

Those eyes that had been sparkling with laughter were liquid now with heat, a kind of breathless anticipation. His mouth went dry as he moved to the next blot of dried paint. But this time it was the velvety moistness of her lip that touched him, burned him. Lips he could still remember plundering in desperation that first pain-hazed night beneath the porch light.

The memory made his fingers go numb, and the rag slipped unnoticed to the floor, his thumb tracing the bit of pink paint he hadn't quite scrubbed clean. He stared at it, there, accenting the corner of those mind-shatteringly sweet lips. Then, unable to stop himself, he slowly dipped his head down to press his mouth upon it.

He felt a tremor go through her.

"The rule was that...that no one was...allowed to taste the paint," she whispered, her eyes half-veiled by the thick sweep of her lashes.

"Ah, but I'm the daddy. Rank has its privileges."

"Is that so?"

She shifted when he touched her and he almost drew away. But she wasn't attempting to escape the caress, only to give him more, offering the full curve of her lips to his.

It was the sweetest kiss he had ever known and the most devastating, seeming to spiral through all his pain, all his doubts, to pierce that part of him he'd thought long dead, the part that believed in miracles and fairy-tale princesses and enchanted castles filled with beauty.

A low groan tore at his chest as he cupped her face in his hands, deepening the kiss, her lips parting beneath his in a tiny gasp of pleasure.

He slipped his tongue into the recesses of her mouth, and felt himself melt. His palms smoothed down the column of her throat and fanned out across the bare slope of her shoulders, and he closed his eyes, wondering what it would be like to chart a path to the narrow band of her top, ease the stretchy material down her breasts, to touch all of her with nothing in between them.

The image was so vivid, so alluring he felt himself harden, and he drew away from her, confused, unnerved, but more aroused than he'd ever been in his life.

For God's sake, he was supposed to be paying the woman her salary for baby-sitting his daughters the past week, and then seeing her to the door—gratefully watching this most disturbing woman exit from his life forever.

He wasn't supposed to be kissing her, touching her. Wasn't supposed to be feeling this gnawing ache of desire that pierced far deeper than mere sexual attraction. She was Melissa's teacher, his children's baby-sitter—not someone with whom he should indulge in a casual relationship.

And this time he didn't even have the convenient excuse that he was strung out on medication to explain why all of his defenses were down.

He raked his hand through his hair, wondering how everything had gotten so damned confusing.

"I'm sorry," he said, his gaze flicking to the kiss-reddened curve of her lips, "I don't know why I did that."

"I don't know, either, but if you promise to help clean up the paint like this every time, I'll start Moey and Sarah's rooms right away."

He wasn't certain what he had expected her to say, feel, but the light words were more soothing than any earnest assurances could be. It was as if she sensed how emotionally naked he felt, how exposed, and was allowing him this time to compose himself.

Her eyes were glowing, tender. "You're a pretty good kisser, Mr. Kincaid. For a daddy."

Damon's cheeks heated, but he felt his lips tug into a grin. "Is that so?"

"Yeah. And you're a pretty good daddy for a daddy, too."

The pleasure he'd been feeling dissipated, and he looked away. "That must be the reason you showed up on my door the night of the Abracadabra party—to tell me what a terrific job I was doing."

"I just think you need a little more time with the girls. Drown your beeper and your answering machine in the swimming pool and nail the doors shut. Or better still, get away altogether."

"That's what I intend to do with the museum trip I planned. They'd learn a lot—"

"So will you if you try to do all those things in one day." Sparkles of green danced in her eyes. "Like I said, I think it would be great for the girls to see those places. But right now, I think you need just to spend time with them. Just to *be* with them, without a lot of confusion or hectic itineraries."

"You mean, just stay at home and—"

"No. I do think you need to get away. I just think you might want to go somewhere quiet, a little more relaxing. Maybe somewhere like...a farm."

"A...I don't think they have many of those in Chicago."

"No. But they do have them in Galena. In fact, I just happen to be going to one next weekend."

"Ariel, I don't understand—"

"I'm a farm girl, City Boy. My mom and dad have a wonderful place just outside of town, with chickens and cows and pigs and horses, seven children and about sixteen grandchildren, all of whom are descending on them next weekend."

Damon gaped at her, aghast at the thought of embroiling himself in such mass confusion. Surely she couldn't be seriously suggesting that he and the girls intrude on a family weekend? Surround themselves with twenty-some total strangers out in the middle of nowhere. Surely this family of Ariel's would be just as nonplussed as he was at the thought of such an intrusion. Not to mention the fact that the presence of a widower with three small daughters in tow would pose about three million questions to anyone who cared about Ariel. It would give the impression that . . . well, that there was some sort of relationship, one far different from the teacher/parent bond that would be considered appropriate.

And in spite of the kiss, in spite of everything, he wasn't ready to examine the ramifications of his time with Ariel yet.

But her family . . . they would be suspicious at best, with a raft full of reservations about him. And he wouldn't blame them a bit. He closed his eyes, imagining Moey grown up, Moey dragging a man like him home, with children in tow, to introduce to her father. The very thought was enough to quell even the slightest stirrings of temptation.

"Ariel, we couldn't come to your parents' farm. It wouldn't be right."

"Of course it would. It will all be very relaxed. And with that many people underfoot, it'll be no inconvenience. No one will even notice a few extras. It would be a perfect place for you to spend some time with the girls. They'd have a great time, and it would be educational, too. Bet we could even get my dad to give them a ride on a hayrack."

"It's very generous of you, but—" He shook his head. "I'm sure your father would be less than pleased. And I wouldn't blame him. I mean, it's not as if . . . as if we . . ."

"Oh." She sobered for an instant, then brightened. "You're afraid he's going to corner you in the chicken coop and demand to know what your intentions are regarding his little girl, eh?"

Trust Ariel to cleave down to the most shadowy, hidden doubts he was having. He grimaced, beginning to feel as if his soul were made of cellophane.

"Ariel, I don't have a clue what's happening between us. And I don't feel comfortable dealing with it—"

"There is nothing *to* deal with. We're becoming friends, Damon. Friends."

He stilled at that simple word, the edginess that seemed to eat inside him suddenly having a name—loneliness. It had always been there—when he was a kid, locked up in that solitary South Side apartment. When he was in college, struggling so hard to stay at the top of his class, to secure his future, that he hadn't had time for the fraternity parties and homecoming dances, the pickup games of basketball and the student-night gatherings in the smoky, college town bars.

He'd had business associates, acquaintances, raquetball partners and employees. He'd had Amanda and the girls. But a friend...?

The gift she was offering was enormous, but as he stared into her eyes, he was afraid that it wouldn't be enough. That he would take from her, just as he had taken from Amanda, and leave Ariel as empty as he'd left his wife.

"Damon, I don't know what you're expecting, but my parents are used to me bringing friends to the farm. My dad...he's always said it's the best place to heal in the whole world. All the land, just acres and acres of it, so quiet, serene. There's something about watching life beginning...lambs and chicks and children. It's good for the soul. I promise you."

She was staring up at him so earnestly, her lips parted, her eyes soft, like the petals of a flower tucked in the cup of a child's hand. And he could feel the pull of those eyes, feel them enfolding him, not battering at his reserve, but rather wrapping around it like a down comforter, warming him through that brittle outer shell.

His voice was roughened with need, with hopelessness.

"No, Ariel. I'm sorry. I can't. I just..." He sighed, suddenly weary. "It would be a mistake."

"You wouldn't even have to stay at the farm if you didn't want to. There are wonderful, quaint bed and breakfasts in town, and hotels you could stay at. You'd be able to retreat to your private sanctum whenever you wanted to. But you and the girls would still get to see the animals and the barn and—"

"Am-in-als?"

Damon whipped around to see Sarah framed in the doorway, a towel bundled around her sturdy little body.

"Does we get to see aminals, Daddy?"

Damon blew out a breath, feeling trapped. "No, honey. Ariel and I were just talking about the place she grew up."

"'Bout the farm? Ariel gots a 'ttack goose an' kitties an' lambikins an' a brother who puts socks on the chickies." She turned soulful eyes up to Damon's. "I'd 'dore to see those lambikins more than anything in the world. Ariel says they feel all fluffy and soft, and sometimes they feed the babies with bottles. And they go get chickies at the snatchery, an' bring them home in boxes."

Damon crossed to where she stood and hunkered down, automatically starting to towel her dry. "I'm sure that it would be really fun to see, Sarah, but—"

"But you're too busy, right, Daddy?" There was such resignation in that small face that Damon flinched. "Well, maybe I could glue cotton balls on my Baby Wet Away, and pretend she's a lambikin. But I don't know what a snatchery looks like, to pretend the baby chicks."

There was something so wistful in that little face. Something that shoved hard at the guilt inside him. She hadn't even waited for him to offer excuses, explanations of why she was to be denied such a rare treat. Sarah had made his excuses herself, and then gone on trying to dream up a way she could make amends, fill up the empty space left by his refusal.

In that instant, Damon knew that nothing could be as bad as seeing his own failure etched so plainly on his little girl's face. Nothing. Not even being overwhelmed by an entire family full of Ariels. Not even fielding probing questions from her parents, or enduring the quizzical glances of her brothers and sisters.

Not even spending the whole next weekend enduring the knife's edge of emotion Ariel seemed to press into his soul?

No. This had nothing to do with him and Ariel. She had made that clear. No strings attached. No expectations. And there was the alternative she'd offered of the hotel room, or the bed and breakfasts—havens where he could get away if things got too intense.

For his children, couldn't he make this little sacrifice? Give them afternoons filled with lazy bumblebees, and wobbly legged lambs? A night filled with the stars Ariel had wished upon as a child?

Surely he could do that much. For Sarah. For Moey. For Ellen. After all the pain he had caused them.

"Tell you what, sweetheart," he said, pulling his little daughter into a somewhat soggy embrace. "You leave me no choice. I can hardly condemn poor Baby Wet Away to life covered with cotton balls. And you've even got *me* curious about this 'snatchery.' We'll go to the farm."

"Honest, Daddy? Honest truly?" Sarah's face lit up.

"Honest truly."

With a shriek of unadulterated glee, the little girl flung her arms around him. "You're the bestest daddy in the whole world!" she cried, punctuating the words with a kiss. "I love you more'n anyfing."

"I love you, too, Sarah Jane." He squeezed the words out of a throat suddenly raw. "More than anything."

"Wait 'til I tell Ellie and Moey! They won't even ever believe it!" In a heartbeat, Sarah had tugged away from him, and was dashing down the hallway. He called out a word of caution as she headed for the stairs, grimaced when she patently ignored him. The room was quiet in her wake, even the tape recorder in the corner silent as he straightened. And he didn't have the slightest idea what to say to the woman standing so close behind him.

He stiffened when he felt her fingertips against the line of his jaw, a soft caress that made him tremble inside.

"You know what?" she asked, and he turned to lose himself in eyes that were shining with approval and so much hope, it seemed to brim in a glistery sheen beneath her lashes. "Maybe you're not the quite best daddy in the world yet, Mr. Kincaid. But you have potential."

Was there the slightest quiver in her voice?

"Yes, sir. You definitely have the potential."

Chapter Nine

The rutted gravel drive wound through ripples of meadow grass and dew-kissed hay reaching for the sun. White wooden fencing bracketed the lane, russet-coated cows and placid sheep dotted the pastures.

Damon gripped the steering wheel of the red BMW, wishing he could feel just a little of that peace. But his palms were damp, his pulse unsteady as he guided the vehicle toward the cluster of buildings just visible on a distant rise, the constant chatter of the girls that had entertained him during the drive suddenly seeming to grate on nerves that had been coiled tightly ever since he'd accepted Ariel's invitation.

His jaw tightened in agitation. Why had he ever agreed to come here? To this place that seemed as far removed from his existence as the Crystal Kingdom that Moey had confided to him about late last night when they'd both been unable to sleep. Three times, Damon had almost called Ariel to cancel the plans for this trip. Once, he'd actually phoned. But when he'd heard Ariel's voice, he'd stunned himself by failing to call things off, asking for more detailed directions instead.

Damon took one hand from the wheel and kneaded the stiff muscles at the back of his neck, disgusted with himself. Why should the very thought of seeing Ariel again disturb him? Deep down, in the hidden currents of his soul?

Why had he wandered around his bedroom, fingering the bottles of cologne she'd shifted aside in order to make room for her own hairbrush and lipstick? Why had he buried his face, time and again in the pillow that still somehow held her subtle fragrance, and dreamed of the way her lips had tasted, her hands had felt against his skin?

When he'd finally surrendered all efforts at sleeping, and had stalked into the bathroom to take a shower, he hadn't escaped Ariel at all; rather, he'd discovered a nightgown she'd forgotten on a hook behind the door. Delicate white cotton, printed with tiny silver flowers, the gown had draped there, the length so short he could picture her in it, could see the way it would brush her thighs, accenting the slender sweep of her legs. He could imagine the way her breasts would look beneath the thin covering of fabric, could imagine the way her skin would feel, heated and eager beneath his hands.

And as he'd stood there, the shower steaming up the room, exhaustion dragging at him, along with frustration and desire, he'd felt like something that had crawled out from beneath a rock.

Ariel had offered him friendship. She'd breezed in and shifted his perspective, shaken him from the emotional coma that had gripped him since Amanda's death, and had forced him to see things he hadn't wanted to see, to deal with things he hadn't felt capable of handling.

She'd given him gifts that had nothing to do with the attraction he'd felt toward her, gifts he was far too grateful for to repay by entangling her in the disaster his life had become. Because she deserved better.

To her, life was a grand adventure, and she deserved to fall in love with a man who saw the world as she did—full of magic and hope and miracles. Damon saw all the harsh edges.

He now gritted his teeth against a welling of something akin to despair. Well, it would be over soon. This visit, this space of time where he'd glimpsed magic through Ariel's eyes. It would be for the better. Everything back to normal, but nothing ever quite the same.

He reached over to where Sarah was seat-belted in beside him, and ran his hand across the silky fall of her hair as the child's chatter distracted him.

"Daddy, is that a cow?" Sarah asked, awestruck. "An honest to really cow?"

"I'm gonna ride one of those cows, Daddy," Ellen piped up. "Just like on the rodeo."

Damon shook his head. That was all he needed when he was feeling so damned edgy—Ellen on a rampage. "Ride the cow and you spend the rest of the visit locked in a suitcase," he warned.

Ellen made a face. "Okay, I won't ride the dumb cow." Her voice dropped low. "At least not until we're about to leave."

"You'd better not do it at all, young lady," he cautioned. "Do you understand me?"

"Yeah, young lady," Sarah echoed in an exact mime of his own stern tone. "Or you'll be in *b-i-g* trouble. Just like at the you-see-'em."

Damon groaned inwardly at the reminder of his outing with the girls two days earlier. An outing, he, for one, would never forget. If the girls had plotted for weeks to find a way to tighten the coil of tension in the pit of his stomach, they couldn't have found a better button to push.

"It's called a *museum*," Moey corrected. "Not a you-see-'em."

"Yeah, so just be quiet, you big baby," Ellen groused.

"But you do see 'em," Sarah said, her voice quivering with indignation. "You see Egypt mummies and dinosaur bones and—"

"Enough, all of you," Damon cut in, the conversation starting to hold all the earmarks of full-scale sibling warfare. "We're going to be guests here, and I expect you to be on your best behavior. No bickering, no calling each other names. No riding on cows—"

Ellen was mumbling an unintelligible reply when his lecturing was lost in Sarah's crow of delight.

The battle with her sister forgotten, Sarah strained toward the window, clapping her hands ecstatically.

"Daddy! Daddy! Look! It's a Hansel house just like in the story! Do you think it gots an oven to push the witch in?"

Turning his attention from his scolding, he looked at the building that had grown significantly nearer during his contretemps with his daughters.

The turn-of-the-century farmhouse was as chaotically lovely as the woman who had grown up there. Blue paint, weathered to a soft patina, covered clapboard siding, dollops of trim as intricately cut as the decorations on the gingerbread house Sarah had chattered about were colored rose pink, while snowy white moldings edged additions that sprawled whimsically in three directions.

Suddenly oblivious to the girls' babble, Damon drove on by sheer instinct, unable to take his eyes off this place where Ariel had grown up.

It was more beautiful than any idyllic familial scene he had dreamed of on the fire escape as a child, from the morning glories baring their throats to the sun, to the prizewinning roses and brilliant petunias that splashed ribbons of color around the building's foundation.

The old-fashioned veranda listed leeward, but it only made the house seem warmer, somehow, more welcoming, the spokes missing from the railing around the porch as engaging as a child's gap-toothed grin.

A tire swing was suspended from a mammoth oak, a tree house nailed precariously on one of the topmost branches. A picnic table was tucked in the shade of a chokecherry tree, while a huge, gallumphing golden retriever dashed around the yard, some unidentifiable object clamped in his jaws. An assortment of children from age four to fourteen raced after the dog in hot pursuit, shrieking at the tops of their lungs.

In their midst he could spy a slender, laughing figure, attempting to collar the excited mutt. Ariel. Everything from her magenta-and-white-striped blouse to her worn blue jeans sang with energy and enjoyment.

At the last possible instant before "Fido" made his escape beneath what looked to be a garden fence, she flung herself onto that furry back, tumbling, dog and all, into a heap on the thick grass. The children tumbled down after her, wrestling with each other and the dog, probably grinding grass stains into their outfits so deeply, a nuclear warhead couldn't have blown the stains out.

Damon strained to see what Ariel was attempting to wrest from the dog's jaws, the purloined object that had undoubtedly been the cause of their grand chase. But as he eased the car to a stop on the gravel drive, he saw Ariel pop up from the middle of the mayhem, her eyes flashing to the car.

Damon felt a sharp tug deep in the pit of his stomach as he saw her eyes widen in pleasure and... could it be surprise?

That split second her attention wavered was just enough time for the dog to make good its escape, scrambling under the fence and streaking away in a blur of golden fur.

A chorus of shouts and groans rose from the children, a few of them climbing the fence, and starting the chase again. But Ariel merely got to her feet, seeming to hesitate long seconds as her hands brushed at the bits of grass and dust that clung to her clothes.

He'd expected her to race to greet them in her usual bouncy, Winnie-the-Pooh's-Friend-Tigger style. But there was something self-conscious about her, something almost shy. Something that made Damon ache way down deep.

The sound of the car door being all but flung from its hinges in Ellen's haste to get out jarred Damon from his thoughts, and also seemed to spur Ariel into movement as his three daughters spilled pell-mell out of the vehicle and ran to meet her. "Hey, you little monsters," she cried. "I missed you!"

"We missed you, too!" Moey grabbed one of her hands.

"I found 'free ladybugs," Sarah chirruped, squeezing a jean-clad leg in greeting, while Ellen all but bowled Ariel over with an enthusiastic hug.

"Yeah, and she ate a monkey biscuit at the zoo, too. I almost barfed."

"So *that's* where you got that long tail, Sarah Jane," Ariel teased, patting the little girl on the bottom. The three girls dissolved into giggles. And Damon knew his daughters well enough to be certain that Ariel had somehow managed to skillfully sidestep a continuation of the argument that had gone on in the car moments before.

He climbed out of the car far more slowly, feeling oddly left out as he heard the girls chattering on, each trying to speak louder than the others as they attempted to tell Ariel everything that had happened in the days since she'd last seen them. And the revelations that were popping out of his children's mouths were less than comforting.

Sarah's piping voice rose above the others, regaling Ariel with the museum trip that had proved to be baptism by fire into the world of involved parenthood.

"—and the guard catched Ellie by the strap of her jumper, and pulled her right out of where the crocky-gator was—"

"It was a stuffed crocodile." Damon felt compelled to interrupt. Ariel turned the full force of her smile on him, and he felt his cheekbones heat. "Sarah had just skinned her knee, and I was trying to find a place with first-aid supplies, and Ellen decided to become a part of the rain-forest display.''

"She was off in search of head hunters, eh, Dad?" Ariel was smiling at him, the clouding of shyness in those huge eyes laced with such understanding and approval his own defensiveness melted into a wry chuckle.

"Exactly."

Sarah was tugging on Ariel's jeans, and she scooped up the little girl, cuddling her close. "Ariel, my daddy was a berry good boy on our 'cation to the you-see-em. He didn't even yell at me when I ated the monkey biscuit and wetted my pants. He just took me over to the lake an' dunked me in.''

"It was real hot out," Damon explained hastily. "She dried off in no time."

"Pretty ingenious troubleshooting there, Mr. Kincaid."

"It's called desperation, Miss Madigan." He stared at her, framed against a backdrop of grass and field, a dark red barn and an oak tree with a swing dangling from it, and he marveled at how she had taken what he'd seen as an unqualified disaster, and made him somehow feel as if he'd earned a Congressional Medal of Honor. He was stunned to find his mouth curving into a smile.

"Next time," he said, suddenly looking forward to the prospect, "I'm packing my own bandages, a fresh change of munchkin clothes and about forty-seven drink boxes."

"Don't forget the aspirin," she teased. "For the headache you are about to receive."

Damon stared down at her, his palm tingling with the need to skim the soft curve of her cheek, to draw her into his arms and feel her laughter as he told her about Ellen's pranks, Sarah's antics and Moey's vivid imaginings.

He swallowed hard, knowing it had been a mistake to come here, but glad as hell that he had done it, anyway. The roar of children around him made him shake himself, turn his attention to his daughters, but in those few moments he had been lost in Ariel Madigan's eyes, all three of the girls had raced off.

Ellen was clambering up the ladder to the tree house with a little boy sporting a shiner that would do Sugar Ray Leonard proud. Moey was enthralled with a girl about her age, who was allowing her to hold a smoke-gray kitten on the porch swing. And Sarah was already spouting her funny little speeches to twin girls of about fourteen, who were looking at her as if she were some wonderful life-size doll.

Damon stared after them, feeling more than a little abandoned. In all his thoughts about this day, he'd imagined the girls clustering around him, a buffer, a shield against the confusing emotions Ariel stirred in him. He'd pictured his daughters clinging to his hands as they had at the museum, dragging him hither and yon to examine the discoveries they'd made.

Time. Precious time they would spend together as a family.

Never once had he imagined that all three of them would zing off on their own without even looking back.

The irony of the situation wasn't lost on him, and he glanced at his wristwatch, wondering how early he could leave without seeming rude.

"Oh, no, Damon." Ariel's voice made him glance up, and he stiffened as her fingers scooped up his hand, making quick work of unfastening the watch. "Relaxation Rule number one—no watches." She slipped the expensive timepiece from his wrist, and stuck it in the car. "You have absolutely nothing to do and nowhere to go until after dark, sir. And I'm not sure I'll even let you slip away then."

Damon's chest constricted, the feel of her fingers still lingering on the inside of his wrist sending tiny, hot sparks through his veins. Attempting to quash the sensation, Damon gently pulled away from her, and turned to the car, grabbing a paper bag from behind the driver's seat.

"Speaking of night . . ." he said, feeling awkward as hell, "you forgot something at my place."

"Did I?" Ariel gave a nervous laugh as she took the bag. "I'm always leaving stuff all over," she said, tugging out the bag's contents. "My sister Carrie says—" The words ended in a choked gasp, as the nightgown spilled out in her hands.

She all but dropped it, and Damon's hand flashed out to catch it before it fell to the dirt. Their hands meshed, tangled in the delicate fabric, the white cotton looking even more sheer, somehow more intimate, in contrast to his dark-tanned hand. The roses that pooled near the veranda seemed pale in comparison to Ariel's cheeks.

"Oh. I—I hadn't even noticed this was...was missing..." she stammered. "I..."

"Don't tell me you're leaving your nightgowns all over Naperville again." The sophisticated feminine voice made them leap apart as if they'd been caught in a heated embrace, and Damon's eyes fastened on a woman striding toward them, with lithe grace.

Her hair was a red-gold color that models would kill for. Her figure equally enviable, set off to perfection by a pair of designer jeans and a black blouse with a smattering of rhinestones at the collar.

She should have appeared as out of place on this farm as Damon himself did, but somehow she blended into the landscape as perfectly as the wren house swinging from the chokecherry's lowest branch.

One slender hand was extended in greeting. "Welcome to Shadylane Farm. I'm Caroline, Ariel's sister."

He took that hand in a firm grip, feeling somehow on the same wavelength as this very self-assured woman. "Damon Kincaid."

"We've heard a lot about you and those three little girls of yours. I've decided they must be the most adorable children ever born, or else so annoyingly perfect I'll have to hate them on sight."

"They're adorable!" Ariel bristled. "Just wait until you see them!"

"Everything small and helpless is adorable as far as Ariel is concerned," Caroline said a little too breezily. "From the time we were kids, she dragged home baby rabbits, orphaned lambs. Once she even brought home a fox cub. Nothing anyone could say would dissuade her."

Damon found himself imagining Ariel as a sunny-faced child, coaxing drops of milk down baby animals' throats, crooning to them in that soft, gentle voice of hers that could be as soothing as spring rain.

"Jake collected fossils, Jesse collected arrowheads. You collected boyfriends," Ariel snapped. "I just happen to collect animals."

"Animals, stray kids. Anything that was hurting." There was a none too subtle warning in Caroline Madigan's forthright gaze. "A puppy got hit on the road out by the school bus stop once. It tore up her hand so badly she had to get stitches, but no one can tell my baby sister anything when it comes to attempting to ease someone's pain. You can warn her, but she won't listen."

Ariel's eyes narrowed, her voice holding an edge Damon had rarely heard. "If I want to get my hand chewed off, it's my business, Carrie."

Ariel's response dissipated any doubt as to what Caroline was alluding to—the fact that she didn't want her sister hurt, not by some stray animal, nor by Damon himself.

"I know Ariel is far too generous when it comes to…easing pain," he said, meeting Caroline's gaze steadily. "You must worry about her being taken advantage of." He paused for a heartbeat. "Don't."

Understanding passed between him and the redhead.

"Of all the—" Ariel sputtered, angry. "Carrie, I didn't coerce Damon into coming here so he could be bored to death with tales of my childhood. I'm going to introduce him to everyone else and then show him around."

With an elegant shrug of her shoulders, Caroline took the nightgown from Ariel's hands. "That'll be terrific," she said, "but I'd better bag this and stick it in our bedroom before someone else sees it. I doubt Dad or Jake or Jesse would be quite so...enlightened about such things as I am." She flashed Damon a smile, not unlike Ariel's own. "In other words, Damon, I'm probably saving you from getting a black eye to rival little Travis's. Everyone in the family is pretty protective when it comes to Ariel."

Damon nodded, understanding more than even Caroline could know. A dreamer... Ariel was a dreamer with a thousand mysteries in those aquamarine eyes that no one else could ever touch. He wanted to stop Caroline, tell her that he wouldn't ever allow himself to be the one to drive those fragile dreams away. But as Caroline Madigan turned and walked away, he was certain that she already knew.

Crickets and june bugs indulged in their nightly concerto, lightning bugs providing footlights against stage curtains of darkness. The children had scattered hours ago to the two spacious tents set up in the farmhouse's backyard—knapsacks with treats and games and fresh flashlight batteries tucked among the sleeping bags their mothers and fathers had laid out earlier.

Damon's girls were among them—fast friends with the children who, on this perfect summer day, had led them on enough farm adventures to last them a lifetime. A day that the girls would never forget. A day Damon would never forget, either.

He sat on the porch swing, alone, listening to the clatter of dishes and the laughter of Ariel and her sisters and mother through the open window as they cleaned up the kitchen for the night. The Madigan women—from six-year-old Anna to Ariel's mother, Meg—were all bright and beautiful and warm, but also unique and wonderful in their own very special ways. They'd fussed over his daughters, and teased him in a way that had soon set him at ease. The Madigan men had taken a bit longer to warm to him—each seeming to be measuring the man Ariel had brought home with some invisible ruler. But after a while, even the stoic

Jake had opened up, including Damon in the brothers' traditional game of touch football, grinning in approval when Damon offered to help with the chores.

He'd provided the Madigan men with more than a little amusement with his citified ineptitude, but his determination had won out, and in the end he'd managed to feel tired but triumphant.

And Ariel . . . Ariel had seemed to be everywhere—taking him to gather eggs, warmed from the hen's downy feathers, laughing when the fowl attempted to peck the thief invading their nests. She'd taken him walking to an Indian burial mound where, as children, she and Jesse had found arrowheads, and had shown him her pet pony—an ancient, mangy-looking creature that looked more than ready for the glue factory, but which Ariel's father kept around because of his daughter's love for the disreputable beast.

She had wandered with him through tangles of berry bushes, and pushed the ripe berries between his lips, so he could taste them, hot from the sun, and sweetened by the touch of her fingers against his mouth.

They had spied on the girls, caught glimpses of Ellen and Travis plotting mischief, and Sarah wearing a flower crown woven by the twins. But most surprising of all had been the time they had caught quiet Moey playing the daredevil— leaping from the barn rafters into soft mounds of hay.

The girls had seemed almost like strangers to him— grubby, happy little urchins, so carefree, he hadn't been able to resist their pleas when Ariel's mother asked if they could enjoy the camp-out with the Madigan cousins.

But now, as he sat with the night breeze whispering, the children's laughter distant, he felt a kind of melancholy wrap around him. This place, these people reminded him with poignant clarity of what he could never have. Of what his little girls could never have. This sense of belonging. Of knowing that white-painted fences would always bracket the lane, that wrens would always nest in the chokecherry tree, that there would always be white lace curtains at the windows, and a comforting creak in the chains of the porch swing. And that when anyone fell, there would always be someone to run to, someone to love away the hurting, and make things right.

With a sigh, Damon dragged his fingers back through his hair, watching the stars glow through the lace of tree branches and rustling leaves. It was so beautiful here, impossibly peaceful. Then why did he feel so damn battered?

The sound of the screen door opening made him shift his gaze, to see Ariel, a bundle of wet dish towels in her hands, her blouse splotched with water. Her hair was tousled from the breeze and her fingers, but her eyes were still shining.

She crossed to the railing, and laid out the towels one by one to dry in the summer heat.

"Tired?" she asked, turning toward him, that shyness that never seemed to leave her face touching him again.

"No. Just watching the stars. I never knew there were so many," he said softly.

Her face lit up, and she caught his hand in hers. "You want to see stars? I can show you a sky full of them. More than you can even imagine."

"Ariel, I—" He started to protest, but she pulled him down the veranda's crooked steps, into the night. Sweet-smelling grass was crushed under their feet, the glowing squares of the house's windows growing smaller as she led him toward where the barn loomed, a hulking shadow against the sky.

She shoved open the door and guided him in, the darkness almost impenetrable, but Ariel obviously knew the way by instinct, drawing him up a ladder into a mow still brimming with last summer's hay.

Pigeons cooed softly in the rafters, straw rustling far below where the animals attempted to bed down for the night, as Ariel curled her legs beneath her and sank onto the musty-smelling hay.

Damon looked down wondering what host of insects were crawling through the stuff, but he was unable to resist sinking down beside her. She lay back, and after a moment, he did the same, feeling oddly more comfortable than he had in years. He stared out at the night, a sweep of sky as wide as eternity, a vastness that made him feel insignificant, and yet somehow awed.

A blur of white smudged the sky, a falling star. And he heard Ariel sigh.

"What was that for?" Damon asked, his voice low, soft.

"What?"

"That sigh. It sounded so sad."

"Didn't you see it? The falling star?" Ariel quieted for a moment. "I used to love them. Loved to make wishes. I'd sit up here, way after dark, and dangle my legs out the window. I'd stay for hours, imagining all the shapes of the constellations, remembering the legends they came from."

She looked up at him, realizing how little she really knew about the man Damon Kincaid, that closely guarded person who had walled himself away from the rest of the world, hidden all his emotions, banished all his dreams. There had been glimpses of the real Damon in the days since she'd met him—flashes of wry humor in those dark eyes, desperate, awed love glimmering through his confusion, his exasperation with his daughters.

She'd seen the pain at once, sensed the scars way down deep. But it wasn't until later that she had marveled at his courage, his resourcefulness, his almost brutal honesty when it came to his own shortcomings.

It wasn't until later that he had buried himself in her heart. She wanted to know everything that was buried deep in his.

"Did you like to watch the stars, Damon?" she asked, watching light and shadow stroke their fingers across those strong-hewn features.

He was so quiet for a moment, she thought he wasn't going to answer. At last he spoke—hesitantly. "You couldn't see the sky where I lived, unless you lay on your back on the fire escape. I used to sleep there sometimes, when it got too hot inside the apartment. Even those times, you couldn't see many stars. The smoke from the factory made it too hazy. By the time I saw a falling star, I'd stopped believing in wishes."

He was looking over at her, the harsh lines of his face gentling. "Somehow I can't imagine that ever happened to you."

Something in Ariel's chest twisted at those words, words almost wistful, from this man who could be so strong. "Oh, I still believe in wishes," she said. "But it's still sad when I see a falling star. My dad got me an astronomy book one year for my birthday. I devoured the thing. Loved it. Until I read about falling stars. They aren't really stars at all. They're meteors that streak across the sky, then burn up as if they were never there at all." She paused. "It seemed so sad to me that something had to die so that I could have my wish. Daddy found me crying one night, and when I told him why I was sad, he said that nothing is forever. That even the sky has to let go of something to make way for what is new."

She shifted against the hay, and was surprised when Damon gently eased his arm around her, pillowing her head on his shoulder. "Damon? What would you have wished for, if you had still believed?"

He looked away from her, and she could feel him tense, feel him withdrawing. But after a moment he spoke. "When I was a kid, all I wanted was a house someplace where the stink of the factory didn't fill every corner. I wanted a yard, with a tree. And something to eat besides soup out of cans. Clothes that the other kids didn't laugh at. And maybe some presents at Christmas. But most of all, I wanted my mother to be home sometimes. Wanted her to be around to talk to me while I had breakfast, and look at my schoolwork when I got home in the afternoon."

Ariel felt her heart wrench, her eyes sting as she imagined the little boy Damon must have been, lying on the hard steel of the fire escape without even a sweep of sky to help him dream.

She'd been so full of preconceptions when she had charged up to his house that first night. Had imagined Damon to be a privileged jerk who hadn't the least idea what it was to want for anything. And when she'd gotten to know him a little better, she'd believed that the pain in his eyes had been put there by the death of a wife he had loved.

But the pain had haunted Damon Kincaid's eyes long before he had met the beautiful woman who was to become his wife. The pain had been there when he was as small as Moey, and as helpless.

He gave a laugh edged with embarrassment. "It was all a long time ago."

Ariel felt him closing himself off, sensed he was gripping at the walls of his defenses, trying to keep them in place. She did the one thing she knew would make that impossible— offering him a piece of herself in return.

"Sometimes I would have given anything to be alone. After a fight with Carrie or Beth, I'd imagine what it would be like to be an only child. To have a bedroom without two other people in it, and not to have brothers tormenting the life out of me every chance they got." She paused for a moment, sensing how full her own childhood had been—filled to overflowing, when his had been so empty.

"I wouldn't have traded the closeness we had as a family," she said. "No. Not for the world."

"I would have loved to have had someone else in my room. Someone, anyone to talk to. My mother worked three jobs just to keep us going, so what little time she *was* home, she was exhausted—or asleep. I guess I was lucky to have a roof over my head. But when you're a kid, you don't see things that way."

"Your father... Where was he?"

"He disappeared before I was even born. It was as if he'd never existed. I didn't even know what a normal family was until I went home on spring break with Amanda to meet her folks. That house was everything I wanted, for myself and for my mom. I didn't want her to have to work so hard anymore. I figured I had forever to help my mom. Years and years to make up for everything she had sacrificed because of me. But she died my last year of college. I'll never forget how angry I was that she didn't give me a chance to take care of her."

Ariel looked into that face that was so rugged, so handsome, so heartbreakingly sad.

"Ariel," he said with soft amazement. "I've never told anyone that before. What it was like for me, growing up. About my mother, and what I wanted for her."

"I'm glad you told me."

He seemed so solitary, so alone, even here, in her most beloved place in the world. A lost little boy with no one to love him. A man, hiding the aching loneliness in his soul beneath a tough, no-nonsense exterior, a hard veneer of affluence and success.

She reached out, clasping Damon's hand, felt his fingers close tight around hers—strong, gentle, just a little bit unsure.

"When I was little," she said quietly, "I made up this game. Whenever I was hurting, I pretended I was carrying whatever bothered me in a little box. And when the stars were out, I would take that box up here and empty it into the night, toss it into the stars. See, with all those wishing stars I felt like there was a whole sky full of miracles out there. And that one of them had to be waiting just for me."

She raised up on one elbow, looking down into Damon's face, the angles and planes limned in the moonlight. "There's one out there for you, too, Damon. I'm sure of it."

There was something unreadable in those dark eyes, such quiet pain in the curve of his mouth. "There aren't any miracles out there with my name on them, Ariel," he said. "But thank you for letting me share yours for a little while."

Her throat constricted, her eyes stinging as he drew her down against his chest, her cheek pillowed upon the steady beat of his heart.

They lay there in silence a long time, his fingers gently stroking her hair.

The garish lights of the city drained the glitter from Ariel's stars, giant buildings thrusting high into the velvety-dark curtain of the night. Damon guided his car along the crowded interstate, feeling as though he were leaving some kind of fantastical oasis of peace, of serenity, and entering another world. One of blaring horns and stressed out drivers, congested traffic and career-minded businessmen clawing their way to the top. His world. The world he'd chosen. The world he'd worked so hard to gain entry to. A world that was far different from the one he would always picture Ariel in from now on.

He reached down to stroke Ellen's hair, his restless little daughter so exhausted from her fun she had fallen asleep with her head pillowed on his lap. The other girls were sleeping, too, dreaming, no doubt, about nests of kittens and riding ponies and the way milk foamed in the bucket when you milked a cow.

The weekend at the farm had been magical. One of those times Damon knew he would remember in vivid detail years from now, when he was fogged in at Heathrow, or attempting to wade through an accounting department's disaster in Hong Kong.

He'd remember how Ellen had raced around, dangling from tree limbs, playing Robin Hood with bows and arrows made of sticks and string. He'd remember Moey, giggling as a dozen little barn kittens tried to steal her ribbons. He'd remember Sarah, cutting her initials in the crust of an apple pie with a butter knife.

But most of all, he'd remember Ariel. Everywhere. In sunshine, at twilight, with dreams in her eyes, and laughter on her lips, showing him what it was like to be alive.

It had been a taste of things he could never have. And yet, he was glad he'd at least touched them once, felt them once, known somehow that they existed. That they were real. It gave him hope where he'd had none. How did you thank someone for giving you so much before you said goodbye?

Goodbye.

The word was bitter, and he swallowed hard, hating the sound of it, knowing that it was necessary. Inevitable. That he had always known it would come to this.

And yet, wasn't this pain for the better? Hadn't it changed him? Touched him? Made him see…see things he'd forgotten, lost somehow?

Ellen stirred just a little, and he lay a hand on her shoulder, murmuring soft words to soothe her back to sleep. Dreams. Ariel had given them back to his girls. He wanted her to know that. Tell her…

He raked his hand back through his hair. Tell her that if he'd met her years ago, when he'd been fighting his way out of the streets, when he'd been driving himself so hard at Stanford, if he'd met her then, before everything got so complicated, things might have been different.

No, he thought, smoothing his fingers down his daughter's cheek. Because if things had been different he wouldn't have Ellen. He wouldn't have Moey or Sarah. And any amount of pain was worth enduring, as long as he had these little girls.

"Daddy?" It was Moey's voice, sleepy, soft.

"What is it, angel?"

"I'm going to make Ariel a picture of the farm, to say thank you. And I'm going to draw my kitty, Rosa. The one Beth and Claire said I could name."

"Ariel would like that very much."

"Daddy?"

"What?"

"Are you going to say thank you, too?"

Damon thought about everything Ariel had done for him. For his daughters. "Yes, Moey. I think I will."

"You could send her 'spensive flowers. Or a diamond bracelet like you got Mommy when Sarah was born. But I think Ariel likes dandy-lions better."

Damon swallowed hard, aware that, for the first time, Moey had spoken of Amanda without that tiny catch in her voice, as if she'd tucked away a large chunk of her grief under the veranda at Shadylane. No. No mere diamond bracelet would do for Ariel. No material thing that could be lost or broken.

"Moey, I think I'm going to call her and ask her to go out to dinner with me."

"You mean like a date?"

"No!" Damon explained hastily. "Just a...a thank-you. So I can tell her how much this meant to all of us. This weekend at the farm. The time she spent at our house." If there was a way to put it into words.

"I think Ariel would like that, Daddy. She always keeps warm fuzzies in her heart."

"Warm fuzzies?"

"Nice things. Special things...like kitties sleeping in your lap, or hugs, or kissing on the forehead to make the nightmares go away. She says she saves them up, and when she's sad she takes them out and wraps herself up in the rememberings, and they make her feel better."

Moey was quiet for a moment.

"Daddy, is it bad for me to feel better? To like kitties, and be glad I cuddled them even though Mommy didn't like them?"

"Of course not, sweetheart."

"Then you could feel better, too, couldn't you, Daddy? You could...stop feeling sad."

Damon's throat went raw. "I love you, sweetheart," he managed to squeeze out. "I love you so much. Go to sleep, now. We'll be home in a little while."

Moey sighed, and he could hear the rustlings in the back seat as she settled back down to sleep. But as he drove on, he heard the echoes of her words.

You could stop feeling sad...

He pictured Amanda, pictured her restless, unhappy. Felt the crushing sting of guilt. No, he couldn't stop the guilt, but he could stop allowing the girls to feel it. He could bury it deeper, help them get on with their lives. And he could give Ariel one night of pleasure, fun. He could take her out and show her the time of her life—and tell her... tell her things that would keep her warm for a very long time.

Chapter Ten

Damon stared at his reflection in the mirror, the handful of antacids he'd choked down an hour ago doing little to calm the gnawing sensation in the pit of his stomach.

He hadn't felt this jittery since his interview at Stanford when he'd been applying for a full-ride scholarship so many years ago. His whole future had teetered in the balance that day. A future worlds away from the cramped, roach-infested apartment deep on the South Side of Chicago. He'd known that he had the brief span of the interview to alter his life forever. And never before or since had he felt that unfamiliar desperation, that twisting in his gut, as if he were holding explosives in his hands, not knowing whether they would burst into glorious fireworks, or devastate him, demolish his hopes, his dreams.

No, not since that day he had waited in the dean's office, a lanky high school kid with amazing scores on his SATs, and the entire high school math department's unrelenting support, had he experienced the feelings he was dealing with now.

Feelings that were ridiculous in their intensity, that made him wary, unsettled, as if each tick of the clock that drew the hour nearer to the time he was to pick up Ariel Madigan was carrying him closer to something he couldn't name.

It was crazy, absurd that he should feel so off balance. This night was nothing more than a token of his appreciation—some small repayment for Ariel's many kindnesses. He'd enjoy her company, drink in her laughter, memorize her voice, her smile, the twinkling mischief in her eyes. And then he would bow to the inevitable and say goodbye.

He shoved away the dragging sense of loss that prospect caused him, never one to shrink from hard realities. Instead, he stiffened his resolve to have the best time possible, make this one night between them filled with pleasure.

"That tie stinks."

The sound of Ellen's voice yanked Damon from his troubled thoughts, his hands stilling on the knot he'd tried and failed three times to work in the length of black silk. Grateful for the interruption, he turned to shoot a good-natured glare at the little girl who had been trundling about underfoot from the moment he had stepped out of his shower.

"Ellen, this is a perfectly acceptable necktie."

"It's boring." Her pert nose crinkled as if she were sniffing Limburger cheese. "Ariel won't like it. She likes purple and pink, doesn't she, Sarah?"

Sarah looked up from where she was busily examining the bottles of cologne arranged on the low surface of his dresser. "Too-Loose the Too-can gots an orange tie," his little daughter offered hopefully. "Do you gots an orange tie for your date, Daddy?"

"It's not a date, Sarah. I've told you that three times," Damon said, almost wishing he had never mentioned the impending outing to the girls—the girls who had then thought it their bound duty to inform everyone they met, from the grocery store clerk to the paperboy, to Mrs. Lefstein next door. And of course, most disastrous of all, to their grandmother who had phoned an hour ago, Eve having returned from her trip to her trendy Florida beach house just in time to register her disapproval of the entire matter.

God knew, he'd been edgy enough about the whole thing beforehand, even without Eve's complaints. The girls had kept up a constant jabbering ever since Ariel had accepted his invitation to dinner. Ariel this, Ariel that.

Ariel, who had taken him up to the hayloft to watch the stars. Ariel, with that mischievous sparkle in her eye, that quick wit and ready humor that made him laugh in a way he hadn't for longer than he could remember. Ariel, whose lips had tasted like cherry candy beneath the sweep of his tongue—a flavor of dreams he had relegated long ago to the memory of his own fleeting childhood. A childhood that really never was.

He quashed the rumblings of emotions that unnerved him, turning his attention once again to the bedroom Ellen and Sarah had reduced to chaos in a matter of ten minutes. A chaos that somehow pleased him, distracted him from thinking too much about the woman he was picking up in forty-five minutes.

Sarah was singsonging an echo of his last words to her, putting them to the tune of "Three Blind Mice."

"Not a date. Not a date," she trilled. Her little forehead furrowed as she grabbed a dark green bottle of cologne, knocking two others over in the process of dragging her most recent selection near enough so she could smell it. When she sniffed it, her eyes widened in delight at the scent. "Daddy, this smells de-lish-iss. Ariel would want to gobble you right up if you weared this on your date."

That was all his rioting nerves needed—a pint-size matchmaker ready to serve him up like the pastry of the day. Damon rolled his eyes heavenward.

"Well, that's what Muffy Addison says when she baby-sits," Ellen called from where she'd disappeared into his closet. "She'd like to gobble you right up because you're a hunk."

"A hunk of what?" Sarah asked, her big eyes turned guilelessly up to Damon's.

"Not a hunk of something," Ellen said disgustedly. "A hunk is a really cute boy."

Damon felt his cheeks heat as he thought of the sixteen-year-old neighbor he'd had baby-sit the girls a few times. He was right. The grandmotherly type was far safer. He winced, vowing that after tonight, he'd never hire Muffy and her rioting hormones again.

"Does Ariel think Daddy is a hunk, Ellie?" Sarah asked.

Damon was nonplussed by his reaction to those innocent words, his pulse lurching as he remembered the heat that had been in those wide fairy-tale blue eyes. He knew Ariel had felt that swift, tightening coil of attraction that he had experienced when he had touched her, seen her smile. He'd never had time to pay much attention to the way he looked—except for presenting the most professional appearance possible.

But as he looked at the man staring back at him in the mirror, he couldn't imagine what a dreamy-eyed Sleeping Beauty like Ariel Madigan could find attractive in the hard lines of his face, the edge of cynicism in his mouth.

And he was surprised at how deeply that disappointed him. He turned away from the mirror, his voice firm.

"I think we've had enough of this conversation."

Moey, hovering in the doorway, said earnestly. "Calling you a hunk isn't anything bad, Daddy. Muffy just says you look like that sports guy in the underwear ad."

"I'm flattered beyond belief. Now—"

"The man in the underwear ad wouldn't wear a black tie." Ellen again. She came trundling out of the walk-in closet, her fist full of neckties. There was an emerald-green one, a bright red one, and one in the shape of a rainbow trout that Joe Jameson had given him as a joke one Christmas.

Damon stripped off the black tie in surrender. "I'm not wearing that fish, Ellen Kincaid, so you can just forget it," he said with mock severity.

But he hunkered down until he was at eye level with his daughter.

"But, Daddy, you have to—"

"I don't *have* to do anything, young lady." He reached out and tugged one of her short curls, then made a great show of examining the remaining ties. "Okay, Ms. Fashion Critic. Which one do you like best?"

"Green."

"All right then, green it is."

"I'll put it on, Daddy. You'll just get it all snarly." Her face a study in concentration, Ellen looped the tie around his neck. Damon watched her, the warmth in his heart welling over.

"I can't tie it, you know," Ellen informed him at last. "You'll have to do that by yourself."

"I'll see if I can manage," he said, serious.

"You weren't doing so good with that black tie," Ellen said doubtfully.

"You were a great help, ma'am."

"Help. Help," Sarah chirruped. "Can I help, too, Daddy? I twisted the cap right off this bottle. I'll make you smell all good."

Sarah giggled delightedly as she poured half a bottle of cologne into her cupped palm and splashed it against his jaw. Damon choked and sputtered as the scent overpowered him. But Sarah was in pure ecstasy. "Yum!" she cried, grabbing the bottle again, and dumping more of the cologne into her hand.

"No, sweetheart. I wouldn't want to smell too good," Damon said hastily, mentally making a note to himself that he should go in and scrub most of the cologne off as soon as Sarah left the room. "We don't really want anyone to gobble me up."

Sarah chortled, and dumped the cologne on her own hair. "Sarah Jane smells de-lish-iss."

"Sarah Jane needs her hair combed," Damon said, scooping the little girl up, and kissing her cheek. "You look like Cousin Itt on *The Addams Family.*"

"You could cut it all off," Ellen said, leveling an appraising look on Sarah.

"Oh, no, young lady. Don't even *think* about it," Damon warned, his head filling with visions of round-nosed kindergarten scissors snipping away at Sarah's curls. But at that moment, he glanced over Sarah's small shoulder, and was suddenly aware of Moey looking somewhat lost, wary as she stood on the fringes of the fun. He set Sarah down, and approached his oldest daughter, smoothing his hand over her neatly plaited hair.

"Well, as long as these two are criticizing everything from my cologne to my tie, you might as well get into the act, too."

"I don't want—want to," Moey said in a voice that belied her words.

"What? No complaints?" Damon teased. "Surely you must be able to find something about me you don't like."

"I like everything about you, Daddy. I like the way your eyes look like chocolate and crinkle at the corners sometimes. I like the way your teeth show when you smile. I even liked the black tie."

"Terrific. Now you tell me," Damon teased gently. "How come you didn't speak up when Ellen, there, was trying to rig me out like something in the latest issue of *Fish Bait?*"

"Mommy said I wasn't supposed to bother you when you were getting ready."

Damon's smile faded. "What?"

"I used to like to sit by the doorway and listen to you whenever you got dressed. You'd whistle pretty songs, and sometimes when you saw me you'd smile at me and call me 'sweetheart.'"

Memories tugged at Damon, of a much smaller Moey, peering at him from the doorway. A little mouse, so quiet there had been times he'd almost tripped over her on his way out the door. A fist closed about his heart. "Is that what you were doing? I never knew."

"I thought you were the handsomest daddy in the whole world. I wanted to come and sit on your bed, and talk to you. Except Mommy said I'd be in your way. That you didn't like interruptions." Moey looked so troubled, torn between her mother's warning and the fun her sisters had been having. Damon felt a swift wave of anger at Amanda for having filled the child's head with such garbage. But he knew he didn't dare let Melissa guess what he was feeling.

He scooped her up, holding her close, and Moey twined her arms around his neck. "I'd like it very much if you'd talk to me, honey. Anytime you want to. You're never in my way."

But even as he said the words, he was thinking how many times he must have inadvertently reinforced Amanda's warnings to the child—how many times he had waved his little girls to silence while he was making business calls, or told them to entertain themselves while he was working at night.

Had there been times during the past year when Moey had wanted to talk to him about her mother's death? Had there been times she had tried to tell him the things she had confided to Ariel? If he had only been listening as closely as Ariel always seemed to.

Guilt. It drove deep. His arms tightened around Moey as if he could somehow protect her from all the hurt, all the loss, as if he could protect her, even from himself.

"Daddy," she whispered in his ear. "I changed my mind."

"About what, sweetheart?"

"About not wanting to change anything about you."

Damon's throat constricted as he thought of a hundred things he would like to change—starting with scooping up that tiny bundle that had been Moey, and plunking her on the big bed when she was as small as Sarah. Getting ready for work on all those lost mornings, entertained by Moey's solemn, funny little pronouncements.

"What would you like to change, Moey?"

"You...well...I think..." She hazarded a glance at Sarah, who was now attempting to feed the pocket change on the dresser to the fish tie. Then Moey seemed to pluck up her courage. She turned her huge dark eyes to peer earnestly into his. "Daddy... you... you smell awful."

Damon couldn't help the laughter that rose inside him—a laughter that hurt, because it held so many echoes of his pain.

She was climbing up a tree, her rainbow-striped skirt a splash of color as it tangled on the low-lying branches, her face a study in concentration as she edged higher and higher. Damon stared at her from the window of the car he had just parked feeling as if he'd tumbled through Alice's looking glass.

A peasant-style blouse clung precariously on her bare shoulders, the tails of the orange scarf knotted around her trim waist fluttering like banners behind her.

One bare foot slipped as she fought for a toehold, the branch cracking beneath her weight, and Damon felt his heart leap to his throat. The idiotic woman was going to break her blasted neck! And after being drowned in cologne, barely escaping wearing a fish around his neck and enduring Eve's diatribe, he wasn't about to let that happen before this nondate had even begun.

He leapt from the car.

"Ariel? What the blazes are you doing?" he roared out. But the moment the words left his mouth, he regretted them, as she instinctively twisted toward the voice, while barely managing to maintain her grip on the branches.

As he jogged toward her, he saw her cheekbones stain a becoming red, and he tried not to notice how sexy her long, slender leg looked with the vivid spill of skirt hiked half-way up her thigh.

"Damon." She sighed fatalistically. "You're early. I should have known."

"What? Were you planning some kind of crazy reception for me? Or do you usually lurk in trees and leap down on your unsuspecting dates?"

"Of course not. If you'd been a few minutes late like normal people, I would have been down from here before you came. But no, you have to be *early*." She said the word as if it was an insult. Damon couldn't help but smile, the knot of nervousness that weighed his stomach like a rock seeming to lighten just a little.

"You'll have to forgive my little foibles. I know it's a nasty habit to be on time, but I can't seem to break it. Now if you'll let me help you down from there before you fall, maybe we won't have to spend another night together in the emergency room."

"No. I can't come down. I have to save him. He's stuck, and can't get loose."

Damon peered past Ariel, attempting to see through the branches of the towering oak, expecting to see the baseball jersey of some little boy whose spirit for adventure had carried him beyond the bounds of good judgment.

But the branches appeared to be empty, except for the exotic Ariel-bird perched just within Damon's reach.

"Who's stuck? Where?" Damon asked, craning his neck farther back.

He turned his gaze back to Ariel, saw her catch at her lower lip with her teeth in that now-familiar nervous gesture.

"It's a baby raccoon."

"Oh, no. Caroline warned me about this," Damon said, reaching up to span Ariel's hips with his hands and pluck her from the branches. "Raccoons have been climbing trees since time immemorial. In fact, I've never heard of one breaking its neck falling out of a tree. Unlike crazed Good

Samaritans in bare feet and skirts that attempt to climb up after them.''

He set her feet gently on the grass, but his hands clung for long minutes to her waist, the warmth of her skin heating his palms through the soft fabric of the sash.

She seemed so tiny as he peered down at her, so fragile. And the knot in his stomach shifted to a dull ache of tenderness as she turned those pleading aquamarine eyes to his.

"You don't understand. The poor little thing is stuck. I've been watching him for ten minutes, and his head...well, it's caught in a hole up there.''

Damon couldn't stop a rumble of laughter. "You have to be kidding.''

Ariel shook her head. "There must be some nuts in the hollow, left over from winter, or some particularly delectable grubs the baby was wanting for dinner. Anyway, he got his head into the hole, but he can't get it out.''

"I suppose you didn't consider calling the fire department, or Animal Control?''

"The raccoon was making these little crying sounds. And besides, I was afraid it would hurt itself even more if I waited.''

"If it was in the middle of the woods somewhere, it wouldn't have you to chase after it,'' Damon said reasonably. "Aren't you supposed to leave wildlife alone when things like this happen? I heard they pick up human scent or something and their mother will reject them.''

"This one is old enough to survive on his own. And young enough to get into major trouble.''

An odd, fleeting memory darted through Damon's mind—the back seat of his rusted sedan—he and Amanda, so young, so naive. They'd gotten into plenty of trouble in the year and a half that had followed. And neither one of them had ever been able to make things right.

It was a ridiculous thing to think of at this moment—an absurd one. He attempted to hide his expression by peering into the branches until he finally located the tiny bundle of fur.

Listening carefully, he could just make out the muffled sounds Ariel had spoken of. And he was surprised to find the baby animal's cries of fright so similar to Sarah's whimpering when she'd had a nightmare, that it wrenched at his own heart.

He gritted his teeth, fully intending to grab Ariel's sandals and propel her to the waiting car, like any intelligent person would. After all, no one in their right mind would even consider risking his neck to release an animal who would probably chew his rescuer's fingers off the moment he was free. Raccoons were notorious carriers of rabies, weren't they? And the thought of a series of painful shots in the stomach was not Damon's idea of a good time.

No, any sane person would merely go to the nearest phone and dial 911....

But at that moment the little animal gave a mewling cry, and Ariel winced as if she felt its terror like a physical pain. The pleading in her eyes intensified until Damon's skin hummed with it.

Cursing inwardly, he released her, and began to strip off his suit jacket. Her eyes widened, a beaming smile setting her features aglow.

"I know I'm going to regret this," he ground out as he eyed the tree with a critical gaze. It wasn't as if he were wary of making the climb. He'd done his share of scaling fences on the South Side—entering barred-off playgrounds, warehouse yards, construction sites. And in the years since he'd moved to Naperville, he'd worked off the stress of his job and his failing marriage in countless gyms in hotels all over the world.

But this time, the trick would be getting down from the tree without that animal scratching his eyes out.

Feeling patently ridiculous, he grabbed the lowest branch and pulled himself into the tree. Hand over hand, he dragged himself into the tangle of leaves, praying that they would block him from view. Knowing with a sick certainty that if anyone he knew should happen by, he'd never live it down.

"Be careful!" Ariel called up. "He's so frightened, he might try to bite—"

"Of course he will. He'll probably chew my fingers to the bone, and then I'll end up with stitches in my hand and a sling on my arm. A week after I got rid of my crutches. Perfect."

As if she'd only now considered the possibilities, he glimpsed her leaning near the tree, peering up at him with a worried expression.

"Maybe we should call the authorities. I wasn't thinking—"

"A common malady with you, Miss Madigan. Forget it. Now that I'm up here, I'm going to get that thing down or die in the attempt."

A ripping sound made Damon look down at his leg—the expensively tailored trousers that he had chosen with such care were graced with a three-cornered tear a teenager would have paid a fortune to have cut into his jeans.

Dark smudges soiled his white shirt, a sheen of sweat making the material cling to his skin. The branches tangled in his hair, the bark shoving tiny splinters into his hand.

He should have been furious, irritated, disgusted. God knew, if Jameson saw him, the man would have him committed.

But as Damon edged near enough to touch the baby raccoon, he couldn't help but feel a wry amusement that tugged at the corners of his mouth.

The coon was a little thing, a ball of brownish gray fur with a little ringed tail. Its tiny paws were still scrabbling against the tree bark, its whimpering so pathetic, Damon couldn't help but reach out and smooth a comforting hand down its little back.

"Whoa, there. Easy big fella," he murmured as the little animal stilled.

"Damon?" Ariel called up. "Maybe this isn't such a good idea. We can call—"

"*Now* you get reasonable—after I'm all the way up here? Forget it, lady. If this little guy and I fall to an untimely death, it's going to be on your conscience, isn't it, buddy?"

He eyed the wood surrounding the hole, grateful to find that it was half-rotted. If he could wedge his fingers into the hole and pull on it, without crashing to the ground, he should be able to break the little guy free. The question was—could he wedge his fingers in the tiny space left by the baby's neck and yet keep them out of the reach of its teeth?

Grumbling to himself, Damon set to work, waiting to become the raccoon's main course. But the animal seemed to sense he was trying to help him—either that, or was frozen with terror.

Within minutes, Damon managed to pry free the entrapping wood, but the raccoon only sat there, so still, Damon was afraid he had somehow injured it during the rescue. Scooping the little guy into his hands, he was enchanted by jet button eyes liquid with wonder in a miniature bandit's mask. By a tiny nose, a pink tongue and pointy little ears that seemed to be listening for something.

But in spite of the fact that the raccoon was so still at the moment, Damon figured that he'd decide to make his grand escape on the way down the tree. Maneuvering the little animal with one hand, he stripped off his shirt, and carefully bundled the raccoon in it, but when he came to covering up its face so it couldn't nip, Damon found he couldn't do it.

Shaking his head at his own stupidity, he tucked the animal in one arm, and then began his descent, Ariel calling out warning and encouragement from below.

When he reached the bottom limb, he lowered the bundle into her outstretched arms, then leapt to the ground.

She curled her legs beneath her, sitting on the grass, the baby raccoon cuddled in her arms. She stroked its tiny ears, and crooned to it, her hands gentle as she eased back the folds of his shirt.

Damon watched, silent as she set the raccoon on his paws in the grass, and stroked him once, twice.

It gazed at her for a minute, then turned its black button eyes up to Damon's before it darted toward a copse of trees a little ways away.

"Do you think he'll be all right?" Damon asked, dubious.

"I think he'll be fine now." Her eyes were glittering. Tears. They were unexpected, and left him speechless.

Gracefully, she swept to her feet, and hesitated for a heartbeat. Then she flung herself into his arms.

If the raccoon had suddenly turned into Cujo, Damon couldn't have been more surprised. His arms closed reflexively around her, the sensation of Ariel pressed against the naked expanse of his chest the most exquisite of pleasure.

He stroked her hair, the warm, moist caress of her breath against his skin sending waves of molten heat to center in his maleness. Heat that put the lie to all his hard-won reasoning, his resolve not to let Ariel touch him any deeper, lead him any farther. Friends, she'd termed their relationship— hell, they'd raced worlds beyond friends, and the realization terrified him.

"Has anyone ever told you that you're wonderful?" Her words were muffled against his chest.

"Not recently." He managed to squeeze the words through a throat thick with desire.

"Well, you are." She arched back her head to smile into his face. "My hero."

A tremor worked through Damon, every inch of his body agonizingly aware of the soft, feminine curves pressed against him, the wide Cinderella eyes whose lashes were spiky with tears. Her cheeks flushed, her hands unsteady as they smoothed up, over his chest, her palms abrading the fine dusting of dark hair. The edge of her little finger just grazed his nipple, and his breath rasped in his throat like a dying man's.

"Ariel." Was that his voice? So ragged, so raw?

He felt her hands move up and her fingertips thread through the dark hair at his temples, saw her lips part. Her lashes drifted shut as she drew his mouth down to hers.

Sweet, delicious, her lips melted into his, reminding him of chocolate warmed in a child's hand. His gut trembled, his hands shook as he cupped her face, those cheeks as soft and smooth as the petals of a calla lily against his hard palms.

The catcalls of a group of teenagers cruising by made Damon still, suddenly aware of the sunshine spilling down around him and Ariel, the cars whizzing by on the street and dozens of windows from which faceless observers could take note of the scene the two of them were causing.

Remembering Ariel's concern about involvement with a parent, he slowly eased her away from him, his hands still curled about the bare silkiness of her arms. He attempted to form his lips into a smile. Found that it was impossible. "I've never had this problem before," he said softly.

"What problem?"

"Needing to kiss a woman so badly, I make a public spectacle of her."

He saw Ariel swallow hard, and she slipped from his grasp, her fingers linking in his large ones. Her thumb smoothed over a scratch a branch had left on his hand. "You don't like that, do you?" she asked.

"What?"

"Making a public spectacle of yourself."

"Not usually. But with you I seem to be making a habit of it." He forced a chuckle. "And believe me, the whistles of a bunch of kids aren't going to be anything in comparison to the sensation I'm going to create when I walk into Armaude's looking like this."

He grabbed up his shirt, and slipped the wrinkled, smudged cotton over his shoulders. The tie Ellen had so carefully selected was nowhere to be seen. When he glanced up into the tree he saw it, dangling from the topmost branch.

He grinned.

"Maybe we shouldn't attempt Armaude's this time," Ariel suggested. "I know a great little Italian place about a block from here. A little mom-and-pop place where they play opera on an old turntable, and serve manicotti so wonderful, even Pagliacci would stop crying long enough to eat."

Damon was surprised at how much more appealing that sounded than the elegant restaurant with its silent, formal waiters, white linen napkins and muted music piped in on a sound system to rival Carnegie Hall's. "That would be great. But I don't know if even a mom and pop would appreciate me coming in looking like this."

"Don't sweat it, hero. I've got something in the back of my car that might fit you. It's Jake's. I gave it to him for Christmas last year and borrowed it back when we were at the farm. I'd *love* to see you in it." Her eyes were sparkling again. She ran lightly to where her car was parked, and pulled out a red sweatshirt.

Damon took it, and read the logo—The Original Bad Attitude. Arching a brow, he looked at Ariel for a moment, then tugged the garment over his head.

"Perfect," she said, trying not to giggle as she studied him with mock-seriousness. "Except for one thing. I know you're a hero, Damon, but I'm afraid wearing laurels on your brow has gone somewhat out of fashion. Unless you want to look like Ben Hur, you'd best let me pluck the leaves out of your hair."

Damon was tempted to run his fingers through his tangled mane, but the prospect of having Ariel touch him again was too sweet to resist.

He leaned down, savoring the feel of those slender fingers feathering through his hair. Her touch was so tender, so gentle. A healing that made his chest ache.

He tried to remember a time when anyone had touched him that way, but there was no one. His mother's touches had always been practical, perfunctory. A little shove against his back to hurry him along when he dawdled, a smack with the flat of her hand when he'd been engrossed in his reading and had forgotten to start dinner. She'd loved him in her way, he knew, but she'd been bitter and hardened by the life she had led.

And Amanda—there had always been something furtive in her touches, even long after their marriage. As if she were still glancing over her shoulder, to see if someone was looking, if anyone knew about the wicked things she was doing with a boy from the wrong side of town.

Damon closed his eyes, wishing it was as easy to rid himself of those memories as it was to brush the leaves away. Wondering if somehow this woman who had blasted through countless defenses could work the kind of miracle on his heart as she had in the hearts of his daughters.

No. Not even a fairy-tale princess like Ariel Madigan could tame the dragons that beset him, and yet...

He remembered his thoughts on his way home from Australia, his decision that it was time to get on with his life, to give the girls the mother they so needed.

Had he ever met a woman more suited for soothing hurts and laughing at child antics than Ariel? Had he ever met a woman he wanted more, with an insatiable hungering for the warmth in her, the giving?

And yet, what could he give her in return? A man surrounded by walls, one who liked the distance he kept between himself and the world. A husband who could never love her with the openness, the honesty that wreathed everything Ariel did.

He opened his eyes, suddenly aware that her hand had dropped away from him. She looked shaken, as if she had somehow read his thoughts, or had fallen prey to secrets of her own.

What the hell did he have to offer a woman like Ariel? A splash of sunshine in a world of drizzling gray? The sound of a gaggle of boys running down the sidewalk scattered his thoughts, and he saw Ariel's eyes shift to follow the children, a smile curving her lips. It was as if those boys were hers, all hers, embraced in her generous heart.

Children.

Damon felt a twisting deep in his loins as he watched a wistful light steal into her eyes. She had surrounded herself with other people's children, lavished them with her love, her laughter.

He could give her children. As many as she wanted. He could supply anything they would need, no matter what the cost.

No matter what the cost...

The words rose up to haunt him, images of his daughters rising in his mind, their tearing grief after Amanda's death, the horrible sense of helplessness that stole over him when he saw their pain, knew that he couldn't protect them from it.

Ariel turned back to face him, the wistful light still a mist in her eyes and he wondered if the cost of sweeping her deeper into his life would be the one thing he couldn't afford to pay.

Chapter Eleven

The stars dangled in the heavens like diamonds upon strings, a soft night breeze brushing cooling fingers against Ariel's skin. She savored it along with the murmur of crickets' song, the flicker of fireflies, the muffled sounds of voices from the older couples who sat out in their yards on lawn chairs, so familiar with each other that they could just sit silently and listen to the secrets of each other's hearts.

She strolled ever so slowly through each puddle of light from the lampposts that flanked the streets, her hand tucked in Damon's strong fingers, her heart fluttering as they walked along the sidewalk that led from Cimirelli's Ristoranteto her apartment.

From the time she'd been a little girl, she'd dreamed of the day that she would be the one sitting like her parents on the porch swing, her hand linked with the man she shared her life with. She had imagined catching lightning bugs in peanut butter jars with her children, and lying on the grass with them to search for four-leaf clovers.

But her childhood dreams had been tucked away, like birds' nests found in springtime, and broken blue shells of robins' eggs.

She'd watched two of her sisters marry in turn, and one of her brothers find a woman astonishingly willing to put up with him. She'd cuddled nephews and nieces, and played godmother to enough babies to stock a hospital nursery. But she had never found anyone she was tempted to spend the rest of her life with. Never found anyone who could share laughter with her, who she could feel comfortable with when she wanted to listen to his silence.

Until now.

She glanced up at the man walking beside her, so quiet ever since that moment by the car—the moment when she had seen something fleeting, unguarded in those dark, haunted eyes. She'd been elated when he'd called and asked her out, the slightest hint of uncertainty in that deep, sexy voice making her melt inside. He'd laid the ground rules as carefully as if he'd been negotiating a business contract. And yet there had been something in the way he spoke, something in the way he hesitated over certain words that had made her hope that this evening they were spending together meant far more than even Damon dreamed.

A hope that grew even brighter as the night wore on. Even the blustery, kind Mr. Cimirelli and his effervescent wife Sophia hadn't been able to shake away the moodiness that clung about Damon's thick lashes and tugged at the corners of those lips that had kissed her until her knees went weak.

He'd given the correct responses, but had stirred his plateful of lasagna around without so much as tasting it, until Mrs. Cimirelli began to take offense.

But Ariel could barely eat, either, unsettled as she was by the way she kept catching Damon looking at her with an intensity that confused her, unnerved her. As if he could say with his eyes words his lips could never form.

And she wanted to know—wanted to understand the emotions he fought so hard to hide. Wanted to reach in and touch the man she sensed lay behind those shuttered brown eyes.

She shivered, just a little, as a slight chill crept over her bare shoulders, and without a word, Damon put his arm around her, his warm palm rubbing gently against her skin. She wished she could think of something to say, something light, something teasing, but for once no ready joke sprang to mind.

She didn't feel like laughing. Didn't feel like making idle conversation that meant nothing. Not with this man, whose quiet pain had touched her more deeply than anyone she'd ever known.

She slipped her arm around Damon's waist and leaned against him. "Damon, what's wrong? You've been so quiet. Even for you. Were you that disappointed about...well, about not going out as planned? I know you went to a lot of trouble, and that Cimirelli's isn't exactly...well, what you had in mind."

"It was terrific. Really...it's just..."

He stopped, and Ariel was disappointed to find that they were standing below the spreading branches of the oak tree he'd climbed earlier.

"Ariel, I'm not very good at this. At saying how I feel. But after all you've done for the girls and me, you deserve to hear it."

A wild, bounding hope slammed against Ariel's rib cage, her pulse pounding with the possibility that he was feeling what she was. That somehow, between the night at the farm, and this moment beneath the stars, he had let go of the past, let go of the guilt, and had become ready to reach out to her, open himself to her loving.

"I want you to know that...that you opened a whole new world for the girls and me. We were all still grieving, closed off from each other. But Moey...she talks to me now. About Amanda. Not just the good things, imagining things more perfect than they were. But the way things really were. Flawed. Confusing. Sometimes happy, sometimes painful. Maybe not everything we would have wished for, and yet . . . still worth remembering.''

"I'm glad. They need to know about their mother. Need to think about her, talk about her. Need to feel as if the subject isn't some dark secret, some taboo too scary and painful and mysterious to touch. And they need to know about you, too, Damon. They need to know who you are, where you came from.''

"I've spent a lifetime trying to forget it. I don't want my childhood to touch them.''

"Touch them? You sound as if it was something to be ashamed of. Your mother was a resourceful woman who managed to raise a son alone. A son who had the intelligence and the drive to get through one of the best colleges in the country and make a success of his life. I'd think you'd want your children to know.''

"Thinking about that kind of poverty would just upset them. Amanda and I decided that with my mother gone, there was no point bringing it up.''

"No point?" Ariel almost choked out in amazement. "Surely she didn't expect you to just . . . just pretend your past didn't exist?''

"In a way, I suppose we both tried to do that. From the beginning, Amanda wanted to know as little as possible about where I came from. It was as if she wanted to pretend it never existed. I made the mistake of forcing her to face it, once. Took her to visit my mother there on the South Side. You should have seen Amanda. I thought she was going to be sick.''

He turned, and walked to the tree trunk, leaning one broad shoulder against it as he gazed through the lacework of branches at the flickering stars. "My mom had gone to a lot of trouble. Made one of those fancy desserts women like to serve. Shined the apartment up cleaner than I'd ever seen it. Amanda spent the whole time looking as if something were crawling under her skin. She never said anything, but she didn't have to. She was revolted by everything—from the water stains on the ceiling, to the plastic flowers Mom kept on the kitchen table. When we left, Amanda cried. And my mom . . . I know she felt like she'd failed me."

"Damon, I'm sorry."

"So was I. But it didn't matter. See, I'd brought Amanda there to tell my mom that we were going to get married. Amanda was pregnant with my child."

"Moey."

"Yeah, Moey."

"How . . . how did you feel about . . . well, about getting married? Becoming a father?" Ariel asked.

"I wanted that little girl more than anything I'd ever wanted in my life. But later . . . I don't know. Maybe it was the biggest mistake I'd ever made."

"You love Moey. All your girls. I know how much they mean to you."

"Yeah, I love them. Wanted them. I wanted someone of my own so much. Especially after my mom died. I wanted to give them everything I'd never had. All the toys, all the clothes. A perfect childhood. And as for Amanda—I wanted her to have anything she dreamed of, too. My way of—of paying her back for having my children."

"Children are a gift, Damon, just like love. Freely given."

"That's just the problem. I didn't love Amanda, not the way I should have. Oh, she was beautiful and intelligent. She was cultured and accomplished. She was everything that had always been beyond my reach. I was fascinated by her, and she . . . she liked the sensation of playing with fire. I was dangerous enough to intrigue her, but safe enough not to frighten her."

"But she didn't love you?"

"She pretended to. Or maybe she really believed that she did. At least for a little while. See, good girls don't have sex. Not without love. And Amanda was good. Far too good for a man like me."

There was no malice in his voice, just regret and self-blame. "In the end, all I could really give her was the children, and enough money that she could attempt to fill up the empty spaces inside her with material things. That...and the only other thing she wanted from me. That I leave her alone. It was easy enough to accommodate her with the demands my job made. And as much as I wanted the girls, I wasn't very good with them, anyway."

Anger pulsed inside Ariel, for this man who had suffered so much. And it cut her deeply to know that he had been made to believe he had so little to offer. "You're wonderful with those children."

"Come on, Ariel. You saw what a disaster things were the first night I met you. It's always like that. I want to be a good father. But, damn it, Amanda was right. I don't know how."

"Damon—"

"I don't." Savage regret seemed to tear him apart. "Look at Moey. I didn't even notice that she was breaking her heart over Amanda's death. That she was retreating to some kind of fantasy world, pretending her mother was there for her. There for her like I never have been. And Ellen—I don't have the slightest idea how to handle her. She's such a great kid. But I have to help her learn to get a handle on her temper." He raked his fingers through his hair. "Or maybe I have to learn to get a handle on *my* temper when she's asserting herself. I know she misses her mother, and I try to be patient. But she keeps on pushing and I get exasperated, and then I don't handle it well. She expects me not to handle it well. I can tell by the look in her eyes."

"The mere fact that you see she's hurting shows what a loving parent you are."

"Sarah's the only one I seem to be able to deal with successfully. And that's just because she's so little, she doesn't remember how much better things were when her mother was alive. Give me enough time, and I'll botch things up with her, too." His shoulders sagged. He looked so solitary, so alone. Lost little boy with no one to love him. A man, hiding the aching loneliness in his soul beneath a tough, no-nonsense exterior, a hard veneer of affluence and success.

What had that woman said to him that had crippled him this way? What had she done to drive him away from his little girls? How selfish had Amanda Kincaid been to place between Damon and his daughters an invisible wall—a pane of glass that separated him from the family he'd created, while giving the illusion that everything was picture perfect. Because he wasn't good enough for the socialite daughter of a family like the Laughton-Smiths.

Ariel could see all too clearly how it must have been—Damon, a mistake the angelic Amanda had made—a sin she'd committed against her social class and her obnoxious mother. A sin Amanda had made all of them pay for because she'd been too weak-willed, too cowardly to acknowledge, even to herself, that she had wanted Damon Kincaid for a clandestine thrill in the back seat of his car. An open, honest sexual relationship—nothing more.

But most unforgivable of all, in Ariel's eyes, was the fact that Amanda Kincaid had made so many people suffer because of her lack of courage—she had crippled her children's relationship with their father. She had used the painful reality of Damon's childhood against him, the most reprehensible weapon imaginable. Ariel felt sick to her stomach when she thought of the damage Amanda Kincaid must have inflicted.

Damon's voice was quiet, stark with torment when he spoke again. "Amanda's mother wants the girls, you know. She wants to take them to Oak Park and raise them. Her opinion of my skill as a parent is even worse than Amanda's was." He sighed. "I don't know. Sometimes I think it might be best."

"Best for the girls to lose their father as well as their mother?"

"Eve would be there all the time. I have to be gone a lot. She knows kids—has raised one of her own."

"Yeah, and look at what a great job she did," Ariel snapped out, then flushed, a little appalled at her blatant criticism of Damon's dead wife.

But he only sucked in a deep breath, released it slowly. "Eve was a decent enough mother. Amanda had every opportunity imaginable. Eve made certain of it. Piano lessons, voice lessons. She was involved in all the right organizations, all the best schools."

"And she had her whole life mapped out for her by her mother." Ariel knew she was crossing lines—plunging into relationships she only half understood—disliking people she'd never even met. And yet the thought of a spoiled, selfish rich girl who had never known what it was like to want for anything, hurting Damon so badly made Ariel's blood boil.

"Maybe it's none of my business, but I don't think you want Moey and Ellen and Sarah to be raised without choices."

He turned, and she saw his brow furrow. Before he could speak, she plunged on. "Think about Moey—so sensitive, dreamy. From what I've seen, Eve isn't going to have any patience for dragon slayers and sorceresses and enchanted castles. Whenever Eve dug her verbal claws into you during Ellen's party, it hurt Moey. Badly."

"I thought Moey had gotten quiet. But she does that sometimes. I never know why."

"Well, that time it was because the child adores you and didn't want to see you hurting. She has such an incredible ability to know how other people are feeling, to know what makes them happy, what makes them sad. Sometimes I'm afraid she hurts for the whole world, Damon. She's such a little thing, and that's such a heavy burden for her to carry. She needs someone to teach her how to laugh."

Ariel's eyes burned, her throat thick with tears. "Do you think she'll learn that with your mother-in-law, Damon? To laugh and be wild and act crazy sometimes?"

"No." It was one word, laced with a kind of wary hopefulness.

"And what about Ellen?" Ariel said, warming to the subject. "Did you hear Eve every time the child asserted herself? Eve acted like it was a crime for anyone under the age of twenty-one to have an opinion in their heads. You think Ellen is wrestling with her temper now—what do you think it would be like for her if she was under Eve's thumb? Ellen would probably spend ninety percent of her time grounded in her room. In her way, Ellen is every bit as fragile as Moey is. Ellen is testing you, true. But you're giving her the answers she needs, Damon. Showing her that you really do care about how she feels. That you'll listen to her, hear her out, even if, in the end, you decide to pull rank on her."

Damon's eyes probed hers, his face like that of a man dying of thirst—thirsting for the hope she was offering him with her words. "Do you really think so? That I'm giving Ellen what she needs?"

"I know you are."

"I'd like to believe you. You don't know how much. But look at why you even came to the house in the first place. Moey was in a crisis and I didn't have a clue. You'd sent home notes from school, tried to contact me, and I wasn't available. I didn't know, didn't suspect."

"But it wasn't that you didn't *care*," Ariel said. "Okay, so you…maybe you are gone more than you should be. And you get overwhelmed sometimes. But everybody does. Kids are every bit as exhausting as they are adorable. Just because you're not perfect, doesn't mean you should give your children to someone else to raise. Damon, you love those girls. I know you do. It's in your eyes every time you look at them. As for the parenting skills you're so worried about—you can grow, learn to be better.'' Ariel's lips curved into a smile, tenderness all but breaking her heart. "C'mon, Whiz Kid. You're supposed to be some kind of hotshot genius. Put all that gray matter to use.''

"Ariel, I don't know how...how to learn. How to love them the way they need me to. I don't...'' Damon lifted his fingers to her face, and with feather-light touches, moved up her cheeks to sift through the silky curls at her temples. "It seems to come so easy to you. So...easy.''

His thumbs skated over her parted lips. "I've never been very good at loving,'' he whispered, and her heart felt ready to burst. "Teach me, Ariel.''

Ariel's trembling fingers traced his cheekbone, the hard line of his jaw. The harsh angles of his face that hid away so much unhappiness.

And as he looked at her from beneath the thick sweep of his lashes with desperate hope, agonizing vulnerability, she knew that sometime between the moment she had charged into the house on Worthington Drive with Houdini in tow, and this moment beneath the oak tree, she had stopped seeing Damon Kincaid as Moey's father, and Ellen's and Sarah's. She had stopped seeing him as one more piece of the world she had to reform, and had started seeing him as a man.

A man whose sensitivity wrenched at her, whose vulnerability saddened her, but whose honesty and courage and dry sense of humor enchanted her.

She loved him.

A flash of panic rocketed through her, then vanished in the wake of wonder. How had it happened? When had it started?

Or had she just stumbled across this love that made her heart ache, race, tremble with a happiness too great to hold? Had she discovered it with the same miraculous serendipity as a child discovering a cluster of springtime's first crocuses tucked upon a pillow of snow?

She swallowed hard, her eyes stinging as she put her arms around his neck, turning her face up to his. There were no words she could say, no way to describe the sparkling wonder that seemed to bubble up inside her. So she drew his head down, her lips velvety soft as she kissed him, tiny, soft, soothing kisses, like the brush of a butterfly's wing. Gentle, healing kisses that she wanted desperately to penetrate deep down inside him, where the raw places lurked, the bruised emptiness life had left inside him.

Damon groaned, his arms drawing her close, holding her as if she were something fragile, precious, some long-forgotten dream he was afraid would shatter beneath his hands.

His mouth moved in answer to her kiss, and the tenderness, the need that seemed to throb beneath the hard masculine line of his lips speared deep into Ariel, leaving her trembling, uncertain. And yet more certain than she'd ever been in her life.

She'd always been impulsive—had flung herself into life with a reckless abandon. But this time, as she stared into the face of the man before her, it was as if she could feel ripples of unease inside her, sense that what she felt for Damon was as dangerous as it was magical, as frightening as it was enchanting.

She pulled away from him, and he stilled, his dark eyes shimmering with soul-deep need.

"Damon, what time did you tell your baby-sitter you'd be home?"

"I didn't say. I left emergency numbers, and..." Damon stiffened, as if thinking how the curfewless night might appear. "I wasn't expecting anything to... well, to happen. I just figured we would be eating at Armaude's and that takes a long time in itself. And then I'd thought we might go for drinks or something. I have this obsessive thing about being on time," he said defensively, "so when I don't know when I'll be home, I just don't say anything."

"I'm glad," Ariel said.

At his quizzical look, her cheeks fired.

"I'm glad—because I want you to come upstairs with me, Damon." Her voice was a breathless whisper. "Please."

Chapter Twelve

Damon stared at her in disbelief, his heart seeming to stop beating, even the crickets seeming to lapse into silence, waiting. She looked up at him, and he drowned in her eyes.

Damon's jaw clenched, her implication as clear as if she'd said the words. And he'd never wanted anything as much as he wanted to take her hand at that moment, follow her upstairs to her bed. It had been so long since he'd been with a woman. There hadn't been anyone since Amanda, and in the time since she'd been pregnant with Sarah, their love life had been all but nonexistent. She'd been his wife, but when she'd offered herself up to him like some kind of martyr, he hadn't been able to stomach the sex.

But despite the fire that was rioting in his veins, despite the generosity, the nervous anticipation that shone beneath Ariel's lashes, Damon couldn't take advantage of her that way.

"Ariel, we can't." The words were the hardest ones he had ever spoken. "I'm not...prepared."

"Prepared?"

"I don't have anything to protect you. And there is no way I'd risk... hurting you."

"What's the matter? Are you afraid I'm diseased?" There were silvery twinkles in the teasing light of her eyes. "I promise you, I've had only one sexual partner. It was my last year in college, and I wanted to find out just exactly what all this fuss over sex was about. I have to say, that from my perspective, it was highly overrated."

"Damn it, Ariel, it's not a joke—"

"I know it isn't," she said, suddenly serious. "And I think you're terrific, for worrying. But I think I can handle that angle of things."

"You?" Damon's brow furrowed.

"Come on." She took his hand, tugging him toward the entry of the sprawling old brick home that had obviously been cut up into apartments.

Even the corridors had a kind of old-fashioned charm— polished hardwood floors covered with frayed hand-loomed rugs. Brass light fixtures from the thirties cast a mellow glow against cracked plaster.

Damon followed in Ariel's wake, his hand so tight on hers, he was afraid he would hurt her, but he couldn't seem to loosen his grip, terrified that if he did, she would melt away, back into the pages of the fairy-tale kingdom she seemed born of.

He knew they were approaching her apartment even before she stopped at the door. Overturned baskets with bright-colored scarves draped over them flanked the door, monster plants, big enough to eat Cincinnati, perched on the wicker tops.

A shiny gold wreath hung on the doorway, cross-stitch letters in purple and red proclaiming a warning to Enter At Your Own Risk.

Damon watched as Ariel inserted an old-fashioned-looking key into the lock and battled with what seemed a recalcitrant door.

He was just about to help, when it gave a squawk of protest and swung wide, revealing the room beyond.

A huge expanse of wood floor stretched the length of the room, the pool of light from the lamppost beyond pouring in vivid colors through stained-glass borders on the old windows. A giant pile of pillows, in rich gold and orange crowded in a window seat and spilled onto the floor. An old rocking chair near a marble fireplace was the only other seat in the place, except for the brass bed aligned against the wall.

It wasn't made up, plain white sheets and a jewel-colored quilt making the bed seem as warm and welcoming as Ariel's arms. The wall was covered with dozens of framed snapshots of the whole Madigan clan.

There was a picture of Ariel and Caroline in bridesmaids' dresses, hugging Beth rigged out in a bridal veil. There was a photograph of a dock in front of a cabin somewhere—the whole family in bathing suits striking funny poses for the camera.

The same porch swing he'd sat in, the night they'd looked at the stars, was framed in another picture, while a much younger Ariel sat perched on it, feeding a baby lamb with a bottle.

He had a fleeting memory of Caroline Madigan's steady eyes, the warning she'd given him that first morning at the farm, but he shuttered it away. This night, this chance, was far too precious to surrender.

Instead, he focused on the collage of pictures, felt his chest ache as he thought of that farm full of animals, hayrack rides and growing your own pumpkins for Halloween. Jesse and Jake, Caroline and Beth and the rest—sisters and brothers to squabble with, to share secrets with, to grow up with and sit, late at night, on holidays, reminiscing about first crushes and creative evasions of chores. Knowing so many stories about each other that the memories would never run dry.

A Norman Rockwell family, with the turkey at Thanksgiving, and stockings at Christmas, and a mother and a father to tend skinned knees and bruised feelings.

He pulled his gaze away, suddenly feeling too raw. Ariel had gone behind a breakfast bar that sectioned off the tiny kitchen area, and was rummaging in a small wicker basket.

He walked over until he was standing behind her and his mouth quirked in a half smile as he saw her going through what looked to be a basket full of junk. Two slingshots, a pocket knife and a homemade bow and arrow set with enough whittled-sharp ammunition to give any parent nightmares were identifiable in the mound of mismatched objects.

"What the blazes is that stuff?" he couldn't resist asking.

"Contraband." She was blushing, soft roses in her cheeks, but she smiled with amusement. "Every year I confiscate a mountain of it from the kids I teach. At the end of the year, I return most of the things, but I keep whatever I think is dangerous."

"I see. And what does this have to do with . . . us?"

She grinned. "I have this little guy named Clark Kent—I know, his parents should be brought up on charges for giving him that name. Anyway, Clark wears pop-bottle thick glasses, and might be able to go nose-to-nose with a cocker spaniel. He's tiny and adorable, and will probably be a rocket scientist someday."

"Off to the planet Krypton, huh?"

"Something like that. Well, he's been experimenting with balloons and paper rockets—trying to find the best propellant. And he brought *this* in. He said his teenage brother told him to try it." She drew something shiny out of the pile, and put it in Damon's hand.

Laughter welled up inside him as he stared at the foil package teenage boys had been optimistically toting around in their wallets for decades as a badge of near adulthood.

"I can't wait to hear what Clark's parents thought about this method of propulsion," Damon said.

"They never found out. Let's just say I've had more than my share of experience with older brothers. I figure Clark's was just waiting to hear the fireworks go off over this little escapade. You know—your typical light-the-fuse-and-wait-for-the-explosion stunt that older siblings take diabolical delight in. So I just sat down with Clark at recess and helped him figure out another way to get his rocket to fly—one that wouldn't land him in Sister Thomasetta's office."

"I bet you didn't bat an eye when you saw that thing," Damon said with an assessing look. "You probably managed to handle the whole situation without a hitch."

She brushed back a stray tendril of hair, and deposited the basket back on the breakfast bar. "You get adept at it after a while. Kids are always coming out with the most astonishing things."

"Are they?" Damon glanced at the foil package, uncertain what to do with it. He wanted nothing more than to hold her, wanted to make wild, sweet love with her, bury himself in her innocence, her optimism. But somehow it didn't feel right to just lead Ariel to the tumbled coverlets of her bed.

He wanted to savor everything about tonight. To luxuriate in every sensation, every smile, every laugh and every sigh.

After a moment, he pocketed the foil square and took her hand, leading her to the mound of pillows that lay in vivid splashes against the mellow glow of the hardwood floor.

"Tell me," he said softly. "Tell me what the kids say."

She sank gracefully to the pillows, and when he followed her down, she curled up next to him, her head cradled against the lee of his shoulder.

The scent of her seemed to fill the room. Damon couldn't help but remember when the stench spewed from factory smokestacks had filled his nostrils, or later, when the expensive smell of Amanda's cologne had seemed to crowd into every corner of his home. He'd known the sterile scent of hotel rooms, and the crisp, metallic one of the administration buildings where he'd spent so many hours.

But as he leaned close to Ariel, she seemed to drive away those hazy memories, filling him with the scent of cinnamon and honey, a scent so wholesome, so alluring, it made his senses spin.

Her voice was soft, quiet. "The night of the Abracadabra party, Moey told me that you were under the spell of an evil sorceress. One who had put up invisible walls that held you prisoner. I was so angry with you when she was alone. I never suspected that what she said was true."

"Invisible walls?" Damon's mouth curled into a smile. His fingertips hungered for the silk of her skin, and he indulged them, burrowing them beneath the fall of her hair to curve around her nape.

She gave a gentle laugh. "Anyone who adores Tolkien the way you do would have to understand evil sorceresses and magic walls. That first night when Houdini tore your living room apart, I saw how you acted. You didn't much care about furniture that must've cost a fortune, or that carpet that's about as thick as the powder in Aspen. But those books...*The Lord of the Rings*...when you saw that they'd been damaged, you looked positively sick."

Damon shook his head, both astonished and yet not at all surprised. "I can't believe you noticed that in all that chaos. No. Of course you did. You seem to see everything, understand everything, like you have some sort of crystal you look through to see into people's hearts. Even when those people don't want you to. Don't want anyone to."

He looked away from her, staring meditatively at the glinting chips of stars just visible through the curtains. "My mom didn't believe in wasting money on things that weren't practical. Birthdays and Christmas were times when I got things I needed—socks, underwear, mittens. One year I got a mattress for my bed."

Damon could feel Ariel's compassion as if it touched him, caressed him, and his voice was halting as he peeled back the layers of his childhood, speaking with her about things he'd never told anyone, things he'd not even allowed himself to think about since the day he had moved out of the tiny apartment forever.

"I loved to read," he continued. "It was my way of filling up the house with friends, with the pets I couldn't have, and the brother and sisters and even a father. It was my way of making things right between my mother and me. I would read and say to myself, there—if we lived in the country, she would be around more, or, if we had our own house with a swing set in back, she would smile at me and wave from the kitchen window, just like the mother in the story I was reading."

"Your mother didn't believe it was important for a child to read?"

"Oh, she didn't mind, if that's what you're asking. There was a library branch three blocks from our apartment building, so I could walk there whenever I wanted to. And the books—I could check them out for free. She didn't mind, but she didn't understand, either. My fascination for what were, to her, just a bunch of black marks on a page."

Ariel's fingers closed around his, and he leaned back against the pillows, tugging her with him. He stroked her hair, and was grateful for the silence she gave him as a gift.

"I wasn't any saint as a kid," he admitted. "And there was a time when I went through a bad period—where I was resentful and angry about the way things were. When Christmas came, I didn't even want to bother—even with what little we had traditionally done. I couldn't see any point in the little plastic tree we stuck up every year. It just made me think about the other kids I knew, with giant trees and mountains of presents. Real presents. Toys and books and candy canes. And my mom...she only sat around feeling sad. My father...he left at Christmastime, and it always made her remember."

He ran his fingertips across Ariel's hair, turned his lips so he could brush them against her forehead. "So, anyway, when Christmas Eve came that year and Mom was getting out the box of decorations, I got angry, said things I'd been thinking a long time. I hurt her. I know I did. And I'd still give anything to change that. I went to bed and cried myself to sleep. I was never sure whether it was because of the expression on my mom's face, or the fear that I'd never know anything better than the life we had in that apartment."

His voice thickened, and he swallowed hard as the memories crowded around him. "The next morning I didn't even want to get up, to face her. When I came out of my room, I saw that she'd put up the plastic tree all by herself, and there was a present under it. It was the Tolkien trilogy. She'd taken back the practical things she'd bought me, and used the money for the books. I never forgot that, Ariel. That one time, that one way that she was able to show me that she loved me."

Damon felt something on his shirtfront, something warm, wet, where Ariel's face was pillowed against his chest. He smoothed his fingertips over her other cheek, gathering up the trail of tears.

She was crying for him, and the knowledge rocked him to his core.

"You must have meant so much to her, Damon," she said in a quavering voice. "She must be so proud of you."

"I told you she died, never knowing that I got out of the South Side. Never knowing that I made it."

"That's not what I meant. Look at you. Look at those children of yours. Look at how hard you are fighting to be a good father. Of any gift you could have given to your mother, I can't think of anything she would have valued more."

Damon's chest swelled with gratitude, and he turned her, gently until she lay back against the pillows, her face exposed to him—every glistening tear, every quiver of her rose-pink lips, every emotion that welled up in those fairy-tale eyes.

She was so beautiful, so giving, and he wanted to give to her in return. He braced himself on his elbow, his hand curving over the skin bared where her blouse dipped low on her shoulder. "You almost make me believe in invisible walls and sorceresses," he breathed. "And you... you'd have to be a fairy princess... a wood sprite... an angel sent here for me." He kissed the tiny hollow above her collarbone, the rapid rush of her breath feeding the fires building inside him.

"Tell me, Ariel Madigan, did you slide down to me on a rainbow? Or was it a unicorn that brought you? Brought your dreams to make me believe..."

"All the unicorns were taken. I had to settle for a pink bug," Ariel said with a shaky laugh.

"I'd like to give you unicorns. And rainbows, Ariel. Enough to drown in, if you'll let me."

He lowered his mouth to sip at hers, as if her lips were the petals of some enchanted flower, filled with a nectar that could make him forget.

Forget all the loneliness, the self-doubt. Forget the ugliness and the rejections and all the mistakes that still scarred his soul.

"I don't want rainbows," she whispered against his mouth. "I just want you. I l—"

Fierce, wild, desire ripped through him. He crushed his lips against her sweet ones, her giving ones, dragging her harder against him. He was burning with need, his hands so hungry for the feel of her, his tongue so thirsty for the taste of her, that he felt like he would explode.

He trailed kisses down her delicate jaw, taking tiny nips at her throat. His hands fumbled with the elastic edging that secured the top of her blouse just above the full swells of her breasts.

All his life, he'd been so damned efficient in everything he'd done. But now, as he struggled with the fabric that concealed Ariel from his gaze, he felt clumsier than he'd ever been in his life. But he didn't care about his fumblings, didn't care about anything except the soft, mewling sound that caught in Ariel's throat.

She looked like a tumbled angel, a mind-shatteringly seductive angel as he finally succeeded in solving the enigma of the blouse, unfastening it to reveal a wisp of nude-colored satin beneath.

The strapless bra that shaped her breasts was embroidered with tiny flowers, and Damon lowered his face to nuzzle against the delicate material, drawing in the subtle feminine fragrance of her, savoring the sensual delight of satin warmed by her skin. Her nipples thrust against the thin material, and Damon opened his lips to pluck at the hardened rosettes, to suckle her through the cloth.

He felt himself swell, harden, where the fly of his pants pressed against the restless column of her thigh, the friction caused by her movements driving him wild with the need to bury his length deep in her welcoming center.

But he forced himself to go slow, resolved to take her to heaven in agonizingly pleasurable stages, until she wanted him with the same wild madness as he wanted her.

His fingers unfastened the front clip of her bra, and the silk drifted apart, the delicate pink nipples peeking at him from the lace edging. God, he wanted her so much, it made him hurt, made him burn; every brush of his fingers across her skin was torture, an agony of hope, of wonder that he never wanted to escape.

With reverent fingers he cupped one breast in his hand, then teased it, ever so softly with the point of his tongue. Ariel groaned, her own hands fighting their way beneath his shirt to find the ridges of his rib cage, shoving the material up beneath his arms until she could touch the hair-roughened surface of his chest.

She was magic in his arms, quicksilver wonder. Every dream he'd never even dared to have. With lightning-swift movements, he pulled away from her, ripping both the

sweatshirt and the cotton dress shirt over his head and toss-
ing them to the floor. Then he drew her close again, the little nubs of her nipples against his chest a delightful contrast,
the taste of her mouth as he kissed her again even sweeter
than he had remembered.

He traced the shape of her lips with his tongue, then in-
sinuated it into her mouth. She opened for him, her own
tongue stealing out to taste him, as well.

"God, you're so beautiful," he praised her, low, urgent.
His hands worked the knot of her sash, the skirt following
to join it on the floor.

He skimmed the impossibly thin band of her underwear
down her legs, leaving her bare, her skin ivory and roses,
shaded with peaches and cream. And he wanted to taste
every inch of her.

"Damon, I want...want to see you, feel you."

The inferno building inside him was set out of control by
those words. He stood, making quick work of his fly, all but
ripping the pants down his legs, kicking them free. They
skidded across the wooden floor to pool beside the bed-
post. And Damon knew that he wanted Ariel there, this first
time, among the soft coverlets, the vibrantly shaded quilt.

He scooped her into his arms, kissing her as he carried her
over, laid her on the bed. His hands couldn't get enough of
her, as he explored the curves and valleys that had tormented his dreams in the endless nights since the first time
he had kissed her.

She was liquid flame in his arms, her kisses generous as
she trailed them down his chest. Her hair, a cloud of sun-
shine-hued silk tormented him with its delicate caress against
the agonizingly sensitive disks of his nipples.

Damon gritted his teeth against a moan. From the time he
was a kid, he had valued control above all else, strived to
maintain it in all situations. It had seemed the only way he
had to make order of his life, the only way to keep things
safe, secure. Even with Amanda, he had kept himself emotionally distanced, despite the physical responses she'd en-

gendered in him. And Amanda had nurtured her own natural walls of reserve, as well. It had been the one thing that they had shared—maybe the thing that had drawn them together in the beginning. This shared understanding of what it was like to want—no, *need*—space, safety zones, when emotions grew too intense for comfort.

But there were no buffers with Ariel Madigan—no boundaries to retreat behind. With every touch, every kiss, every word she breathed hot against his skin, Damon could feel her encircling him, engulfing him, plumbing depths inside him he'd never suspected existed.

And even as he felt himself racing toward a release more mind shattering than he'd ever known, he sensed the accompanying terror, the feeling of dangling from a precipice by his hands, watching, helpless as Ariel slipped his fingers from the edge one by one.

He gritted his teeth as those small, warm fingers dipped low to curl around that part of him that was swollen, pulsing. She explored him there with the same joyful abandon, the same delight she brought to everything she embraced. And Damon arched his head back, fighting to maintain his sanity.

When he couldn't bear the excruciating ecstasy a moment more, he pulled away, groping for the pants that lay close to the bed. He fumbled with the pocket, and when he shoved himself back upright on the bed, he felt his cheeks burn as he met Ariel's gaze.

"I had to...to..." Christ, he didn't know what the hell to say. The foil package cut into his clenched fingers.

But Ariel only smiled, a smile so contagious, he felt his own unease ebbing. "You had to head for the phone booth, huh, superhero?"

Her teasing was so gentle, so loving, Damon felt his heart lurch, the emotions he felt for this woman cutting him so deep, he couldn't stand the pain. The pain of wanting her—not just sexually, although God knew he wanted her so badly in that way he burned with it. But rather, the pain of wanting Ariel in ways he could never have her—wanting to lose himself in her laughter, her loving. Wanting to bury himself in the world she saw with that vision of hers that was as magical as any fantasy world any spinner of legend had ever created.

A vision that Damon was certain he could never share. Because he knew...knew that magical world was only illusion.

As if she sensed him withdrawing from her in ways that had nothing to do with the heat of his body, Ariel's fingers closed on his, gently peeling his hand back from the protection he held.

Lovingly, so lovingly, she wisped it over his length, making it seem like the tenderest of gestures. Then she drew him down until he lay on top of her, her legs parting to welcome him, cradle him against that warm, downy haven he craved. Ever so gently, Damon reached between them, touching that velvety place that was as warm and giving as the rest of her. A shiver of pleasure racked Ariel, and he felt it to the core of his soul.

"Damon," she said with a whimper, arching against his hand. "Now. Please, now."

He eased his hand away, centering his throbbing length in its place.

He felt her tense, heard her cry out with ecstasy even as he slowly, torturously buried himself inside her.

Pleasure. Pain.

Had there ever been anything like the sensation he felt as the contractions of her release tightened around him? Had he ever known anything as beautiful as the expression on her face as her head tossed against the pillows, her lips parting in a cry of joy. He held himself still, just watching the wonder of her pleasure until those thick lashes fluttered open, revealing eyes wide, beautiful. Both more loving and more terrifying than anything he'd ever seen. He closed his eyes, burying his face in the soft lee of her throat.

"Ariel," he rasped. "Oh, Ariel."

Then, unable to bear the exquisite torture another moment, he grasped her hips in his hands and thrust. Beads of sweat broke out on his brow as Ariel's hands stroked him, her voice urged him, her body welcoming him again and again. She was everything he could have dreamed, everything he could have wished for what seemed a lifetime ago. Before Amanda, before he'd sacrificed the last of his dreams, preferring the emptiness to the pain.

And now . . . now it was too late. Too late to drink in Ariel's joy. Too late to share that wonder-filled glow in her eyes.

Too late.

The certainty of that devastated him as he drove himself deep one last time.

He stiffened, shuddered, every muscle in his body quaking with what he had just experienced. His throat constricted, his eyes burned, and he kept them buried against the pillow of her hair.

She'd won.

Defeated the dragons, broken the spell. The walls were down, a ruin about his soul.

But how could he tell a dreamer like Ariel that in defeating the dragons, they had lost? How could he tell her that what remained was too raw, too fragile to trust even into her gentle hands?

Chapter Thirteen

He was quiet. So quiet.

Ariel cradled Damon against her, wishing desperately that he would say something, anything, to break the silence. His breath had slowed, stopped rasping, harsh with the exertion of their passion. His heart had stopped thundering where it was pressed against her breasts. But he hadn't moved, hadn't stirred as she threaded her fingers through the tousled silk of his hair.

What had he felt? What had he experienced as they had touched each other, kissed each other? What thoughts had been hidden beneath those thick, dark lashes, those wary eyes?

Even though Ariel's own experience with sex had been limited, she'd known instinctively that what had passed between her and Damon was rare. And yet that certainty was frosted with the chill knowledge that now something was terribly wrong.

Was it possible Damon was regretting this? That he was thinking of Amanda and the disaster that had resulted the last time he had given himself to a woman?

She swallowed hard, stunned at the depth of the pain that possibility caused her.

She loved him.

Loved him in a way that his wife had never loved him. Loved that part of him that was uncertain, unsure. Loved the part of him that had searched for stars from the fire escape on the South Side.

She loved the man who still treasured the tattered books his mother had given him so long ago. The man who had struggled so desperately to make sure Ellen's birthday party was wonderful.

She loved the man who stared all of his own faults square in the face, who judged himself so harshly in the wake of his wife's death.

And she was furious, outraged that Amanda Kincaid had done everything in her power to deaden the dreamer inside Damon. The dreamer that had escaped the poverty of his childhood and accepted the bitter reality of being forced into marriage with a woman who didn't love him, could never love him. A woman who hadn't flinched at sabotaging his relationship with his children—the only dream that Damon had had left.

But the most unforgivable thing of all was that Amanda Kincaid had succeeded in killing any dreams Damon had had for himself, and would most likely have succeeded in destroying his relationship with the girls, as well, if she hadn't died.

Ariel felt a momentary surge of something ugly inside her, a kind of relief that the woman had been thwarted. And yet, Ariel knew it wasn't death she wished on Amanda Kincaid, but a kind of gladness that Damon at least had a chance—this chance to make things right.

Ariel's throat constricted as she held him, stroked him. She wanted so much to reassure him, to help him to see the beauty she had found in him. She wanted so much for him to know what this time with him had meant to her. But were there any words that could express perfection? Magic? Were there any words to explain the sensation she had known, of reaching high into a night-shrouded sky and holding the glittering brightness of a star in her hands?

Yes, she thought, a kind of panic jolting through her. There was one way to tell him. And yet, of all the things she could say to him, she sensed that those words were the ones he was not yet ready to hear.

I love you.

She mouthed the words silently against his temple, hoping that deep in the most secret, guarded part of his heart he would hear her, know that it was true.

But at that instant, he shifted away from her, as if her very thoughts had shoved him away. Ariel shivered, feeling the loss of the cocoon of warmth, contentment that had enveloped her in the aftermath of their lovemaking.

She had wanted him to open up to her—wanted him to expose that hidden part of his soul to her, certain that she could heal it because she loved him so much. But now, looking into those haggard features, she wanted to close her eyes against what she saw.

Savage guilt, merciless self-blame and a hopelessness so barren that it made her hands tremble because she sensed that here, in the tumbled coverlets of her bed, she had just added a hundredfold to those emotions warring inside Damon.

"Ariel, I..." He drove his fingers through his hair, squaring his shoulders as if preparing to take a blow. "Ariel, I think we need to talk. About this. About what just happened." His eyes were smoldering, not with passion now, but with regret and responsibility.

And in that moment she knew that he blamed himself for something he couldn't name, that he was once again taking on himself the weight of all the guilt for something that had happened.

Guilt. Blame. When she had felt only wonder, waves of beauty and joy and fulfillment so intense, it still shook her soul.

She battled the hurt that stung deep, and reached out her hand to tentatively touch one rigid shoulder. "It's all right, you know," she said, groping for some way to ease his pain. "If you're worried that I was...was making more of this than you were ready for, I wasn't. I don't expect anything from you."

He looked at her, his face stiff, confusion and a shading of anger lighting his eyes. "What the blazes is that supposed to mean?"

"I just don't want you worrying that I'm expecting you to tell me you love me or—or talk about forevers."

The dark flush that spread across those chiseled features lanced deep in Ariel's chest. She tried to ignore the sinking sensation in the pit of her stomach, and rushed on.

"I mean, this...this was beautiful." Her voice quavered just a little. "I can't even begin to tell you how much I loved making love with you." She forced a tiny laugh. "Believe me, it changed my perspective on the entire undertaking completely. But there's no need for you to feel obligated to make more of this than there is. People do this all the time, for all kinds of reasons, Damon. Lust. Love. Just for...well, the thrill of it. And sometimes—" Ariel's voice dropped "—just to take comfort. Because they need someone."

His features had gone ice white, a muscle in his jaw knotted. "I see." His voice was so level, so cool as he climbed out of the bed that it terrified her. Ariel watched him grab up his pants and shirt, drawing them on with controlled violence. She felt her stomach lurch with the certainty that somehow she had just made things far worse.

How? she wondered numbly. She'd seen the wariness in his face, sensed the edginess, the unease. All she'd wanted to do was make it easier for him to deal with this wellspring of emotion that seemed bent on drowning them both.

She'd just wanted to give him a chance to get used to what they had shared—not physically, although that in itself had been incredible. But what they had shared emotionally, the secrets he'd told her, the corners of himself he let her glimpse before he'd shuttered them away.

Yet somehow, in the very act of offering him the space he needed, she'd wounded him even more deeply. "Damon, I...I know how hard this whole night has been on you. I know you're feeling raw. It doesn't come easily to you—opening up, talking about...about your pain. But you did it tonight. And you did it with me. I can't even begin to tell you how precious a gift that trust was."

"So precious that you were even willing to hop into bed with me? What? As a reward, like those damn stickers you sent home with Moey?"

Ariel flinched at the bitterness in those words. "Of course not. It wasn't like that."

"Oh, it wasn't, was it? You tell me that what just happened between us didn't mean a thing to you. That you don't *expect* anything from me. But you've only had one other lover, Ariel. One other man. So you obviously don't go impulsively leaping into bed with just anyone."

For a heartbeat Ariel thought of flinging the truth at him, telling him that she loved him. But the thought of him, bitter, angry, disgusted at her confession, made her swallow the words. "I don't appreciate being analyzed like some company's pay log, Damon."

"Terrific, because I don't appreciate being analyzed, either. Come on, Ariel. Why? Why did you invite me up here? With protection conveniently tucked in that basket full of kid's stuff? Did you go to bed with me in hopes that I'd crack even further? That I'd bare my soul to you?"

"I didn't think about that. I..."

"Maybe you were hoping I'd tell you the truth about Amanda and me. But believe me, Cinderella, the reality would be a sight too ugly for those fairy-tale eyes of yours. For years I resented her. I was tempted—hell, yes, I was tempted to have an affair. Be with somebody who didn't shudder every time I touched her. Not only that, but I've even sunk so low as to consider giving up my daughters. Giving them to Eve to raise because I get so damn exhausted sometimes, I can't even see straight. Because when I look at them, I see how badly I failed them. I have to face all my mistakes, and know that I'm making new ones every day."

"Damon, don't." The plea was soft, wounded.

"Don't? Come on, Ariel, isn't this what you *expected* when you had sex with me? Didn't you figure it would be so much better for me to get it all out? Well here it is, Miss Fix-It. Only it's not quite as easy to stick a bandage on a grown-up's wounds, is it?"

There was enough truth in the words to make her cringe. She was in love with him, had made love with him because of that. And yet, hadn't she also wanted to help him deal with the guilt, the confusion, the grief that was tearing him apart? Hadn't she wanted to reach past his pain and somehow make things right for him?

But that was what love was about, wasn't it?

Tears stung her eyes, and she tugged the quilt close around her, as if she could use it to block out the misery suffocating her now. She closed her eyes, knowing she had no choice but to tell him.

"Damon, I wanted to help you. I won't even try to deny that. But the reason I asked you up here...the reason I touched you, held you, wasn't because I felt sorry for you or wanted to force you to tell me things you weren't ready to say. I made love with you because...because I love you, Damon."

Silence. It stretched so long, Ariel couldn't stand it. She opened her eyes.

His features were drawn, pale, his eyes twin pools of pain. His mouth was twisted with an anguish she knew she'd put there.

"Don't love me, Ariel." He looked away from her, his voice savage, tortured. "It would be the worst mistake you ever made."

"I don't believe that. There's so much love inside you, Damon. I can feel it. Trust me with it. I'm not like Amanda. I promise, I—"

"It's not you, Ariel, it's me. Everyone I've even tried to love I've hurt. My mother, Amanda, my children. And now you."

She started to protest, but he stopped her, laying his fingers on her lips. "I can see the shadows in your eyes, now, Ariel. Shadows that weren't there when I first met you. I put them there. I did. And I'm going to fill them with even more. Because I used you." A bitter, strangled laugh came from his throat. "God, I must really be the monster Amanda thought I was. Taking so much from you when I knew—damn it, I *knew* I didn't have anything left to give."

"I told you I didn't expect anything."

"You might not have expected it, but you sure as hell wanted it. And you deserve it, Ariel. The whole damn storybook ending. Everything you dreamed of. But I can't be the one to give it to you. I knew that from the beginning."

"I knew you didn't believe in miracles," she whispered, feeling her dreams wither and die. "I guess I just thought I could change that."

He paced over to her, his hand gentle as he touched her cheek. "I'm sorry. I'm sorry any of this ever happened."

"Don't be." She was breaking into tiny pieces. "Don't be sorry. I can stand anything but that."

She looked into those eyes that had been exasperated when he'd climbed to rescue the baby raccoon, the eyes that had been so intense, so haunted as they had walked back from Cimirelli's, a sky full of wishing stars sprinkled over their heads.

She had been so eager to bring the dreams back into his eyes, but the sherry-dark depths only reflected how torn he was, bruised, destroyed as certainly as the rose she had ruined as a child. And no amount of regret, or magic, or even imagination would ever be able to make it right.

It was over. The certainty filled Ariel with grief and anger and soul-numbing despair.

"I'd like to see the girls one more time," she said softly. "I sort of... promised them that I'd take them to the park sometime."

"I know you've grown close. But... I think they've been getting pretty used to having you around. Maybe a little dependent. It might... might be better if..."

"If I didn't see them anymore?" She couldn't keep the catch from her voice.

Damon's fist knotted, as if he'd just taken a blow. He walked to the door of the apartment, then rested his hand on the knob. He didn't look at her. He didn't have to. The image of what she had done to him was seared forever into Ariel's heart.

"I am sorry, Ariel. I'll never forget you," he said softly. "What you tried to do for me. Do for the girls..." His voice trailed off, and she saw his shoulders tremble. "I'll never forgive myself for hurting you this way. Goodbye, Cinderella."

She closed her eyes against the anguish, the emptiness, as he pulled the door shut behind him, the last of her dreams crumbling to dust.

Chapter Fourteen

The cluster of little faces at the kitchen table was unnaturally subdued, with even Sarah's accustomed bubbling curiosity quelled somehow between the time Damon had left for his "nondate" and this morning. He regarded his daughters uneasily, wondering if they had somehow picked up on his own agitation. Wondering if they knew how mixed-up he felt inside, how confused and yes, damn it to hell, how blasted scared he'd been from the moment he'd looked into Ariel's eyes and seen a future, possibilities he'd been afraid even to hope for.

Possibilities that would leave him far more vulnerable than his relationship with Amanda ever had. That would leave his daughters vulnerable, as well, when they'd already suffered so much pain.

He'd been falling in love with her. Falling so fast, he'd barely caught hold of his sanity in time. Hell, he'd been wanting her a dozen times a day, dreaming about her, tumbled in his big bed. And when she'd offered him what he'd been craving for so long—offered him a taste of her lips, her creamy-smooth skin, offered him her warmth, her starry-eyed wonder—he hadn't been able to fight it anymore.

He'd taken her. Buried himself in Ariel's dreams for just a little while. But they had turned into a nightmare, when he had lifted his face from the cloud of her hair and had seen what he had so carelessly done. Destroyed her. Disillusioned her. Taken those fairy-tale eyes and forced them to see harsh realities that had snuffed out the wonder in them, the joyous anticipation.

Oh, God, what it had done to him to see her that way. To know... know that it had been his fault.

But then, hadn't it always been? With Amanda? With the girls? With his mother? Hadn't it always been him who had been unable to give them what they needed? Who hadn't been able to open up his heart wide enough to let them in?

Wasn't that why Amanda's death had devastated him so? Because he suspected that he might have been the reason she'd slammed into that overpass—that she hadn't had the will to fight to live because she'd been so drained, so weary of the arguments and the coldness and the loneliness.

But he'd been weary, too, damn it. And so blasted lonely. And most of the time his daughters had been half a continent away from him. Chirrupy disembodied voices at the end of a telephone line. Wary-eyed waifs who had seemed content to avoid him as much as possible when he intruded on their well-ordered world. Amanda's well-ordered world.

All his life, he'd been fighting to belong somewhere. But maybe he didn't deserve to. He was selfish. Impatient. And despite Ariel's reassurances, he didn't know a damn thing about how to make his daughters happy.

Then maybe you should let them go, a voice wrenched deep inside him.

The pain that gripped him was agonizing, and he shoved away from the table and stalked over to the refrigerator, pretending to search for more orange juice. But when he opened the door, even the blasted juice pitcher—the plastic

one she had bought while he'd been away—reminded him
of Ariel.

If you don't want something to break around kids, she
had teased him, *you'd better make sure it can bounce.*

But hearts didn't come in plastic. And breaking them was
so damned easy.

He schooled his face into a facsimile of his usual expression, not wanting to frighten his daughters. Then he turned
with the pitcher in hand, and began refilling Ellen's glass.

"Did Muffy talk you girls out last night?" he forced
himself to ask, desperate for the morning chatter that usually made him half-crazed before he'd had his coffee.
"You're awfully quiet."

Moey flinched as if he'd lit off a firecracker under her
chair. She set to work stirring her bowlful of instant oat-
meal as if she were attempting to start a miniature whirl-
pool.

"Nana comed here," Sarah confided, looking unsettled.
"She drop-ted off our Florida presents."

"That's...nice." Damon kept his voice level, stealing
another glance at Moey.

Sarah turned troubled eyes back up to Damon's. "Daddy,
is Ariel gonna be my new mommy?"

Damon set the pitcher down so abruptly, juice sloshed
over the side. "What?"

"Ellen said Ariel's gonna be our new mommy. I don't
think Nana liked that berry much."

Ellen looked stricken, but she jutted her chin up. "I don't
care!" she cried. "I *do* want Ariel to be our mommy! She
reads to me an' lets us help make cupcakes and she laughs,
Daddy. Ariel laughs. Mommy never ever did."

His heart seeming to twist from his chest, Damon reached
for his little girl, wanting to pull her into his arms, but Ellen shoved him away, rejecting the comfort he offered, as
certainly as he had rejected the haven Ariel had offered him
the night before.

"Daddy..." Moey's voice broke in, soft, tentative. "Why didn't Mommy like you anymore?"

Damon reeled at the question, feeling as if a fence post had just slammed into his gut. The knowledge that his children had sensed that things were wrong with him and Amanda was crushing. Desperately wishing for Ariel's ability to comfort, console, Damon groped for the right words to explain something that was beyond explanation, beyond understanding.

"Mommy and I...we made choices...some wrong choices, Moey. We didn't mean to. We didn't want to. But we did." He looked down into that solemn little face. "It hurt Mommy and me, hurt us both sometimes, because we wanted different things, and we couldn't seem to talk about them with each other. You know how it is when you get in disagreements with your sisters, and you can't seem to work things out?"

"Mrs. Bea makes us go to our rooms 'til we can love each other again," Sarah offered, her mouth pursed with seriousness. "Couldn't you and Mommy have goed to your room?"

"Sarah, you're so stupid!" Ellen snapped. "Nobody makes grown-ups go to their rooms."

"Maybe someone should have," Damon said. "I don't know. The only thing that I *do* know is that we had three precious little girls that we both loved very much."

"Ariel loves us berry much," Sarah piped up. "She didn't even care when I wetted the bed the night the monsters sneaked under the closet door. Ariel said *she* might have wetted the bed, too, if she'd seen those spooky claws."

Damon's throat ached as he pictured the scene as it must have been—Ariel, tumbled from sleep, climbing out of his bed, padding down the hall to where Sarah was crying. He could see Ariel's hands, gentle, as they freshened Sarah up, slipped on a clean nightgown. Ariel would have been smiling, that tender, secret smile he had seen her smile so often when she was with his daughters.

She would have handled it all so perfectly, soothed Sarah's fears, eased the little girl's ruffled dignity after the accident. Then she would have carried Sarah into the big bed, and watched those big brown eyes grow heavier and heavier as she told the little girl stories of fantasy worlds where there were no monsters lurking in the closets. Where mommies always laughed and daddies never went away.

But that would be a world that his daughters would never experience, any more than he had when he'd been small, and scared and lonely.

Damon ground his fingertips against his eyes, hating the desolation that stole over him.

Would it have been such a crime to ask Ariel to marry him? Ever since he'd gone to Melbourne he had been toying with the idea of finding someone to be his wife. Someone to fill the empty spaces in his children's lives. It would be the most practical, most logical thing to do. And he'd spent a lifetime pointing out to international companies the most expedient ways to remedy their problems.

Wouldn't marrying Ariel, asking her to be a mother to his children, be the most reasonable solution of all? He would have been able to give her security—any material thing that she wanted. And the sex—it had been beyond anything he'd ever imagined.

But more than that, he'd learned so much since Amanda's death, faced so many hard truths about himself. He could be a better husband this time. He and Ariel could be friends, partners. They could share each other's lives and be content. And could anyone really ask for more?

They would have the children. The children . . .

Damon gritted his teeth. Hadn't he made that mistake once before? Marrying for the sake of a child? It had been a disaster. Ruined Amanda's life, made his little girls suffer.

How could he be so reckless as to risk such a thing again?

Ariel wanted to be loved, deserved to be loved as unreservedly as the love she gave, and Damon knew that if he lived a hundred years, he would never be able to give her that gift. No, it was better this way. Better to end it and give her a chance to find another man—one who wasn't so damned battered inside, who could play the noble prince to her Sleeping Beauty.

But the thought of another man sharing forever with Ariel was like an acid searing deep in Damon's soul.

He battled to hide the emotions roiling inside him, and looked down at Sarah, stroking one hand down her silky curls. "I think Ariel does love you. Very much. But Ariel and I...we decided that it would be better if..." He sucked in a deep breath. "Ariel's not going to be your new mommy, girls. It just...just wouldn't work out."

"Why?" Ellen demanded, her lower lip trembling. "Did you yell at her?"

Damon winced, remembering the scene in Ariel's apartment. "Yes. I guess I did. But that's not the reason—"

"You yell at me sometimes, and I don't care at all!" Moey burst out. "I love you anyway."

Damon's throat felt thick, his eyes burned. "I love you, too, Princess."

"Ariel won't be our mommy because of me," Ellen broke in. "Because I'm stubborn and bad and I call Sarah 'stupid' sometimes."

"No! No, Ellen, don't even think such a thing."

"That's why Mommy was so sad all the time! Because of me! She said I was...was just like...you." Her voice shattered on a sob. "Was that bad, Daddy? To be like you?"

Fury. It sliced so deep, Damon couldn't breathe.

I'm the stubborn girl, Ellen had claimed that first night at her birthday party. He'd been afraid that he'd been the one to give her that perception of herself. Barring that, he'd been sure it must have been the baby-sitter. Never once had he suspected that it might have started long before, with Amanda.

Rage sickened him, seething resentment making his stomach churn. How could she have done such a thing? How could she have been so damn cruel, wounding Ellen that way?

Oh, God, why hadn't he seen? Why hadn't he suspected what was going on? From the first, Amanda had seemed a little taken aback by their middle daughter—a daughter that was so much like the husband she loathed.

The possibility that Amanda had somehow taken out her frustrations with Damon on Ellen was more than he could stand.

But wasn't that his fault, as well? That he'd hurt Amanda so badly, failed so miserably in being the husband that she wanted, needed, that she wasn't able to deal with Ellen?

What if he'd been home more? If he'd been around long enough to see . . .

No. He'd just have bungled things even more. Made things worse, the way he had now with Ariel.

"Oh, God, Ellen," he choked out, gathering the child into his arms. "I think you're wonderful. You're so brave and bright. And you're never afraid to go after what you want. Sweetheart, someday you're going to be one formidable young lady."

Ellen was clinging to him with all her might, snuffling against his shirt, the dampness of her tears searing hot against his skin. "D-do you really think so?"

"I think you are very special, Ellen Johanna Kincaid. So special that I can't wait to see what happens when you grow up. You'll be able to do anything, be anything you want to. Something wonderful. I just know it."

He glanced over at Moey, sitting in her chair, so dreamy, so vulnerable. "And you," he said, reaching out to grasp her hand, "you're going to make the world a wonderful place someday, Melissa. Imagine things that I could never even dream of."

"What 'bout Sarah Jane, Daddy? Can I be anyfing I want, too?"

He felt his littlest daughter clambering at his shoulder. He smiled, love for the little girl weighing his heart. "Yes, Sarah Jane. You can be anything you want."

Her eyes widened with delight. "Then maybe I'll be a ladybug. Like the ones Ariel's goin' to paint on my walls."

Moey's voice broke in softly, sadly. "I don't think Ariel's going to be doing that anymore, Sarah. But maybe I could help you imagine it."

Damon felt the shadow that stole over their faces as if it were the first snow of winter.

"Maybe... maybe I could try it. Try to paint it for you," he offered. "I've never been great at drawing, but if you girls are willing to help, we can try it when I get back from my next business meeting."

"You goin' away again, Daddy?" Ladybugs forgotten, Sarah peered up at him with sad eyes. "Mommy wented away. Then Mrs. Bea. An' Ariel. An' you. You always go 'way." She stared at the floor, a little waif in her teddy bear robe. "Ev'rybody always goes away."

They looked at him, three somber oval faces, each so different, so precious. Fragile. Each of them terrifyingly fragile in their own way. Each of their faces still carrying the shadows of grief.

Loneliness. It shrouded their features, showed in their eyes. God knew, Damon recognized that particular childhood monster. He'd faced it himself often enough. And now it was obvious he'd passed it on to his children, along with his dark hair and eyes, and the stubborn jut of Ellen's chin.

Hell, Damon thought wildly. He could just throw it all away—Kincaid Jameson, the fast-paced job, the crazed lifestyle. He could stop and get a job in Chicago, where he could be with the girls more. Wouldn't have to be gone. He could fix things. Make things right.

But how? How would he fix things? He didn't know how. Didn't know how to nurture them. And he loved them far too much to subject them to any more of his parental fumblings.

Ev'rybody always goes away. Sarah's words echoed in his mind. Eve wouldn't go away. She would be there, twenty-four hours a day. Constant. Secure. There would be Grandma's face at the breakfast table instead of a baby-sitter's. There would be Grandma taking them shopping and to the park. Grandma, always there for school functions, or birthday parties or the million and one crises that seem to cluster around small children like bees to a honey pot.

Ev'rybody always goes away....

Maybe it was time to give them one last heartache, one last parting so that they never had to suffer another.

Maybe it's time to let them go.

His shoulders slumped, and he buried his face against Ellen's hair.

Chapter Fifteen

Ariel sat, curled on the window seat, staring down onto the yard below. A half-dozen neighbor kids were playing stickball, the window of the lady across the street already numbering the first casualty.

Two little girls were pushing baby buggies down the sidewalk, dress-up finery borrowed from their mothers trailing along behind them. The oldest one had slapdash, honey-brown braids streaming down her back, and Ariel couldn't help but remember how Moey had always come to school, her braids almost militantly precise.

She hadn't known then, that it had been Moey's father who had plaited her hair. Hadn't been able to picture Damon, his face taut with concentration, taming the wayward strands. But now, every time she saw a little girl who was Moey's age, or Ellen's or Sarah's, she would feel a jab of pain, and would torture herself with bittersweet imaginings of Damon tending to his daughters' needs with that endearing mixture of competence and confusion that had made her love him.

Love him. The cardinal sin, the one thing above all others that Damon couldn't tolerate. Because he could see nothing in himself worth loving.

How many times in the past three days had she thought of calling Damon. Picking up the phone, just to see if he was all right. How many times had she wanted to find out what the girls were doing—whether any monsters had slipped out of the closet, or any knights from the Crystal Kingdom had been victorious over the dragons?

How many times had her fingers ached to skim over Damon's hair, his face, her mouth aching for the kisses that had been at once desperate and hungry and so agonizingly tender?

It had been the hardest thing she'd ever done, accepting the finality in Damon's voice when he'd left her. But he'd made himself perfectly clear. He didn't want her love. Couldn't stand the pain of risking his heart.

No. There wouldn't be any miracle this time. No happy ending where the fairy princess broke the knight free of the enchantress's spell and gained his love in return. There wouldn't be any more lemonade stands on Worthington Drive, or any more birthday disasters with cakes obliterated by bunny feet.

And no matter what the future held, Ariel wouldn't be there to see it. Wouldn't be there to kiss away Sarah's nightmares, or laugh Ellen out of a fit of the sulks.

She wouldn't be there to bully Damon into going to the emergency room if he was ever hurt again. And she would never know what it was like to wake up in the middle of the night, curled next to him, so that she could watch the moonlight streaming from the window to bathe his face.

But as wrenching as that knowledge was, the thing that hurt her most of all was the fact that she knew that no one would ever be there to hold Damon, to love him. Because he'd never allow that to happen.

If she could just have believed that someday he would be able to open up to someone who would love him back. Someone who would show him how warm he could be, how loving, how tender. She would almost have welcomed that— some other woman who could give Damon the things he needed, but wouldn't accept from her.

But after the scars she had dealt him to deepen the wounds left by his wife, she knew that Damon would never again risk reaching out to someone, never again risk feeling such pain.

She loved him, but she'd hurt him far worse than his wife had. She'd forced him to face the fact that she loved him, knowing he wasn't ready yet. Knowing it was too soon. She'd made him accept the fact that he refused to love, even when it was offered to him. She'd laid the responsibility squarely in his hands, and forced him to throw love away.

It had been inexcusable. Cruel. An unforgivable mistake.

One she would have given anything to be able to correct. But there were some things that couldn't be fixed once they were broken, no matter how much one might want to make them right. There were some consequences you had to live with forever.

The ring of the phone made her glance wearily over at the receiver. She'd been ignoring it for the past few days, unable to face talking to anybody. But it was time she started pulling herself together. She couldn't keep avoiding the rest of the world forever.

She let out a sigh and took up the receiver. "Hello?"

"Ariel?"

Alarm shot through her at the sound of Moey's voice, a voice so lost, unsteady, as if the child were attempting to hold back the tears.

"Moey, what is it? What's wrong?"

"Ellen and Sarah and me—we've been waiting a long time for you to come and see us. Aren't you coming anymore?"

Ariel had believed she couldn't feel pain any more deeply, but the little girl's words made her throat squeeze shut, tears burn at her eyes.

"No, sweetheart. I think maybe it's better if I don't come anymore."

"You never said goodbye. Mommy never said goodbye, either."

"I...I wanted to. It's just that...it's so hard to explain."

Moey was quiet for a moment, and Ariel could feel the hurt welling up in the child as if it had crawled into Ariel's own heart.

"You remember when I told you my mommy made the cupcakes? The ones with pink frosting?"

"I remember."

"She didn't. She didn't like pink frosting because it stains your clothes. And cupcakes get crumbs all over everything. I just...just wanted her to like pink frosting and not care about the crumbs, so I sort of made believe that she did."

Ariel gripped the phone in white fingers, trying not to cry. "It's okay to pretend sometimes, Moey, to try to make things seem better than they are."

"We're going to have to do that a lot from now on," the child said in a lost voice. "Me and Ellen and Sarah. I heard Daddy talking to Mrs. Applebea. After he gets back from his trip, we're going to go live with Nana."

"Y-you're going to what?" Ariel asked, feeling dizzy, afraid she was going to throw up.

"Live in Oak Park with Nana. Daddy says he keeps makin' mistakes, and he doesn't like to make mistakes. He told Mrs. Bea it's so we'll have someone there that loves us all the time, even when he's gone."

Tears were streaming down Ariel's face, searing her with guilt. "Moey, I... Oh, God, I don't know what to say."

"Oh, it'll be all right I guess. I mean, we'll get used to it. But Ellen and Sarah and me, what we really hoped was that you could stay with us. That you could...well, be like our mommy. But Daddy said that you couldn't come live here. Maybe he thinks you'd get sad like my mommy did."

Sad? Her heart was breaking. Had she hurt Damon so much that he was even going to give up his daughters? When she had forced him to open up, had there been so much pain inside him, that he couldn't see what a wonderful father he had become?

Even in the short time that she had known him, he'd made such strides in learning to deal with the girls. But more important than that, she'd known how much he loved them, how deeply he wanted to do the right thing for each of them. They had been the one thing he'd been able to rescue from the emotional rubble of his relationship with his wife. The one thing that had given him some sort of hope. And now he was surrendering them, as well, because he didn't think he deserved them.

She had to do something. Find some way to make him see that giving up his children wouldn't be some honorable, noble sacrifice, but rather, would be a horrible mistake, one that he would regret for the rest of his life.

"Moey, is your daddy home? Can I talk to him?"

"He's back in Australia. Or maybe he's in London, now. He's supposed to call, but last time, his voice got all crinkly, and he had to get off."

Ariel closed her eyes against the image of Damon, listening to his children's prattle, knowing that when he came home he would be emptying his house of their antics, their laughter, leaving it quiet, dead, as dead as Amanda, as dead as his dreams.

"Honey, when do you think your daddy will be back?"

"Not for a long time. Weeks and weeks."

The racing panic inside Ariel dulled, fading into a numbing sense of resignation. And for once she was glad that Damon was gone, at least for this brief period of time. Gone so that she had time to check the impulse to race back into his life, into the lives of his children, to try to mold things to suit her, force him to do what she believed was the right thing.

Hadn't she learned anything? She'd already done enough damage. Failed him in ways that were inexcusable, that would leave so many inner scars, she couldn't bear to think of them.

She gripped the phone in bloodless fingers, aware of the silence, unable to break it.

"Ariel?" Moey said softly at last.

"What, sweetheart?"

"If I live at Nana's house, I won't be going to St. Gen's anymore. I'll be going to a new school. I'm going to miss you a lot. And I'm going to miss Houdini and the games we played at Abracadabra. You're the best teacher in the whole world. G'bye."

Ariel fought to hold back the tears that were choking her as she listened to the phone go dead. She let the receiver dangle from limp fingers as the sobs shook her.

You're the best teacher in the whole world, Moey had said. But that wasn't true. She wasn't even a good teacher, not even a competent one. She'd made the most grievous mistake of all, was responsible for the pain in Moey's voice, the anguish that must have prompted Damon's decision to let his mother-in-law take his children.

She remembered the night of the Abracadabra party, Nancy's warning about getting overly involved with Melissa Kincaid's case. Nancy had cautioned Ariel that such involvement could hurt Moey. Could damage what little progress they'd managed to gain. She'd insisted that the interference could upset the balance in the family. Throw it into even deeper turmoil.

And Ariel had ignored her. Had been so certain that she was right to go charging off on Moey's behalf, indignant, outraged, ready to force Damon Kincaid to see the wrong that he had done.

But in the end, she had been the one who was wrong. Wrong about Damon. Wrong to believe she could only make things better for Moey. Fatally wrong. Irrevocably wrong. And those three little girls and their father would pay the price for her mistake for the rest of their lives.

Feeling as if she'd aged a hundred years, Ariel dragged herself from the window seat and walked into the kitchen. There was only one thing she could do.

She shifted the basket of contraband from where it sat on a sheaf of paper. Taking up a pen she sat at the breakfast bar, the paper poised in front of her.

All her life, she'd wanted to be a teacher. Had worked toward it. Dreamed of the day she would have charge of her own classroom. And from the moment she'd begun teaching, she'd always taken away anything she believed was physically or emotionally dangerous to the children. She'd always done her best to protect them from anything that could hurt them. And there was nothing more dangerous, in her opinion, than a teacher who had been incompetent.

Her only choice was to make certain that she could never cause such damage again.

With trembling fingers she began to write.

Chapter Sixteen

Damon sat in the darkened hotel room staring out the window at the sky. The meetings for the day were over, Joe and some of the company bigwigs had gone out on the town. But Damon had been no more tempted to join them tonight than he had any of the other nights that he had spent here, alone in his room.

The posh suite that had been his home the past two weeks was worlds away from the apartment on Chicago's South Side. The plush velvet chair was sinfully comfortable, the mahogany table with its bottle of Dom Pérignon gleamed in the moonlight. But as he sat there, alone, he felt the same yawning emptiness that had stalked him when he had curled up on the hard metal slats of the fire escape twentysome years ago.

Only this time, the emptiness was far deeper, far more miserable because he knew now that it could be filled. Filled with laughter and teasing, those tender, careless caresses Ariel seemed to lavish on everyone from children, to baby raccoons, to Damon himself. Touches that were infinitely precious because he'd never experienced them before.

Gestures of love—given without thought, so openly, with no fear of rejection, no thought that they might be unwanted or rebuffed.

Touches that Damon had played over and over in his mind these past weeks, remembering how they had soothed him, warmed him, and when they had turned passionate, how they had inflamed him.

He stared up at the twinkling stars, feeling the wrenching tug of Ariel's magic. A sky full of miracles, that was how she saw them. Endless possibilities, each one more beautiful than the last.

She had changed him forever.

He could see the stars now. They'd always been there—outside his hotel rooms, dappling the night sky above the yard on Worthington Drive. But he hadn't bothered to look at them. Hadn't wanted to. Because he'd stopped believing in wishes. He'd stopped believing in miracles. He'd stopped believing in anything except the driving need to make certain his daughters were never without all the things—the tangible trappings of security—that his own childhood had lacked.

But somehow, in his quest for what he thought his children needed, he had missed what really mattered. To him. To them. He'd missed seeing the Crystal Kingdom through Moey's fantasy-misted eyes. He'd missed laughing over Ellen's relentless practicality, her blunt, head-on method of charging into life. He'd missed Sarah's babyhood, her first smile, her first step.

Where had he even been when those momentous milestones had passed? In Athens or Paris? Tokyo or Geneva? He couldn't even remember. Why? Because those places, those companies, those business coups that had seemed so blasted important at the time, didn't matter a damn.

Even the mistake he had made right after Amanda died, the one that had cost Kincaid Jameson so much, the mistake that had undercut his self-confidence and sent him plunging deeper and deeper into his business affairs to make things right, had, in the end, been far less important than the mistakes he'd been making at home.

The chaos, the confusion, the laughter, the tears. The triumphs and the total catastrophes that were far more draining, but also far more rewarding than anything he'd ever found out on the road.

He was certain if he lived to be a hundred, he would never forget Ellen's fifth birthday. How that rabbit of Ariel's had turned the whole house into a disaster rivaling any hurricane the national weather service had ever named. He'd never forget how delighted the girls had been when they'd turned Ellen's walls into a painted menagerie. How their eyes had shone when they'd run, in paint-splattered delight, under the sprinkler that Ariel had rigged.

And he'd never forget how wonderful it had felt to hold his children, feel Sarah cuddled close against him, sorrowfully confessing that she'd "eated" the chocolate frosting. He'd never forget how small, how precious Moey's hand had felt slipping into his. He'd never forget how his throat had constricted those times his restless little Ellen had snuggled in against him, her battle with the world put on hold for a little while.

He felt a sharp stab of panic when he thought of how close he'd come to giving up those things forever—how close he'd been to giving his children to Eve, to raise in that cool, orderly, sterile house in Oak Park. To be groomed and shaped into perfect debutantes with perfect manners and plastic smiles.

It had seemed like the right thing to do—giving them into Eve's custody. Until Sarah had clamored to go to the airport with him, to watch him take off for "Stralia," and Ellen had ordered him to bring her back a kangaroo to keep as a pet in the garage.

But it had been Moey who had made his heart wrench the most savagely. Slipping up to put a tissue-wrapped package in his hand. "You can't open it 'til the plane takes off," she had insisted wistfully. "It's a goodbye gift, so you won't forget us."

He had done his best to reassure her, telling her how much he loved them all, that he could never forget them. He was only going to be gone a little while.

But Moey had stared up at him with those wise, dark eyes that seemed to probe far too deeply for such a little girl. Though he'd been disturbed by Moey's expression, he'd done as he'd promised and opened the gift just as the plane was taking off. Beneath the crumpled tissue was a frame made of flat wooden sticks, drowned in an ocean full of glitter. It surrounded a snapshot Ariel must have taken of the three girls in front of their lemonade stand.

A delightfully devilish Ellen was making bunny ears behind Moey's head. A tinfoil crown encircled Sarah's curls. There was a streak of marker on Moey's nose, and she was smiling so widely, Damon could almost feel the shivers of delight that must have been going through her.

It was as if, in that single picture, Ariel had captured how much his children loved him, needed him. There would be no bunny ears tolerated at the house in Oak Park. No bright splashes of marker left on noses, testament to a day full of fun.

But he could make certain that there were wooden sticks and glitter and tinfoil crowns. He could make certain that there were smiles and laughter and bunny ears.

That knowledge had been Ariel's gift. She had reached deep inside Damon to the little boy who had sat on the fire escape, and had brushed away the curtains of smog and dirt and ugly street noise. Like the magic in *Peter Pan,* she'd not just shown him the sky, the stars, but she'd taken his hand and flown with him into the center of all the beauty, all the magic that had seemed forever beyond his reach.

And he'd been terrified. So scared of flying, that he'd torn away from her, raced back to the familiar bleakness he'd always known. But wasn't it more terrifying still to be forever trapped in that cage of loneliness? The fire escape that led nowhere, except down into the streets that could be hostile and filled with hopelessness?

Love was pain. He still believed that. But wasn't it also wonder and warmth when he'd been cold for so long? Wasn't it also hope when he'd all but given up years ago?

He was scared. So damned scared. Scared of hurting his children. Scared of failing Ariel. But mostly he was scared of letting the walls inside him tumble down, and finding only the emptiness, the ugliness Amanda had seemed to see in him.

No. Ariel had already looked behind those walls, slipped through the solid stone like some fairy enchantress. And she'd loved him. All of him. Even the faults that he knew were there.

Maybe he wasn't everything she deserved. But she loved him. Loved him. And he ... blast it, he loved her.

A streak of white blurred in the sky above him, and Damon watched it disappear into the darkness. A falling star. Memories of the night at Shadylane Farm, when he had sat in the barn with Ariel haunted him, the wistful tone of her voice as she'd told how sad she'd been when she realized that stars die.

What was it her father had said to comfort her? That even the stars have to let go of something to make way for what is new?

Wasn't it time to let go of the bitterness? The doubts? Wasn't it time to reach out and take the magic, let it flush away the emptiness? Time to take a chance?

A chance on aquamarine eyes that could sparkle with mischief. A chance on laughter and long nights making love in his big bed. A chance on belonging.

A chance far too precious to let slip away.

Damon levered himself out of his chair and went to the closet, dragging out his suitcases. He'd head home on the first flight out in the morning.

He left a message for Joe to call him the minute he got back to the hotel, so he could give him the news. Explain.

Explain? Damon could almost laugh. Joe would think he should be committed, racing off in the middle of a business deal this way. He'd be irritated as hell at Damon's abrupt departure, but it didn't matter. Damon had carried the weight of the company for over a year now—prodded by guilt. And even before that, he'd done more than his share. Both he and Joe had been leery of admitting any new partners. They'd spent years teaching other companies how to delegate work advantageously, and yet they hadn't done so in their own business.

It was time to make a change. Time to hire some of those hot-eyed college graduates who were so anxious to secure a position in the company.

And as for Joe . . . he could carry the ball on this deal or drop it. Damon didn't care. Nothing mattered except getting home.

He had just jammed the last of his clothes into the bags when the phone jangled.

He dived for it, expecting to hear Joe's voice, muzzy from the pitcher of martinis he'd doubtless sipped over his filet mignon. When he heard the crackle of long-distance wires, his stomach plunged to his toes in panic that something was wrong.

"Damon?"

Eve's voice, sounding far too smug to be bringing tidings of disaster. Damon sucked in a steadying breath, somewhat relieved.

"Eve. What is it? Is anything wrong?"

"Not anymore, it would seem. Melissa just gave me the news, and I must say I'm delighted that you've finally come to your senses."

"News? What news?"

"That you've decided to see reason. Even before the accident, I told Amanda that you would. You're not cut out to be a family man. These little adjustments are painful, but necessary sometimes.''

''Adjustments?''

''In fact, sometimes I think if Amanda had just been honest with you, she wouldn't have been so distracted. She was such a nervous child, underneath it all. So unsettled. I told her that you'd be reasonable and see that it was best for everyone concerned. But she seemed to think you'd be averse to being separated from the girls. And with your temper, well, she was afraid to risk speaking of it. Not that things could have gone on so much longer.''

''You're not making any sense.''

''I'm sorry. It's just…all this time, I've been reluctant to admit that Amanda had any culpability in what happened. You were not a good husband, Damon, gone all the time. It was no wonder she got lonely and met someone else. And I'll never say anything other than that the affair was your fault.''

''Amanda was having an affair?'' He should have felt something. Anger. Betrayal. Instead he felt as if somehow he'd always known. And he couldn't help being a little glad that she'd found some happiness before she'd died.

''If only she'd told you, I know things would have worked out. I'd even agreed to take the children while she got her life settled. That's why it's so tragic to realize, now, that you would have been happy to give them up.''

''Give them up?'' Damon exclaimed.

''Now, I know you weren't planning to make the change until you returned from overseas, but there's really no point in putting it off. I mean, since they are going to be coming here anyway, there's no sense in the girls spending the next month with that baby-sitter.''

''What? You want the girls to come for a visit? You know, I told you at the beginning of the summer that it would be fine. I just wish you would have given me a little more notice as to when you wanted them.''

"Well, it hardly makes any difference now. I mean, this way I'll have time to enroll them in classes—dancing, piano. And Ellen could certainly use one of those white gloves-and-party manners courses they offer for children."

"Eve, I appreciate your concern, but it's not necessary for you to go to all this trouble. Just take the girls to your country club's pool. Or turn on your sprinkler system and let them run through it. They'll be perfectly content."

"Trouble? It's no trouble. You know how much I wanted this. I've been planning it for months. And schools. I'll have to check into what school to enroll the girls in next fall."

Damon's fingers clamped on the phone, his head swimming with confusion. "Schools?"

"Yes. You certainly don't think I'd allow any grandchild of mine to go back to that hideous St. Genevieve's."

"I hardly think that the girls' schooling should be any of your concern."

"Damon, I'm going to have to insist that you give me complete control of those sorts of decisions. I am much more practiced in making them than you are."

"They're my daughters, Eve."

"So they are," she said in such conciliatory accents that warning bells went off in Damon's head. "It's not that St. Genevieve's was...totally unacceptable. I know that Amanda must have had her reasons for choosing it."

"Eve, what the hell are you talking about?" Damon roared into the phone.

"Don't use that vulgar tone with me, Damon. I'll not tolerate it. Melissa told me that she had overheard you speaking to Mrs. Applebea about transferring custody of the girls to me. And when I spoke to the baby-sitter, she confirmed it."

The entire conversation suddenly jerked into horrible focus. His head reeled as he imagined Moey hearing such a thing. That was why she had looked so sad. Why she had said goodbye to him with tears in her eyes. That was why she had given him that picture so he "wouldn't forget" them.

Cursing himself a thousand times over, he snarled into the phone, "I'm not giving up my children, Eve. I love them and they love me."

Eve's gasp of outrage carried through the phone line.

"But Mrs. Applebea assured me that you have spoken about it. That you had been quite certain that it was the right thing to do. And it is, Damon. You can't raise three little girls. You don't know the first thing about children."

"I know that there are monsters in the closet. They come out at night if the door is left open. And I know that there is a sorceress in the Crystal Kingdom who builds invisible walls. And I know that Sarah wants to be a ladybug when she grows up."

"A—A what? Of all the ridiculous—"

"No, Eve, it's not ridiculous. Not when you're three years old and ladybugs are your most favorite things in the world. Anything is possible then. It's even possible for your daddy to realize how wrong he's been. How much he loves you. Ariel showed me that."

"Ariel? That—that person from St. Genevieve's? Damon, surely you can't mean to pay any attention to what that woman has said to you! Why, I heard just the other day that she is so incompetent she'll no longer even be teaching—"

"You heard *what?*" Damon couldn't breathe, disbelief streaking through him.

"She's been thrown out of St. Genevieve's. Terminated from their employ."

"Son of a bitch! When the hell did this happen?"

"Last week. Marilyn Von Damme heard it from her daughter-in-law..."

"This is my fault," Damon raged.

"What?"

"I have to go. Goodbye, Eve." He slammed down the phone and punched Ariel's number. No answer. Furious with himself, he scrawled out a message to Joe and raced to grab a taxi.

The jovial driver eyed Damon curiously as he flung the bags in the trunk.

"What time is your flight, mate?"

"As soon as I can get one."

"You don't have a ticket?"

"No. But I have to get back to the States tonight. I'll charter a damned plane if I have to."

"Something that important, huh?"

Damon thought of Ariel, alone, devastated by the loss of the job she loved, the children she adored, the man she'd opened her heart to.

"Yeah. It's important," he said quietly. "The most important thing in my life."

The house was quiet. Too quiet, as Damon maneuvered his luggage through the door. It was Mrs. Applebea's knitting time—that sacrosant hour when she went into the study to knit, sometimes afghans for local nursing homes, or lately clothes for her daughter's baby.

The living room was immaculate, the entryway devoid of the clutter of tennis shoes and jackets and toys that had been there when Ariel had been in charge of the household. He hesitated a moment and listened, astonished to discover that he was longing to hear music drifting out of Ellen's tape recorder, or longing to hear Ariel's laughter, punctuated by the girls' eager voices. All of them talking at once, laughing at once, their hands sticky with paint, and anxious to run to him and hug him.

For a moment he feared that Eve had come to take the girls in spite of the phone conversation. But at that moment he heard a soft rustle from somewhere deep in the interior of the house. Easing his bags to the floor, he followed the sounds, only to find that they led to his bedroom.

He peered inside. Three little figures were sitting on his bed, Moey in the middle, with her sisters pressed against either side of her. They were pristine—the way Amanda had always kept them, their hair ribbons as precise as the scalpel path of a surgeon, their outfits crisp and pressed. And he found himself searching for smudges and spills, colorful badges of a day spent playing, a day full of adventure.

But the only splash of color to be seen was in the faded pages of the book Moey held, pillowed on her lap. Her forehead was creased with concentration as she pointed to figures in an illustration, attempting to weave a story about them for her sisters.

They looked so subdued, so sad, clustered in their little circle. Damon cursed himself for his part in that sadness, and swore that he'd make certain from now on that their lives were filled with laughter.

Quietly he slipped up behind them, listening as the oblivious Moey spun out her tale.

"And this . . . this is the fairy princess Ariel, who came to get the ring from the evil wizard. 'Cause then she could break the spell and marry the prince."

"Prince Daddy," Sarah supplied.

"Uh-huh. But the wizard had magical powers and he made the prince so sad, he went far away into an enchanted forest with trees that had faces and wolves and snakes. And he was lost forever and ever."

"Not quite forever." The words were quiet, his eyes stinging, his throat aching.

"Daddy!" Ellen cried, Moey gasping in surprise. But not even Sarah flung herself at him in her usual exuberant hug, all three girls looking uncertain, wistful.

He sank onto the bed next to them, taking the book from Moey's hands. "Do you know that my mother got that for me when I was a boy? One morning I woke up and found this under the Christmas tree."

"A 'drate big Christmas tree?" Sarah asked.

"No. It was only this big," he showed her with his hands. "It was made out of plastic, with tinfoil decorations and white paint spattered on it to look like snow."

"You could've left that tree up 'til Valentine's Day, and watched it sparkle," Moey said, awed.

"I suppose we could have. But we didn't keep it up very long. Our apartment was really small, and we needed all the room we had."

"Could you fit many presents under your Christmas tree?" Ellen asked. "I get lots of presents. Even when I'm bad."

"No. I didn't get a lot of presents. But this one was so special, I didn't mind. It was the most wonderful gift I had ever gotten, and I read it . . . read the whole thing before we went back to school after Christmas vacation. I read it so many times, that I learned parts of it by heart."

"I'd like to hear the story." Moey stroked the illustration longingly. "The pictures are so pretty. But the words are too hard."

"We'll read it together. Make it a bedtime story, if you'd like. It's full of imaginings, Moey. And adventures for Ellen. And there's a magical ring sparkly enough for you, Sarah."

"It'll take a long time to read through all three books if you only read to us when we come and see you from Grandma's house," Ellen complained.

"No, it won't because you're not going to live at Grandma's house. You're staying here, with me."

Moey's eyes widened, her lip quivering. "But I heard you talking to Mrs. Applebea, and you said—"

"I didn't mean for you to hear that, Moey. It was a mistake. A mistake." He cupped her face in his hands, hating the hot trickle of her tears against his skin. "Daddies make mistakes, sometimes. So do mommies. We get confused, and angry, and sad just like you do. I wanted to do what was best for you three. I've been gone so much. I don't think that it was good for you, and I know it wasn't good for me."

"I missed you terrible bad," Sarah confided, snuggling close. "But if I went away to Grandma's, I'd miss you even worser. See, here we can come in your room and sniff your smelly bottles and hug your fish tie. And Moey can tell us stories out of your special book, and pretend like you're listening, too.''

"You won't have to pretend anymore, Sarah. Because I'm going to be right here, as much as I possibly can. We're going to be a family, now. A real family.''

"Like Travis at the farm?'' Ellen asked, perplexed.

"Absolutely.''

"But...but real families have a mommy,'' Sarah said hopefully. "Mommies who laugh and catch ladybugs and make lemonade stands so their little girls can get lots of quarters.''

"Is that so?''

All three girls nodded vigorously.

"You wouldn't happen to know anyone who does all those things, do you?''

"Ariel does!'' Ellen said eagerly. "But I wouldn't even care if she didn't do any of them, 'cause she gives us hugs and loves us and never yells. I think she'd like to give you hugs, too, Daddy, if you'd let her.''

Damon thought about the night he'd spent in Ariel's apartment—how generous she'd been, not only with her body, but with her spirit. How stunning, how humbling, how terrifying it had been to see all that love shining from her eyes.

She'd told him she believed in miracles. And he'd told her there were none left for him. This once, just this once he had to reach for it, try to see if he could find the most precious miracle of all.

For Ellen. For Moey and Sarah.

But most of all, for himself.

Chapter Seventeen

Ariel balanced on the stepladder, tugging the last of the poster-board characters from on top of the tall metal cabinet in the corner of the room. The almost surreal quiet of summer clung to the halls of St. Gen's, the halls smelling of wax newly applied to floors that had been scuffed all year long. Fresh paint was being brushed onto the classrooms in the east wing by a team of fathers who had volunteered some of their vacation time. And a pair of plumbers were rattling around in the boys' bathroom, attempting to fix a faucet that had been leaking off and on since the first day Ariel had come here three years ago.

She swallowed a lump in her throat, remembering the day she had first come to St. Gen's, as starry-eyed and eager as any of her students. She'd clutched a box full of the games and teaching aides she'd made during her stint of student teaching, her head filled with so many ideas she was eager to try, that it felt ready to explode.

Even Sister Thomasetta had smiled at her, telling her that she hoped Ariel would still be this enthusiastic after her first turn at recess duty when there was three feet of snow on the ground.

But Ariel had loved it—loved it all. Loved it so much that it had filled her life for the past three years, so totally, so completely that she hadn't needed anything else. She hadn't needed the dates that were so important to her friends. She hadn't needed parties or candle-lit dinners. She'd been happy—fulfilled. Her dreams of a family of her own put temporarily on hold.

Until Damon Kincaid had come into her life, and she'd suddenly wanted so much more.

She struggled to quell the dragging sense of loss that had engulfed her for the past weeks, and climbed down the ladder to sort the bulletin-board characters into the row of boxes she had lined up against the wall. Each box was labeled with another teacher's name, and she'd spent the past three days sorting through her materials, dividing them between the colleagues who had admired them or borrowed them or attempted to copy them over the years.

She'd wanted nothing more than to take everything and dump it into the trash hopper at the back of the school. Had just wanted to finish the agonizing task of cleaning out this classroom, obliterating any sign of herself from it so that some new teacher—still starry-eyed and confident—could take her place.

She'd just wanted the pain to be over. But in the end, she hadn't been able to just throw away everything she'd worked on during her stay at St. Gen's—not when she'd already lost so much.

She felt her eyes burn, and wiped them impatiently on the sleeve of her pink T-shirt. No. No more tears. She felt like she'd shed enough to fill Lake Michigan. From the time she'd been a child, her parents had taught her that you had to take the consequences of your mistakes. And no matter how hard it had been for them, they had always allowed their children to stumble, to fail, to experience not only the love of that huge, boisterous family, but also some of the knocks that were inevitable in life.

Always before, Ariel had been resilient, able to look at her mistakes, but not dwell on them. Make reparation, but not languish over the guilt. But ever since she'd talked to Moey Kincaid, realized the scope of this mistake, there didn't seem to be any energy left inside her. Nothing to fight back against the sense of defeat she'd never experienced before.

The sound of footsteps approaching made her wince at the thought of making small talk with one of the fathers or answering some question from the custodians or the plumbers, but she turned around, resigned.

At that moment a tall, broad-shouldered figure filled the doorway, and she froze, staring into Damon's haggard features.

Her fingers tightened on the comical caricature of Columbus she'd been about to put into Sister Floria's box, her heart slamming against her ribs.

She'd never thought she would see him again, except in the night dreams when she tortured herself with the beauty of the one time they had made love. But she drank in the sight of him, more than willing to relive the hurt of watching him leave again if she could just see him, touch him, hear his voice one more time.

He looked as if he hadn't slept in days—his clothes were crumpled, his jaw shadowed by two days' worth of beard. His eyes were red rimmed with exhaustion, filled with regret and a tender reproach that made her throat squeeze shut as he quietly closed the door behind him.

"Ariel, why didn't you tell me? Tell me about this." He gestured to the evidence of her packing that was scattered about the room, his eyes holding hers with such intensity that she had to look away.

She shrugged. "I guess I figured that we said all we had to say to each other that night at my apartment. This has nothing to do with you."

"Like hell it doesn't! When Eve called me, told me about the trouble you were in, I grabbed the first plane out of Melbourne. This is my fault. And I'm going to fix it. I'll go to the school board. Explain things. Damn it, they can't just fire a teacher who is as gifted as you are."

"They didn't fire me, Damon. I resigned."

He took a stumbling step back, aghast. "Resigned? Why in God's name would you resign? You love this job. Love the children."

"Unfortunately that's not enough. I used to believe it was, but I was wrong. People warned me. People who had been in teaching a lot longer. But I thought I knew better."

"You're the most gifted teacher I've ever seen. Your instincts with the girls are always perfect, the way you love them, nurture them—"

"The way I barged into their lives and made them miserable."

"Miserable? What are you talking about? Just look what you did for Moey. For me. If it hadn't been for you—"

"If it hadn't been for me, you wouldn't be giving your daughters to your mother-in-law," Ariel said, her voice cracking. "You'd be keeping them with you where they belong."

"Ariel, I—"

"Don't, Damon. Moey told me everything. And I know that you've made the decision to give them up because of me. Because of the way I pushed you before you were ready. Made you confront feelings you weren't ready for. Unfortunately you can't just throw a kid away the way you can toss out an adding-machine tape if you make a mistake figuring up a company's gross annual product. You can't just slop white-out across the figures and start over again. When you make a mistake with a child, alter the course of that child's life by something you've done, it's permanent. No one can afford to make that kind of error, Damon. The price is too high."

"Ariel, the girls are staying with me."

She shook her head, confused. "But Moey...she said..."

"She overheard a conversation between me and Mrs. Applebea. I was feeling really low at the time. Hopeless. Because as much as I loved the girls, I thought I wasn't good for them, didn't know how to make them happy."

"But they love you! They need you! I told you that—"

"You told me a lot of things, but you showed me much, much more. You showed me it didn't matter if I was a perfect father, if I did everything right. What was important was that I loved my children, was trying to do my best. At first I couldn't believe you. I didn't... God, it was so hard."

Ariel felt tears wet her cheeks as his voice broke. He came to her, framing her face in his hands, skimming away the moisture with the edges of his thumbs.

"But I know now that my little girls love me. Whether I deserve it or not. For some reason, in spite of how bad things were with Amanda . . . in spite of how many times I screwed up, all the times I was gone when they needed me...Ellen and Sarah and Moey still want me. What I need to know now is . . . do you still want me, too?"

Do you still want me . . . ? Ariel flinched at the pain those words caused her. *Want* not *love.* He might have said the same thing to Amanda when she'd told him she was pregnant. Being the man he was, he must have rushed to Amanda's aid, too, promising his life away, giving up his future to give his name to the child they'd conceived.

From the moment he had entered the classroom, he had made it clear that he had rushed back to the States the moment he heard Ariel was in trouble. He had believed that she was suffering repercussions over their relationship and he had determined to find some way to fix things for her, the way he had for the frightened Amanda so many years ago.

But she didn't want noble sacrifices from this man. Didn't want to spend a lifetime looking into his eyes and seeing the places he kept locked against her, against everyone. She couldn't stand the loneliness of knowing that she loved him, and that he could never love her back.

"I'm glad you've...you've worked things out with the girls. And I'm so glad that you've realized how much they need you. But I..."

She tugged away from him and went to stand by the window, turning away because she couldn't stand to look at him, couldn't bear to let him see how much she wanted to fling herself into his arms.

"Damon, you don't have to feel responsible for my resignation. You don't have to try to make up for everything that happened the way you tried to make up for conceiving Moey with Amanda. This isn't your responsibility."

"This isn't about responsibility. It's about miracles."

She felt his hands close gently on her shoulders, turning her around to face him.

"Ariel, I never learned how to show love. I wanted to." He raised his eyes to the ceiling, and she saw them glimmer, overbright. "God, I really did. Even when Moey was a baby, I tried to...but I didn't know how. Or maybe Amanda was so unhappy by then she couldn't allow me to. The girls were her whole world, and she didn't want to let me in. But then..."

He threaded his fingers through her hair, and the wonder that filled those dark eyes shook Ariel to her very soul. "Then Cinderella showed up at my door. She didn't wait for the glass slipper. She just swept into my life and filled it with laughter, with love. With hope." His voice dropped, low. "Magic, Ariel. The magic that touches everything you do. It made me...believe."

He tipped her face up to his. "Even before I knew about your problems, I could feel the walls inside me crumbling. Knew just how much I wanted you, needed you. It was hard to face it—the risk... But every night I would sit by the window watching the stars. And I would wonder if you were watching them, too. If you were seeing miracles." His voice was a hushed whisper. "I was afraid that I'd taken them away from you."

"I couldn't see past the mistakes I'd made. *I* had made, Damon. Not you."

"But don't you see? They weren't mistakes. It just took a little while for your miracle to find me."

His mouth drifted down to melt against hers, agonizingly tender in a kiss filled with every dream she'd ever known. When he drew away, her breath caught at the emotions radiating from those dark lashed eyes.

"I love you, Cinderella," he said. "I want to marry you. I want to laugh with you over Ellen's antics and Moey's dreams. I want you to be there when Sarah has a nightmare, so we can snuggle her between us and make her feel safe. And I want to fill up the house with more children. Yours and mine, Ariel. A little piece of the magic that we can keep forever. Don't you want that anymore?"

"I do. I want it so much. But I... Damon, don't you see? I was wrong. I could have cost you and the girls so much. When I told Nancy and Sister Thomasetta what had happened, they didn't want to accept my resignation. They insisted on tabling it until August, hoping that I would change my mind. They told me that everyone made mistakes. That you had to learn from them, and do better the next time. But I couldn't forgive myself."

"No one understands that feeling more than I do," he said gently. "But there is still time for you to change your mind. You belong in the classroom, Ariel. You belong here, helping kids in Abracadabra, doing magic tricks with that demonic rabbit of yours and making the kids' grief disappear."

"But when I think of what almost happened—"

"Think of what *did* happen. The gifts you gave to all of us—Moey and Ellen and Sarah. And me, Ariel. Think what you've given me. You've given me my children, when I almost lost them. You've given me my life back. Let me try to give you something in return."

"Damon, I—"

"Believe, Ariel. Believe in the magic. In this. I do." He kissed her, kissed her until she felt all his pain melt away, mingle with her own.

"I believe," she whispered, holding him, loving him. "I always did." She hugged him tight, then drew away. "Let's get out of here," she said in a choked voice.

"Where do you want your coach to take you, Cinder-ella?"

"To the girls, Damon. I've missed them so much. Al-most as much as I've missed you."

She hadn't believed his face could hold more joy, but it seemed to spill over, lighting his smile with such devastat-ing beauty she felt it plumb the depths of her soul.

"We'll have to get married in a hurry," he warned her. "No long delays or anything. You know Ellen. The kid has no patience, and she'll be driving us crazy, trying to hurry things up. In fact, when I stopped home to tell them that they were not going to Eve's and that they were stuck with their father forever, they wouldn't give me any peace. See, I told them I was coming here to see you…ask you…" He glanced away for a moment, sheepish.

"You told them? About this?" Ariel asked, incredulous. "You must have been pretty sure of yourself."

"No." He stroked his fingertips down the curve of her cheek, his mouth tipping into a tender smile. "It's just that for once in my life I wanted to believe so badly. Maybe you're not the only one who can dream."

Ariel turned her mouth into the cup of his palm, kissing him. "I knew you were a dreamer all along. You just got lost for a little while."

The creak of the door made Ariel turn to find a small face peering through a narrow crack. "Daddy, are you finished yet?" Ellen demanded, her eyes so nervous, so hopeful, Ariel's heart swelled with love. "You're taking forever and ever."

"It's only been ten minutes, Ellen," Damon chided in-dulgently. "You promised to wait in the hall."

"I been waiting. And it's making me feel all crinkly inside. Is Ariel going to be our mommy?" Ellen turned her gaze to Ariel's, the child's eyes brim full of pleading. "Are you going to marry my daddy and come and live with us and make Daddy let us keep the bunny forever? I'll be good if you do. I'll never be stubborn, and I promise I won't call Sarah names."

"I love you just the way you are, Ellen Kincaid. And the only way I'm going to be your mommy is if you promise never to change."

Ellen's eyes were round with delight. "I promise! I... Moey! Sarah! Did you hear?" she called out to her sisters, still waiting somewhere in the hall. "Ariel's going to be our mommy!"

Whoops of excitement echoed down the corridor, accompanied by the sound of running feet. But Ellen wasn't about to wait for her sisters to join the celebration.

Damon held out his arm to his daughter, and the little girl hurtled against him, drawn tight into the loving circle of Damon and Ariel's embrace.

"You're the most deliciously impatient little person I've ever met, Ellen Kincaid," Damon teased, stroking his daughter's hair.

"I wonder where she gets that trait?" Ariel shot Ellen a conspiratorial wink. "From her father, maybe?"

"Yeah. From her father," he smiled, and there was peace in that face that had been haunted for so long. "The father who loves her. The man who loves you. Forever."

Epilogue

"Melissa Kincaid, if you don't stand still, I'm going to use this string of pearls to tie you to a chair!" Ariel laughed, attempting to calm her antsy daughter. "You're worse than Ellen before we went on Space Mountain last summer."

"You can't have a play about Rapunzel without a Rapunzel, Mom." Moey grinned. At eleven, the wistful little girl Ariel had fallen in love with so long ago had blossomed, leaving in Ariel a tender ache as she saw the shadings of the young woman Moey was about to become.

"I can't help being excited," Moey said. "The tower Daddy built is awesome, and my dress...it's perfect! And Uncle Jesse promised me he'd get seats in the first row for Aunt Caroline and Grandma Meg and Grandpa John and Nana."

She tugged away from Ariel for the third time in as many minutes, twirling in delight as her medieval-style costume of cherry-and-rose velvet swirled around her. "Everybody is going to be there!"

Ariel couldn't help laughing, pulling Moey into her arms. Everyone in Moey's world would be there—a world that had become so rich in love the past three years that the child had thrived on it, becoming as bright and beautiful as any fairy-tale princess.

Moey squeezed her tight, then suddenly pulled away, brushing Ariel's distended stomach with a kiss. "You won't be able to see the play yet," Moey said to her prospective brother or sister. "But Dad and Uncle Jake are going to tape the whole thing, so soon as you're born you'll get to see it."

"Threaten that kid with the Kincaid family home videos in utero and it'll refuse to be born."

Ariel wheeled at the sound of that low masculine chuckle, and her heart tightened with love as she saw Damon framed in the doorway. His hair was just a little mussed, as if two-year-old Tommy had been playing with it, a smear of something white was on his fingers, while a video camera was slung by its strap over his shoulder.

"How's my favorite princess?" He went to his daughter, taking over the weaving of the pearl string into her hair as deftly and capably as he did everything else.

"Daddy! I can't wait. I feel like . . . like I'm just going to explode in a jillion pieces. I still can't believe I got the lead in the play instead of Stephanie Walker." There was a glint of pure satisfaction in Moey's eyes as she spoke of her personal nemesis—the most popular, most obnoxious girl in the fifth grade. "Isn't this the most wonderful thing in the whole world?"

"Absolutely," he said with a final twist of his wrist. The braid Ariel had been attempting to fix for half an hour gleamed in glossy contrast to the rich glow of the pearls. But even more beautiful was the shining of Moey's eyes.

"Did Scott pick up that package of stuff for Scotland yet?" she asked, suddenly concerned. Scott Jefferson, Damon's new associate, was an eager, brilliant twenty-five-year-old kid who adored traveling.

"You *did* tell him not to bring Ellen a bagpipe, no matter how much she begs, didn't you?" Moey went on with dramatic flair. "I couldn't *bear* it if she got those things!"

"I threatened him with death. The boomerang he brought her back from Australia took out half the windows on the block. All I need is for Mrs. Lefstein to call the police because Ellen's disturbing the peace."

Peace.

The very word made Ariel's chest tighten as she looked into the face of her husband. She never stopped marveling at how different these years had made him. He was still every bit as dazzlingly handsome, carrying that powerful aura of success, but the dark shadows of guilt, of loneliness had vanished from his eyes, to be replaced by bright sparkles of anticipation, of amusement. She'd long ago stopped worrying that he missed the excitement of the life he'd led before—that he regretted limiting his business trips to three a year, spending his time in Kincaid Jameson's home office, managing projects through kids like Scott instead.

She knew Damon had never regretted his choices. It was evident in everything he said, everything he did. He was almost as bad as the children—devouring every minute to make up for all those years that he had stood on the fringes, alone.

"You're giving me that look, again." His voice was whiskey dark as it jarred her from her thoughts, his eyes dusky with half-hidden desire.

She felt the familiar tingle go up her spine as he crossed over to her and took her in his arms. "Mmm," he growled, kissing her ear. "What kind of part will I get next play if I fool around with the director?"

"The same part you had *this* time, Whiz Kid. What you're best at."

He wriggled his eyebrows wickedly. "Really?"

"I meant *professionally,* Mr. Troubleshooter. Wouldn't want that Stanford education to go to waste."

"No danger of that happening. Two snowbirds got in a fight and one ripped her tights. It was a crisis beyond imagining, until I figured out a way to disguise the gaping hole."

He was waiting to be prodded, and she didn't disappoint him.

"White tempera paint. I just brushed it on her knee and, *voilà*. No knee sticking through the costume. And then there were the vines Jake and I spent the last fifteen minutes stapling up. We couldn't figure out why they were falling down until we noticed *your* daughters picking out the staples. It seems when they were at Caroline's last weekend, she showed them how to link staples together to make necklaces. You know how Sarah is when it comes to sparklies. But that wasn't the worst, by far. Your son . . ." He paused for effect. "Spilled his entire bottle of apple juice down Eve's ice-blue suit."

Even Eve had calmed down considerably during the past years, largely due to Meg Madigan's intervention, Ariel's mother having an innate gift for soothing people's egos and cutting them down to size at the same time. Still, Ariel couldn't stifle a giggle at the image her husband's words had created.

"You probably sabotaged that bottle on purpose!" she said. "Two-year-olds cannot unscrew the lids on their bottles. Their fine-motor coordination isn't developed—"

"Hey, the kid's a genius. Takes after his father."

"Mrs. Kincaid . . ." Sister Thomasetta stood in the door, her black habit flowing in intimidating waves about her portly form, her eyes twinkling with enjoyment. "I realize that in all your years in my employ you have never been particularly concerned about the time, but the curtain is about to go up, and there isn't a Rapunzel in sight."

With a shriek, Moey made a dash for the door, but Sister Thomasetta stopped her. "With dignity, Melissa. Dignity. You are, after all, a princess."

The two of them vanished, and Damon started to follow, but Ariel pulled him back into her arms.

"The play," he protested. "It's going to start any minute."

"I know. But before you go, I get to kiss the prince."

She threaded her fingers through his hair, reveling in the familiar melting sensation deep inside her as his lips caressed hers, tender, so tender.

Damon slid his hand down to where the new life they had created nestled, safe inside her. "Looks to me like you've been kissing the prince pretty often, Cinderella."

"That's because I love him. So much."

He groaned, dragging her close, and she could feel the heat blaze inside him. But before his lips could take hers, a sudden crash, a sudden shout made them leap apart, their eyes meeting in amused horror.

"It's the tower!" Ariel wailed. "I know it's the tower! If it didn't smash the entire enchanted forest it'll be a miracle!"

His laughter rang out, rich, beautiful.

"It's going to be fine. After all, miracles are what you're best at, Ariel Kincaid," he said with a parting kiss. "No one knows that better than me."

* * * * *

Silhouette

SPECIAL ✦ EDITION®

™

VOWS
A series celebrating marriage
by Sherryl Woods

To Love, Honor and Cherish—these were the words that three generations of Halloran men promised their women they'd live by. But these vows made in love are each challenged by the tests of time....

In October—Jason Halloran meets his match in *Love* #769;
In November—Kevin Halloran rediscovers love—with his wife—in *Honor* #775;
In December—Brandon Halloran rekindles an old flame in *Cherish* #781.

These three stirring tales are coming down the aisle toward you—only from Silhouette Special Edition!

AMERICAN HERO

Every month in Silhouette Intimate Moments, one
fabulous, irresistible man is featured as an American
Hero. You won't want to miss a single one. Look for
them wherever you buy books, or follow the
instructions below and have these fantastic men
mailed straight to your door!

In September:
MACKENZIE'S MISSION by Linda Howard, IM #445

In October:
BLACK TREE MOON by Kathleen Eagle, IM #451

In November:
A WALK ON THE WILD SIDE by Kathleen Korbel, IM #457

In December:
CHEROKEE THUNDER by Rachel Lee, IM #463

AMERICAN HEROES—men you'll adore, from authors
you won't want to miss. Only from Silhouette Intimate
Moments.

What a year for romance!

Silhouette has five fabulous romance collections coming your way in 1993. Written by popular Silhouette authors, each story is a sensuous tale of love and life—as only Silhouette can give you!

SPRING FANCY
Three bachelors are footloose and fancy-free...until now.
(March)

to Mother with Love
Heartwarming stories that celebrate the joy of motherhood.
(May)

SILHOUETTE SUMMER Sizzlers
Put some sizzle into your summer reading with three of Silhouette's hottest authors.
(June)

SILHOUETTE Shadows
Take a walk on the dark side of love—with tales just perfect for those misty autumn nights.
(October)

Silhouette Christmas Stories
Share in the joy of yuletide romance with four award-winning Silhouette authors.
(November)

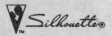

A romance for all seasons—it's always time for romance with Silhouette!

PROM93